"*Deep Water* is an intriguing and original thriller, with the serious issue of medical ethics at its core. Christine Poulson describes her fenland setting with palpable authenticity in this pacy, thought-provoking tale."

Kate Rhodes, author of the *Alice Quentin* series

"I found it difficult to put *Deep Water* down. An intelligent, thought-provoking read, with engaging and believable characters. It gripped me from the start, and didn't let go."

Sarah Rayne, author of *What Lies Beneath*

Previous Books by the Author

Dead Letters (Murder is Academic, US)
Stage Fright
Footfall
Invisible

Christine Poulson was born and brought up in North Yorkshire. She studied English Literature and Art History at the University of Leicester, later earning a PhD. She went on to work as a curator at Birmingham Museum and Art Gallery and at the William Morris Society at Kelmscott House in Hammersmith before becoming a lecturer in Art History at Homerton College, Cambridge. As well as writing fiction she has written widely on nineteenth-century art and literature, and her most recent work of non-fiction was *The Quest for the Grail: Arthurian Legend in British Art, 1840–1920*. She lives in a watermill in Derbyshire with her family.

www.christinepoulson.co.uk
Blog: www.christinepoulson.co.uk/a-reading-life
Twitter: @chrissiepoulson

Christine Poulson

DEEP WATER

ONE MISTAKE AND YOU'RE DROWNING

LION FICTION

Published by Lion Fiction
an imprint of
Lion Hudson plc
Wilkinson House, Jordan Hill Road
Oxford OX2 8DR, England
www.lionhudson.com/fiction

ISBN 978 1 78264 214 5
e-ISBN 978 1 78264 215 2

First edition 2016

A catalogue record for this book is available from the British
Library

Printed and bound in the UK, September 2016, LH26

To Joanna Bellamy (1953–2013)

"Precious friend hid in death's dateless night"

Shakespeare, Sonnet 30

"The past isn't over. It isn't even the past."

William Faulkner

"La lutte elle-même vers les sommets suffit à remplir un coeur d'homme. Il faut imaginer Sisyphe heureux."

[The struggle itself towards the summit should be enough to satisfy the human heart. One can imagine Sisyphus happy.]

Albert Camus

Prologue

Ed was nervous and he hadn't expected that. When he'd talked it over with Melissa, she'd been the one who was uneasy, and he'd argued in favour. But now, as he looked around the sterile little bedroom, small and white and clean like a room in a budget hotel, he would have given almost anything not to be here.

His hand went up to his hairline and traced the line of a scar. It was thirteen years since he had taken a header over the handlebars of his new bike. It had been his eighth birthday. It was the one and only time he'd been in hospital as a patient. You take good health for granted and he'd been lucky, no doubt about it. That was one reason for taking part in the clinical trial: giving something back.

As he unpacked his overnight bag, he reminded himself of what he had told Melissa. There was virtually no risk. This was the last stage in a lengthy process. The therapy had been tested on mice and then on monkeys. Medical students took part in trials all the time.

He discovered a bar of chocolate that Melissa must have slipped in his bag that morning. He smiled: after all, he'd only be away from her for two nights. And with the money he was earning, they'd be able to have a holiday for the first time in ages.

There was a knock on the door. That would be Tom, who had signed up first and persuaded Ed to come along: a chance to revise for their finals. Ed often found himself agreeing to do things with Tom and then half-regretting it. On the face of it, they were an oddly matched pair. They'd first met when they had found themselves in adjacent rooms in their hall of residence. Ed was short and dark and thoughtful, and his idea of a good time was a concert at the Festival Hall or a foreign arthouse movie. Tom was a roaring extravert, a big burly blond who spent his weekends hurling himself round the rugby pitch. Ed wanted to specialize in psychiatry after he'd qualified. Tom planned to be a cardiac surgeon.

"So you persuaded Melissa to let you off the leash," Tom said, as they walked down the corridor to the ward.

"No, I'm wearing an electronic tag and she's put me under curfew."

The teasing had started after Ed and Melissa had announced that they were getting married after they qualified. There was something unkind about it, an implication that Ed had settled for Melissa too soon and could have done better. Ed had wanted to have it out with Tom, but Melissa had told him to chill out. She said, "Remember how Tom dropped everything to drive you home when your father was taken ill? And have you seen him with those kids in the paediatric ward? No, under all that bluster Tom's got a heart as big as a bucket. He's lonely. That's his problem."

"Lonely! He has a different girlfriend every term!"

"Exactly. We're the lucky ones to have found each other so soon. Tom would love to have a woman who cared enough to boss him around. He's jealous, that's all."

Ed had laughed. "Perhaps you're the one who should be a psychiatrist."

"No, no. GP training for me. Easier to fit round all those babies we're going to have."

Ed pretended to look doubtful. "I'm not so sure about that."

Melissa pursed her lips. "Think you might not be up to it?"

"Might be as well to get in some practice now?"

"Oh, I think so."

And she'd pulled him down onto the bed...

"Ed, Ed," Tom hissed.

Ed came to himself with a start.

They were in the ward now. Tom nudged Ed in the ribs and raised his eyebrows in the direction of the doctor who was conducting the trial.

She was a young Chinese woman with long black hair so straight that it might have been ironed. Ed caught his eye and shook his head as if to say "naughty-naughty". Tom grinned.

Ed stole a glance at the others: all male, all young. He recognized one of them as a fellow medical student whom he'd met at the chess club and nodded to him across the room. The others were probably students too.

Dr Chan's voice broke into his thoughts. "I'll be delivering the injections one at a time at half-hour intervals. That's in case there's an unfavourable reaction to the drug. It's highly unlikely, but we have to follow protocol." Dr Chan glanced at her clipboard and then at Ed. "I think we'll take you first. Ed, isn't it?"

He nodded and rolled up his sleeve. His mouth was dry and he was annoyed with himself for feeling a frisson of – what? Not anxiety exactly, more a shrinking back, a reluctance to go first. He reminded himself again that it was very, very rare for anything to go wrong. That was why it made headline news when something did.

When Dr Chan slid the needle into his arm, he had an idiotic impulse to grab his throat and roll his eyes, but of course he didn't and in fact no one was watching. A couple of the guys were chatting about the prospects of their football teams. Another was playing on his iPad. One was leafing through a copy of *New Scientist*.

As for Tom, he had equipped himself with a James Patterson novel.

Ed settled back on his bed. Now that he'd actually had the injection, he felt fine. Why on earth had he been so worried?

"What about revision?" he asked Tom. They'd been planning to go over things together.

Tom grinned. "Plenty of time for that later."

Ed shrugged. He propped himself up on the pillows and resolutely addressed himself to his revision notes. He was soon deep in endocrinology.

At one point Ed was aware of someone else being injected and later that it was Tom's turn.

He couldn't have said how much longer it was before he looked up, disturbed by something unexpected.

It was the sound of Tom's book hitting the floor.

"Tom?" Ed said.

Tom turned his head. He stared at Ed with his eyes narrowed. It was as though he had seen something in the distance and wasn't sure what it was.

A bleeper went off. Heads turned all over the ward. Dr Chan was standing by one of the other men, a syringe actually in her hand. She was about to inject a fourth subject. She dropped the syringe with a tinkle into a tray. She started over towards Tom.

"Tom!" Ed swung his legs off the bed. "What's the matter?"

Later, when Ed tried to recall what had happened next, the memories were disjointed and he couldn't even be sure what order they came in. He saw Dr Chan's face as she bent over Tom, serious, absorbed. Tom was struggling, trying to pull off the electrodes, to brush away the people who were crowding round his bed. Ed caught a glimpse of his face – it was not fear he saw, he thought afterwards, but bewilderment.

Another alarm went off.

There was the rasping sound of Tom trying to get his breath.

Then Ed and the other subjects were hustled out.

Two days later, when Ed got round to unpacking his backpack, he came across the James Patterson novel. He had no idea how it had got there.

He stared at it, weighing it in his hand as though he'd never seen a book before.

"Plenty of time for that later," he heard Tom saying.

But there wouldn't be plenty of time later. There wouldn't be any time at all. The long years of friendship that might have lain ahead had been wiped out, deleted.

Big, brash, wise-cracking Tom, who only a few days ago had been making bad jokes about carving people up, was lying in the hospital mortuary, awaiting his own post-mortem.

Chapter One

Two Years Later

The bed was rocking and someone had their elbow in Daniel's ribs.

He clung to his dream, but it was dissolving, slipping away. He knew only that he was young, everything in front of him, and a beloved woman was beside him. He tried to get back to her, but it was too late. He broke the surface of his sleep. Only the aura of the dream remained, a sense of being warm and cocooned, and yet there was something wistful about it too.

He wasn't as young as he had been in the dream, he knew that. He was thirty. But no, he wasn't. *I'm nearly forty*, he thought with a pang of regret. *How did that happen? How did I get to be this old?*

The bed *was* rocking, or it had been; it was just a very gentle motion now.

It came back to him. He was married to Rachel and the elbow in his ribs belonged to their four-year-old daughter, Chloe, who yet again had climbed in between them in the middle of the night. How could he have forgotten Chloe for a single second, even in a dream? And with that thought he was fully awake. He was on the boat. It was the wake from some passing cruiser that had rocked the bed. He eased himself up onto his elbow and looked at the clock: 7.00. They were on holiday. No need to get up yet.

On the other side of Chloe, squashed against the hull of the boat, Rachel murmured and shifted in her sleep. She turned over, pulling the duvet with her. He tugged it back, rearranged Chloe's sprawling limbs so all three of them lay like spoons in a drawer, and tried to settle back into sleep. But it was no good.

15

Gently, he disengaged himself and slipped out of bed. He pulled on a heavy woollen jumper over his pyjamas. He padded into the galley and put the kettle on. Who was the woman in the dream? It hadn't been Rachel. He felt vaguely guilty – but he wasn't responsible for his unconscious, he told himself. It didn't really *mean* anything. Just a bit of flotsam and jetsam tossed up to the surface. Just debris.

He got out the map to plan that day's journey. They had stretched the holiday out as long as they could, but they had to be back in Ely that evening. That still left plenty of time to meander back along the waterways.

The kettle switched itself off. He spooned ground coffee into the cafetière, and filled it up with boiling water, relishing the fragrance. He took his cup of coffee to the wheelhouse, shivering in the chill of a November morning. Mist was rising from the water. A startled moorhen paddled rapidly away.

He let himself have a few minutes before the demands of the day began, then he went back for his iPhone and brought it up on deck. The deal with Rachel was that he only switched it on once a day, and fair enough, they were trying to have a proper break. It wasn't as if anything urgent was likely to come up. He was a lawyer, yes, but not the kind whose clients were liable to need him at any hour of the day or night. Specializing in patents tends to be a nine to five thing.

When he switched it on he was surprised to see that it was clogged with text messages and voice mail and emails.

Most of them were from the office, but one phone number appeared increasingly and his heart gave a jolt. Dad. He had rung every quarter of an hour from ten the previous evening and the last call had been at one o'clock in the morning. The fact that he was still up at that hour wasn't in itself remarkable. Since Mum had died a few years ago, he had become more and more nocturnal. But what could be so urgent that he was ringing so late? Though of course if anything had happened to his father, he wouldn't be ringing himself.

Daniel listened to the most recent message. All it said was, "Ring me as soon as you get this, son, whatever time it is," but he heard the anxiety in his father's voice.

He returned the call.

His father picked up on the third ring. "Daniel!"

"What is it, Dad? What's the matter?"

There was a hesitation at the other end. "You haven't heard, then?"

"Heard what? Dad, what's going on?"

"It's Jennifer."

"Jennifer?" he echoed. It was the last thing he was expecting – that she'd be in touch with his father. "What did she want?"

"Not... it's not... she's not... you won't have been following the news. I know this is going to be a shock, son. She's dead. Jennifer's dead."

Dan groped for the bench that ran round the wheelhouse and lowered himself onto it. "How? What?"

"A car crash. Sunday evening. I saw it on a news website."

How many times had he told her that she was driving too fast? He felt that he had always known something like this would happen. At the same time it was incredible, fantastic... Jennifer dead... no...

"Was there another car involved?"

"It seems not. It had been raining. The road was wet. Looks as if she took a bend too fast. She came off the road and hit a tree."

There was a sound behind him. He turned to see Rachel climbing up through the hatch. She was wearing a heavy woollen dressing gown over her nightdress and her short hair was ruffled from sleep.

Her smile froze when she saw his face.

"Dan, what is it?"

"It's alright." He turned back to the phone and heard his father say, "Is that Rachel? Give her my love. And Chloe."

"I will, Dad. Thanks for letting me know."

"I didn't want you to hear about it from someone else – or see it on the news."

"Look, you did right. I'll ring you later, OK? Rachel sends her love too."

"What's happened?" Rachel said. "Is he alright?"

"He's fine." Daniel ran his hand over his unshaven chin. "He rang to tell me that Jennifer's been killed in a car crash." Even as he said the words, he thought that it couldn't really be true. This kind of thing didn't happen to people you actually knew. But then, didn't everyone think that?

Rachel stared at him.

He could see she was wondering what this would mean to them, to him and Rachel. He was wondering that, too. And the truth was that he didn't know what it meant. It wasn't something he could take in all at once. It was too big, too unlikely...

"A car crash..." Rachel said. "How?"

"She ran her car off the road."

Rachel came over to stand by his side. She slipped an arm around his waist.

The phone buzzed. Another call was coming in. It was from his secretary. He had forgotten about the backlog of calls from the office.

He answered the call. "Alison?"

"I thought I'd never get hold of you. Everyone's running around like headless chickens. Can you get into the office for ten?"

What had this to do with Jennifer? He couldn't make sense of it.

"Haven't you listened to my messages?" she said. "We had a call from Lyle Linstrum yesterday."

"It's not about Jennifer?"

Now it was her turn to sound bewildered. "Who's Jennifer? Daniel, Lyle Linstrum's flying in from Texas overnight. He'll be in the office at ten and it's you he wants to see. Mr O'Donnell

18

said I *had* to track you down." In as far as Daniel had a boss, it was O'Donnell, one of the senior partners. "Daniel, you *can* be there?"

"I'll ring you back, OK?" He looked at his watch. Amazingly, it was only 7.30. "Ten minutes max."

During the conversation Rachel had gone back inside.

Of course: Alison had only been working for the firm for a year. Even if she'd seen the news about Jennifer, there was no reason why she should have connected it with him. There was no question that Daniel would have to go into the office. And in practical terms getting back was no problem – a taxi would get him back to Ely in less than half an hour, which would leave him ample time to go home and get into a suit.

Rachel came back with a cup of coffee in her hand.

"That was Alison," he said. "They want me in the office. It's urgent."

"Had she heard about Jennifer?"

He shook his head. "A new client, an important one – if he throws business our way it'll be huge for the firm. He wants to see me in the office at ten."

She frowned, but he guessed that she was simply working out what it meant and what adjustments would need to be made to the day. It was a relief to be back on the solid ground of solving little problems and making practical arrangements.

"Would you be able to manage OK getting back to Ely?" he asked, though he knew that she would. They were at the Lazy Otter moorings at Stretham, only about five miles from Ely, and there weren't any locks. It was her boat – she'd been living on it when they first met – and she'd have no trouble managing it for that distance. But in this, his second marriage, he tried not to take things for granted.

She nodded, acknowledging his tact in phrasing it that way, and answered the question he'd really been asking. "I don't mind. It's the last day anyway."

"Chloe..."

"I'll tell her I'm promoting her to first mate. She'll be thrilled."

"I'll go and shave," he said.

"Daniel?"

He turned. "Yes?"

"Are you alright?"

"Yes... no..."

"Stupid question, really. It's bound to be a shock."

He shook his head, at a loss for words. That it should end like this. The golden girl – that was what he used to call her. How could someone so full of life just be gone, snuffed out in a moment of carelessness?

As he ducked his head under the hatch to go down to shave, vestiges of his dream came back to him: that beloved female presence; had it been Jennifer?

Chapter Two

Daniel locked the door of the little Regency house on Waterside, near the quayside where Rachel would later be bringing the boat to its winter mooring.

On his way back to Ely in the taxi he had tried to turn his thoughts to the coming meeting with Lyle Linstrum, but had found himself obsessively combing the internet for more information about Jennifer's accident. There wasn't much more than his dad had told him.

As he headed up the hill towards the Market Place, he glanced at his watch. He'd be meeting Linstrum in quarter of an hour.

The towers of Ely Cathedral came into view and Daniel found himself wondering where Jennifer's funeral would be held. Not that he'd be there, but – there'd have to be an inquest, wouldn't there, first? And a post-mortem. He had a flash of memory: Jennifer naked, getting into bed, and now that body was lying in a mortuary somewhere, and – his thoughts swerved away. A wave of dizziness came over him and dark spots appeared before his eyes. He stopped abruptly and a man bumped into him. The man scowled; Daniel muttered an apology. A few deep breaths and he was alright again. He continued up the hill, more slowly this time.

Ely was a sleepy little market town, remarkable only for its cathedral, and on the face of it seemed a strange place for a firm of patent lawyers. But it was very well placed for the phenomenon that was known as Silicon Fen or the Cambridge Cluster, one of the most important technology centres in Europe. The area was home to over a thousand high-tech businesses focusing on software, electronics and biotechnology, many of them with connections to Cambridge University. It was a magnet for venture capitalists, big consultancy firms, bankers – and lawyers.

As Daniel walked into his secretary's office he was struck by the scent of lilies, a smell he had always disliked. Today it made him feel nauseous. Alison was arranging a huge sheaf of them mixed with pink and white roses in a vase on her desk.

She looked up. "He's already here, drinking coffee in your office."

"And those?" Daniel nodded at the flowers.

She nodded. "By way of an apology. He was, well, let's say he was rather pressing on the phone yesterday."

Daniel raised his eyebrows. The look she gave him acknowledged that, yes, it was a cheesy gesture, but on the other hand, the flowers were gorgeous.

He squared his shoulders, took a deep breath and opened the door to his office.

Linstrum was sitting in an easy chair by the coffee table, a cup of coffee in his hand. He unfolded himself and stood up. He was long and lean with a leathery face and hair that clustered on the top of his head with a little quiff that made Daniel think of Tintin. Some famous people look shorter in the flesh; Linstrum looked taller. He had to be at least six foot four, and the cowboy boots added to his height. Daniel recalled a photo of him in the *Financial Times* rounding up steers on his ranch in Texas. Linstrum liked to present himself as a latter-day cowboy and he dressed the part, inviting jokes about John Wayne and Clint Eastwood. But there was a hell of a lot more to him than a bolo tie and a pair of cowboy boots.

Linstrum held out his hand. "Sorry to haul you in off your vacation."

Daniel nodded. He didn't make the mistake of saying that it didn't matter.

They shook hands. Linstrum's grip was firm to the point of discomfort. His hand was hard and calloused.

Daniel gestured for Linstrum to sit down again and took a seat opposite him.

"OK. Let me get straight down to business," Linstrum said. "I need a lab book report in a hurry."

"When you say 'in a hurry'?"

"I've got an interference proceeding in a little over two weeks and disclosure before that. Needless to say I'm willing to pay whatever it takes to make this happen."

Two weeks! That would mean putting everything else on hold, offloading work onto other people. And even then it would be tough. Was it even possible?

"Tell me more."

"A few years ago, Honor Masterman was principal investigator for a postdoc who stumbled across a discovery that had huge potential for a therapy to combat obesity. The university started up a company to manage it – that was Calliope Biotech – but they just didn't have the resources to develop the therapy and I bought them out. It was all looking great, but then – disaster."

Daniel remembered that. The potential of the therapy had made front page news. And so had what happened next. Six healthy young men go into a clinical trial and one of them ends up dead.

"I had sleepless nights over what happened," Linstrum said. "Still do, truth to tell."

Details of the therapy were coming back to Daniel. "I seem to recall it worked by using an antibody designed to target fat cells?"

"Yup, that's right. We attached a cytotoxic payload to the antibody."

"A virus that kills fat cells? Remind me what went wrong."

"The antibody was designed to home in on the fat cells by identifying a specific marker on the surface of the cells. What we didn't know – and couldn't have known – was that a tiny subset of people express this marker on their heart cells as well as their fat cells. And that was the case with Tom Manners." Linstrum's face was sombre. "Poor guy. Hell, we'd tried it on mice, we'd tried it on monkeys, and it had worked just fine."

They were silent.

Linstrum said, "I don't need to tell you what an effective therapy would mean. An estimated 64 per cent of Americans are overweight or obese and here in the UK you're catching up fast. It's a leading cause of premature death in the developed world – 336 million cases of Type 2 diabetes worldwide, not to mention heart disease, cancer... They could all be cut at a stroke, and in commercial terms..."

Yes, in commercial terms the sky was the limit.

Linstrum went on. "The enquiry found that the trial was carried out properly and concluded that the mishap couldn't have been foreseen. So, with a therapy like this," he spread his hands, "where the fundamental molecular structure is sound..."

Yes, with a therapy like that, even a death wouldn't halt its development. It was just too important, too much was at stake, so many lives could potentially be saved.

"We went back to the drawing board. We're pursuing two lines of research: a test to screen out the vulnerable subset who have that marker on their heart cells, and a way to identify a different marker. We're fighting on both fronts, and things were going just fine until a few weeks ago when we were given notice that another US company intended to challenge our patent for the antibody. They're claiming that someone in one of their labs got there first."

Daniel let out a long, low whistle.

In Europe, including the UK, it was first past the post. The winner was the one who got to the Patent Office and filed their papers first. In the US it was the person who actually made the invention first who was entitled to the patent. That was set to change in a couple of years. The US was planning to adopt the European system, but for now the principle still held. And

Linstrum's company, Calliope Biotech, had its headquarters in the US, so they were subject to US patent law.

"Yeah, that's right," Linstrum said grimly. "I've sunk all I've got into this. And I'm not the only one. I've drawn heavily on venture capital, and my backers are riding me hard. They're getting jittery. I need to raise more funds and this couldn't have come at a worse time. And that's why I'm here. I want you to go through our guy's lab books."

Daniel frowned. There was something that didn't stack up here. Lawyers should have been trawling through the lab books weeks ago to establish the exact date that the discovery had been made. Why was Daniel coming in so late in the day? There could be only one answer.

"You must have had someone else working on it," Daniel concluded.

"Oh, for sure," Linstrum said. "I should have mentioned that earlier. We had Jennifer Blunt."

Daniel stared at him.

Linstrum went on. "Terrible thing, losing her like that. A car crash. It's shaken us all up. If I were a superstitious guy, I might think there was a hex on this project."

He broke off, looked closely at Daniel. "You don't look so good. I guess you must have known her? It's a small world in your line of work. Don't tell me you hadn't heard?"

Daniel's head was swimming. "I'd heard." He leaned forward and put his head between his hands.

"Hey, are you OK?"

Daniel took a deep breath and straightened up. He poured himself a glass of water.

"She was a friend?" Linstrum asked.

"Not exactly. She was my ex-wife."

"Oh gee, that's tough. I'm sorry."

"It won't be a problem," Daniel said, answering the unspoken question. "I've remarried and that's all in the past."

"So you'll take the job?"

"I'll have to clear it with my colleagues."

There was really no chance that they'd want to turn down this kind of work and Linstrum knew that too. He reached over and they shook hands again.

Daniel expected him to leave, but instead he sat in thought for a few moments.

"Something I'd better tell you," he said. "Jennifer thought there was something wrong somewhere."

"Can you be more specific?"

"No, dammit, I can't. She didn't want to talk about it on the phone or in her office. We planned to meet at her house in Cambridge. She was on the way there when she died."

Chapter Three

"No, Mummy, no. Please, Mummy!"

Chloe was sitting on her bed in her nightie with her arms around her legs. Her face was scrunched up, tears were welling in her eyes.

Rachel was sitting next to her, the needle in her hand. Daniel sat on the other side.

"Come here, little chicken," he said. Gently he unwrapped Chloe's arms and lifted her onto his lap so that she was sitting sideways. Daniel's heart contracted at the sight of her spindly legs and knobbly little knees. Was there anything more vulnerable and touching than a little girl's legs?

Chloe turned her face into Daniel's shoulder. She knew there was no escaping it and she didn't resist as Rachel swabbed her thigh. Her acquiescence hurt him more than her protest. Chloe had been diagnosed with Diamond-Blackfan anaemia at birth. Her body could not make red blood cells. She needed blood transfusions every three or four weeks and this had the side effect of laying down too much iron in her body, especially in the heart and liver. If it were allowed to build up, it would eventually kill her. Five times a week she had to have subcutaneous infusions to shift the iron deposits. The needle went into her leg or waist and an infusion pump was attached to deliver the therapy overnight.

When the needle went in, Chloe flinched and gave a little moan. Daniel tightened his grip on her. Then it was over and she relaxed against him. Rachel taped the infusion pump to her thigh.

"All over now," Daniel said. "Story time."

Rachel leaned over to kiss the child goodnight, but Chloe

shook her head and burrowed deeper into Daniel's shoulder, rejecting the parent who had hurt her.

Rachel kissed the back of her head. "Night, night, sweetie-pie," she said. As she straightened up, Daniel saw the pain in her eyes. He'd had this treatment, too, and it was part of the reason why they took it in turns to deal with the infusion. It wouldn't be fair or good for Chloe for just one parent to bear the brunt of it. Bad cop, good cop, was how he thought of it.

Rachel went off down the stairs.

Daniel swept Chloe's hair back and kissed her forehead. "What'll it be?" he asked, already knowing the answer.

"Rumpy, tilt, skin," she said, separating out the syllables.

"Rumpelstiltskin it is. Hop into bed, then." He reached over to the bookcase and pulled down the big pink book of illustrated fairy stories. The book fell open at the familiar page.

Chloe snuggled under her duvet and put her thumb in her mouth. Daniel propped himself up on a pillow beside her and she leaned against him. She adored fairy tales. In fact, she adored fairies, full stop. They decorated every possible surface: her duvet cover, her nightdress, even her wellingtons. For Daniel it was all part of having a little girl, and he relished her femininity. Rachel found it all a bit much. He had tried to console her by pointing out that Chloe was keen on Lego too and they hadn't started to make that in pink yet. Rachel had snorted. "Don't you believe it! It's the latest thing. Chloe just doesn't know it yet."

The pink-shaded bedside lamp cast a soft light and Daniel began to feel sleepy as he read the story of the little man who turned straw into gold for the miller's daughter and the terrible price he tried to exact, claiming her first-born child unless she could guess his name. The story exerted a curious charm over him, too. Was it something to do with the repetition, the way everything had to happen three times? And he liked the way it ended with the plucky girl turning the tables: "The little man came in, and asked, 'Now, mistress queen, what is my name?'

At first she said, 'Is your name Conrad?' 'No.' 'Is your name Harry?' 'No.' 'Perhaps your name is Rumpelstiltskin?' 'The devil has told you that,' cried the little man, and in his anger he plunged his right foot so deep into the earth that his whole leg went in, and then in rage he pulled at his left leg so hard with both hands that he tore himself in two."

He had wondered if this was too much for Chloe, whether he ought to tone it down a bit, but Rachel said no, she thought it was a mistake to censor everything. And it was true that Chloe didn't seem at all disturbed by it. In fact, it was her favourite story.

He looked down at Chloe. Her thumb had dropped from her mouth. She was asleep.

Carefully, he disengaged himself. He pulled the duvet up and tucked it round her.

He sat down in the little nursing chair that had belonged to his grandmother and was now Chloe's. Above him, a mobile of floating fairies shifted lazily in the heat from the bedside lamp.

At intervals during the day he had managed to put Jennifer to the back of his mind, only to be ambushed all over again, brought up short by the stark fact: he would never see or speak to her again. Had it always been there, then, unacknowledged, hidden even from himself, the hope that their story hadn't really ended, in spite of all the evidence to the contrary?

It seemed no time at all since he had first met her at a postgraduate seminar. She had given a paper and he could see her now – totally absorbed – so absorbed that she had flung out an arm and knocked her papers all over the floor. He got down on his hands and knees to pick them up for her and she'd thanked him, blushing and laughing. She had the most amazing blue eyes. When the seminar was over, they had walked out together, gone for a coffee, and then a meal. They couldn't stop talking. They had spent the night together, and the next, and the one after that. Six months later they got married. They had been so young, so unblemished, untouched by life...

Perhaps if she hadn't dropped the papers, he wouldn't have fallen in love with her. The entire course of their lives was decided that day. Only one thing has to be different for everything to be different. If he had known how it would turn out, would he have let someone else pick them up?

"Dan, Dan?" Rachel was calling softly up the stairs.

"OK, I'm coming."

He got up and went down.

Rachel was sitting on the sofa, working on the quilt she was making. Her hands were never idle.

There were two gin and tonics on the coffee table in front of her.

She gestured towards them. "I thought we'd need these." He sank down beside her and reached for his glass.

He took a gulp. "You couldn't be more right."

"It was on the news. They said there's a child," Rachel said.

Daniel knew that. A few months ago he had glimpsed Jennifer at Cambridge station, getting off a London train. In the small world of Cambridge and Ely, it was hard to avoid someone completely. He didn't think Jennifer had seen him and he hadn't mentioned it to Rachel.

In most marriages there are things that by common, unspoken assent are not discussed. They had never really talked much about Jennifer. When Daniel first met Rachel, he had been living alone in the little house near the quay where he had moved after Jennifer had left him. He had still been too raw to tell her more than the bare outline of what had happened. And Rachel hadn't probed. Later it might have helped to talk about it, but he had sensed her reluctance, her jealousy even.

Daniel cleared his throat. "A funny thing happened. Lyle Linstrum, the man who I went in to meet? The case he wants me to take over – it was Jennifer's."

"It was Jennifer's?" Rachel echoed. "You mean – "

"She was in the middle of a very important case to do with a patent for an obesity therapy."

In the silence that followed he could hear the tick, tick of the bubbles in the gin and tonic.

Rachel put her quilt aside. She turned in her seat and looked at him. She pushed her glasses up her nose, a characteristic gesture that told him she was disturbed.

"I've said yes," he admitted.

Rachel thought about it. "Are you sure you're OK with this, Dan? Wouldn't it be better if someone else did it?"

"No one else specializes in this particular area. I can't justify turning it down. It's too important for the firm." He turned to her and took her hand. It lay inert in his. "Look, love, when all's said and done, it's just a job, like any other."

There was a sound behind them. Chloe was on the stairs, her eyes drowsy, her old cloth rabbit trailing from her hand. "Mummy..."

Rachel got to her feet. She knew and Daniel knew that it was the first of many reappearances and that she'd spend most of the night in bed with them.

She went across and picked Chloe up. "Come on, little monkey." She hoisted her onto her hip and Chloe's arms went round her neck. Rachel took her upstairs.

Daniel got up, went to the window, and parted the curtains. If he looked to the left he could just see the edge of the moorings and the gleam of lights on the water. He swirled the gin round in his glass so that the ice cubes clinked.

He'd been disingenuous, he knew that. How could it be a job like any other, when Jennifer was involved? What he'd said was true: it was a huge thing for the firm, but that wasn't the only reason. He felt drawn to the case, compelled to pick up where Jennifer had left off. There had seemed to be an inevitability to it, a rightness to it that he couldn't explain. He just knew that he had to do it.

He heard Rachel's footsteps on the stairs. He turned and

watched her pick up her glass. She walked over and joined him at the window.

She said, "I'm having lunch tomorrow with Katie Flanagan."

It was his turn to demur. "I hope you haven't taken on too much there."

All the same, he was relieved. This meant that for now she'd dropped the question of the case. A fortnight ago, Rachel had joined the board of a charity that raised money for research into childhood blood disorders and this lunch was part of her effort to get up to speed.

She shook her head. "Better to be doing something, anything."

He nodded. They had to fight on, had to believe there was hope of a cure.

"And it makes sense for me to be the one to go, now she's moved to that lab near Ely."

There had been a serious setback a month or so ago. Professor Goring, the principal investigator for the research the charity were sponsoring, had collapsed and died. The lab he had run was broken up, leaving Katie Flanagan, the sole researcher on the project, without a home – and this with only a few months of her two-year grant still to run. A place had been found for her in Professor Masterman's lab; the same one, Daniel now realized, where the obesity research was being carried out.

He reached for Rachel's hand and twined his fingers in hers. She squeezed back. She had strong supple fingers – her work saw to that.

"Better to light a candle than to curse the darkness," she said.

That was Rachel all over; she was not one to sit around and brood. She was a doer, so intensely practical, and he loved her for it.

He leaned forward and pressed his lips to hers, tasting the sweetness of the gin on them. "Let's have an early night," he said.

Chapter Four

"It's a real pity you didn't get a better result with the western blot," Paul said. "Something we could publish."

Katie was sitting beside him at his desk in his consulting room at the hospital. Her lab book was open in front of them. She'd come in early so that he could fit her in before his nine o'clock clinic. And she'd been in the lab even earlier.

"The band's in the right place," she pointed out.

"It's just too faint. I'd hoped you were on the verge of a breakthrough here. You'll try again, of course. You've got enough antibody?"

Paul O'Sullivan was tall and gangly with big hands, had to be in his early forties to have got to this position, though the short, cropped hair and fashionable, heavy-framed glasses made him look younger. On the filing cabinet was a school photo of two little boys, one of them with a gap-toothed smile. Did parents find that reassuring, Katie wondered, knowing that he had children of his own?

He was a consultant in paediatric blood disorders – and a full professor too, meaning that he had reached the top of the ladder in not just one, but two spheres, the clinical and the academic. To do that it wasn't enough to be exceptionally able; you had to be exceptionally driven too, and driven people could be difficult people. She hadn't made her mind up about him yet. This was only her second meeting with him.

"I *am* on the verge of a breakthrough," she said. "There's enough to run it a couple of times if necessary. I'm in the middle of doing that right now."

He turned the pages of the lab book, initialling pages as he went.

She wasn't going to tell him that she'd made a mess of it the first time round and had had to start again. It would be a long time since he'd done any lab work – if he ever had – and he'd have forgotten how easily things could go wrong. Yesterday she put her starter culture into the flask and it had spent the whole night in the shaking incubator. This morning she'd been able to tell just by looking at it that it hadn't worked. The broth should have been dense and cloudy with E.coli, but it was just as clear as when she'd put it in. It was a simple enough procedure – a first-year biology student could do it – and she'd done it herself hundreds of times. She didn't understand what had gone wrong. This particular batch of E.coli was resistant to ampicillin, so that was the antibiotic that she'd put in the broth to kill the other bugs, the ones that she didn't want to grow. Had she picked up the wrong bottle, put the wrong antibiotic in? Or had she forgotten to put it in altogether?

Paul nodded, closed the book, and handed it to her.

"We're running out of time and money. Looks like it'll be down to the wire on this one."

As if she didn't already know that. Still, at least he'd said "we". Perhaps he was OK after all.

"Let me know what happens when you run it again," he said.

"Of course."

"Talk to me before you write it up." He wasn't quite meeting her eye.

She wasn't sure that she'd understood what he was saying.

He glanced at his watch and she saw that the meeting was over. His clinic was about to start.

She got up to leave.

He said, "Did you arrange to meet – what's her name?"

"Rachel Marchmont. Yes, I'm having lunch with her today."

"Good. It's important to keep the sponsors happy."

She went out through the waiting room. There were clusters of people: children with their mothers, who had often brought along their own mother for moral support, and sometimes Dad was there too. Families came from all over the country to see him.

Their eyes followed her. They were wondering who she was and whether she was someone that mattered. When they took in her jeans and T-shirt and scruffy shoes, they lost interest. They weren't to know that she was the person who might find a cure for the disease that afflicted their child – if she could only get her act together and stop making silly mistakes.

A lot was riding on this for her. She was nearing the end of the life-cycle of a postdoctoral researcher. However much you loved bench work you couldn't go on doing it indefinitely, because as you got older and more experienced, you became more expensive, *too* expensive. At the most you had three or four cycles of grants of two or three years before you had to try for some kind of permanent post: a lectureship, maybe – though those were very hard to come by – perhaps science writing or patent work. What she really wanted to do was become a principal investigator herself, applying for her own grants and supervising her own postdocs. She could kiss goodbye to that if she didn't make a success of this project.

She had a cup of tea and a bacon sandwich in the hospital café. Then she drove back towards Ely across the Fens. The fields had been ploughed, ready for their winter crops, and pigeons pecked the rich dark earth.

She pondered over what Paul had said. Surely he couldn't have been suggesting that if the result wasn't good enough, she shouldn't write it up? She replayed the conversation in her head. He hadn't come right out and said it. But then he wouldn't. Because what he was suggesting, if he *was* suggesting it, would be the equivalent of falsifying research results, even if it were just by omission.

Of course, Big Pharma did that all the time. A drug company might run four different drug tests. If only one of the four was positive, that was the one they would publish. They would quietly bury the others and that was perfectly legal. They were under no obligation to make the results public. When Katie had first learned about this as an undergraduate she had been incredulous and, as a scientist, deeply affronted. She still felt exactly the same. But even if she hadn't felt like that, for her the rules were different. She wasn't allowed to ignore inconvenient results and Paul knew that. If she failed to record an experiment that went against her earlier findings, and she was found out, it would be career death. In this game, she had the most to lose. But it *was* frustrating. The procedure *did* work. It was just the final piece of evidence that was missing.

She had to pull it off next time, that was all there was to it. She couldn't afford to be making mistakes at this late stage. Paul was right: she was running out of both time and money. And now she'd have to waste some of that precious time sweet-talking one of the sponsors.

She thought of Michael, her old supervisor, and tears pricked her eyes. He hadn't been just her principal investigator; he'd been a friend and mentor. A month ago he had been cooking roast chicken for his wife and teenage son in the kitchen of his house off Parker's Piece. He had just sat down at the table and was reaching for the carving knife. "Now who wants..." He'd stopped in mid-sentence and his wife looked up from the bottle of wine she was opening. Later she told Katie that she actually saw the light leave his eyes. His son caught him as he slumped sideways. A massive heart attack. It had come completely out of the blue. He was only fifty-six.

She could still hardly believe he had gone.

His death had left her orphaned professionally. Most researchers were part of a team, but Katie was working on her own, funded by a charity, and she was left in the lurch when Michael died. After a couple of weeks of uncertainty, she'd had a lucky break. Lyle Linstrum was the father of one of her best friends and he had come to the rescue. He'd pulled some strings and she'd been offered a bench in Professor Masterman's lab.

It was on the outskirts of Ely, miles away from her old lab in the centre of Cambridge. But on the plus side the building was only a few years old and the facilities second to none.

I'll do it, Michael, she promised, as she drove into the lab car park. *I'll crack it. I'll be the one to find a cure for Diamond-Blackfan anaemia and it'll be thanks to you.*

It was only when she got back to the lab that she realized she hadn't got her lab book.

Chapter Five

The chisel slipped and bright beads of blood sprang up on the back of Rachel's hand.

"Oh, damn!"

She grabbed a handful of tissues, pressed them onto the wound and walked over to the sink. She turned on the cold tap and let the water run over her hand, washing the blood away. Just a scrape, luckily. She got the first-aid kit, cleaned the wound, and put a long strip of Elastoplast on it. She couldn't remember the last time she had had an accident like this. She was normally so careful.

She went back to her workbench. No blood on the trumpet she was carving, thank God. She ran her hand over the dark oak, stroking it as you'd stroke the fur of an animal. This was the sort of job she loved, restoring two baroque angels that belonged to the organ case of a church out in the Fens. They had been found stored away in the loft of the church hall, battered, dismembered, and covered in treacly brown paint. One of them was missing a wing and one a trumpet. She had stripped away the paint and now she was doing the part she liked best: making good the damaged or missing pieces. It was at times like this that she felt close to the original craftsman. Her aim was to add her voice to his: to produce something so much in the spirit of the original that only another woodworker would know the difference.

She spent three or four mornings a week in her studio while Chloe was at her playgroup. Their lovely GP had persuaded her not to give up work altogether. Chloe should have as normal a life as possible. "It won't do Chloe any good to have you anxiously brooding over her the whole time. She needs other children and you need to have something else in your life." Daniel had thought that, too.

Her studio had become a refuge, somewhere to escape from her preoccupation with the relentless round of blood transfusions and overnight infusions that kept Chloe alive. Here she could lose herself in the work, her hands busy, her senses fed by the feel and smell of the wood.

But today she just couldn't settle. She decided to knock off for the day.

She had about forty minutes before she had to set off to meet Katie Flanagan. She quickly tidied the studio and put on her good coat and her favourite scarf: yellow chiffon with swirling organic shapes in crimson and black and orange. It made her think of paintings by Matisse. She was already wearing her one pair of smart trousers. As a board member of a charity supporting research into Diamond-Blackfan anaemia she felt she had something to live up to. And she was nervous about meeting this very clever young woman. Her own scientific education had stopped with GCSE biology.

She locked up and set off up Back Hill. She was lucky to have her studio so close to the centre of Ely, and only five minutes' walk from their house on Quayside.

The cathedral tower came into view, and just the sight of it brought a sense of calm. This had been a place of prayer and worship for 1,300 years, and the thought of that always made the hair rise on the back of her neck. Over the centuries so many people had gone there with their problems and their sorrows and found consolation, and today she was following in their footsteps.

As she turned the corner into The Gallery, a blast of cold air hit her full-on. She gasped and hunched her shoulders. It was like having icy water dripped down your neck. These Fenland winds: however well you wrapped up, they somehow worked their way under your clothes. She hurried on past the King's School and the Bishop's House. She reached Minster

Place and turned right into the shelter of the cavernous porch of the cathedral.

Her footsteps echoed on the stone floor. She lifted the iron latch of the small oak door set in the larger one, and pushed it open.

She passed the café and the gift shop and reached the ticket desk. As a resident of Ely she had a pass that allowed her in free, but she didn't need to show it. The woman on duty smiled and waved her on. Rachel came so often – once a week at least – that they all knew her.

The nave stretched ahead, immensely long and narrow, the pillars soaring to a breathtaking height. Beyond was the dark tracery of the screen, the dimness of the choir, the golden glow of the altar, and far away at the very end of the cathedral, a glimmer of stained glass. It was a sight that Rachel usually rejoiced in. The glorious space made her feel at once very small and yet infinitely cherished. But today as she made her way down the centre of the nave, the clip-clop of her shoes loud in the stillness, her thoughts churning, she was scarcely aware of her surroundings.

Rachel had never met Jennifer, had never even seen her, but she knew what she looked like. A few months ago she had picked one of Daniel's books off the shelf and a photo had dropped out: a snapshot of the young couple outside a register office. As she scrutinized it, her first feeling was one of relief. Jennifer wasn't as beautiful as she had imagined. Her second thought was how very young they were. Daniel's face was so open, so innocent, so undefended. The man she knew had been approaching middle-age when she met him, a little worn, more than a little guarded. She'd sensed how terribly he had been hurt.

She couldn't understand Daniel wanting to take on the case. It wasn't fair, the way Jennifer had come back into Daniel's life – into *their* lives. It was as if she had crooked her little finger and he had come running. A flash of anger was followed instantly by a pang of guilt. No one deserved to die so young and in such a terrible way, leaving a child behind.

She had reached the transept underneath the octagonal tower. Without pausing to look up, she turned left and made her way down the dark passage that led off the transept and, footsteps echoing, emerged into the airy space of the Lady Chapel with its high vaulted ceiling. There seemed to be as much glass as stone and marble so that even on the dimmest days the room was full of light. Once the Lady Chapel had glowed with colour, but during the Reformation, the windows had been smashed, the pedestals emptied of their saints, and the delicately carved figures defaced.

Rachel sat down on one of the stone seats set in niches around the wall. A couple of tourists, a middle-aged couple with guide book and camera, were wandering around, but soon they left and Rachel had the place to herself. She let the silence settle around her. She gazed up at the statue of the Virgin Mary. Her arms were raised in exultation, and golden hair flowed down her back. She wore a dress of a wonderful lapis lazuli blue with a golden girdle. Rachel had been raised as a Quaker, but over the last few years she had grown to understand the Catholic veneration of the Virgin. If anyone could understand the joy and pain of motherhood, it had to be her.

Chloe had been three months old when she was diagnosed as severely anaemic. When she didn't respond to treatment, they carried out a battery of tests, and at nine months Chloe was diagnosed with Diamond-Blackfan anaemia. Wandering around Ely in a daze of misery with Chloe asleep in her pushchair, Rachel had gone into the cathedral and found herself in the Lady Chapel. She read the placard describing its desecration: *It is a place of brokenness, reminding us of our broken world.* She had lit a candle for Chloe.

The next few months had been a roller-coaster ride of hopes raised and dashed, and Rachel had returned to the Lady Chapel many times. Yes, Chloe had Diamond-Blackfan anaemia, but a bone marrow transplant might offer a cure. Yes, Rachel or Dan might be a suitable match but, no, it turned out that they weren't. But yes, the chances of finding an unrelated donor were high. Ah, but no, they weren't because Chloe had a rare tissue type that she had inherited from Dan, and there were no matches on the register of bone marrow donors.

Someone was practising on the organ. Trills and runs of notes floated into the Lady Chapel.

Daniel is married to me now, Rachel thought, *and that's all that matters*. The birth of Chloe had turned them into a family and that was something he had never had with Jennifer. Jennifer had been a mistake and the way that she had betrayed Daniel showed that.

Rachel got up and went over to where the candles were kept. She lit a candle for Chloe and stuck it upright in the stone bowl of sand. She gazed into the flame and lost herself for a few moments in a wordless prayer for Chloe. Then she did put into words her prayer that God would be with everyone who was trying to find a cure for Diamond-Blackfan anaemia, in particular Katie Flanagan. Today she hesitated, then she lit another candle. She didn't know the name of the little boy who was now motherless, but she could still pray for him. Silently she told Jennifer that she was sorry and would pray for her soul.

The light in the chapel changed. A cloud must have passed over the sun. Rachel glanced at her watch. If she didn't hurry, she would be late for her meeting with Katie Flanagan.

Chapter Six

Daniel had spent the morning clearing his desk, handing over cases to colleagues, and now his secretary had instructions not to let any calls through unless they were about the new case. The papers relating to it were brought over by Jennifer's secretary. Daniel promised to call Linstrum at the end of the day. By then he would have reviewed Jennifer's progress and he'd be able to give a preliminary report on how long the remaining work was likely to take.

One thing: he could trust her to have done a good job. Good as Daniel knew he was, Jennifer had been even better.

Daniel's first degree was in Biological Sciences. He'd gone on to do an MSc in Molecular Genetics, but he'd decided against a career in research. Life in the lab wasn't for him, and the long-term prospects were precarious even for an outstanding student – which he wasn't. Turned out, though, that he was a first-rate lawyer. Patent law suited him perfectly. He was endlessly fascinated by other people's research and he liked the rigour of the law, the way even the most complex questions were in the end settled according to criteria that could be reasoned out and justified.

Much of Jennifer's report had come on memory sticks, but there was also a folder of handwritten notes. The sight of Jennifer's handwriting, the knowledge that she had touched these papers, unsettled him. For years they had worked for the same firm, but six months before the break-up Jennifer had moved on. It had seemed reasonable at the time: the rival firm had held out the prospect of a partnership and she did, in fact, become a partner soon afterwards.

Later Daniel wondered if she hadn't already been planning

to leave him. What made it worse was that Nick was a close friend, and an old one: he had been at school with Daniel. He was married, too, and the two childless couples had often socialized. When Daniel found out about the affair, Jennifer said, "You must have guessed that something was wrong," but he hadn't. It was true that they hadn't made love as much lately, but they were both very busy, and he thought... But it didn't matter what he thought. Nothing had prepared him for the pain that swept over him, the sheer incredulity that this could be happening, the sleepless nights that went on for months. There were moments when he thought he was going mad, other moments when he thought that surely she would change her mind and tell him that it was all a mistake. He would have had her back in a heartbeat.

But eventually he understood that she wasn't coming back and that a clean break was the best thing. He knew that she was living with Nick in Newnham in Cambridge, and after a while a casual acquaintance happened to mention that they had a son. By then he was with Rachel and she was pregnant with Chloe...

He came to himself and found that his hands were clenched. Ten minutes had passed. He shook his head. He didn't have time for this.

Jennifer's secretary had prepared a checklist of the documents and PDF files that she had handed over. He worked his way down it, ticking off each item as he located it.

Everything seemed to be present and correct, and yet... He frowned. There was something not quite right here.

He turned to the pile of lab books and checked the dates on them. Yes, there was a gap in the sequence. One of them was missing. He ran his finger down the checklist: it wasn't on there either.

He rang through to Alison and asked her to call Jennifer's secretary and track down the missing lab book.

He was deep into his preliminary reading when Alison

buzzed through to say that Jennifer's secretary had checked and she couldn't find it.

Daniel sat back and thought it over. A missing lab book would really put a spanner in the works. But maybe it had been returned to the lab for some reason.

He rang Honor Masterman. She was pleased to hear from him, said she was glad he was picking up the ball, but when she heard about the lab book, her voice grew serious.

"Which one is it, which dates?" she asked.

When he told her, she said straightaway, "We haven't got it. And I can be sure about that because I know which one it is. It covers a key period."

They were both silent for a moment or two.

Daniel said, "Most likely it'll still come to light. But just in case, can you ask your researcher, what's his name..." He shuffled his papers. "Orville, Will Orville, if he kept other notes?"

"I don't think he did, but I will, of course."

Daniel put the phone down, thoughtfully. It wasn't unknown for lab books to get lost. They weren't supposed to leave the lab, but scientists were as fallible as anyone else. They took work home with them, they left their briefcases in the pub or in unlocked cars. But he was surprised that Jennifer should have been careless. She had been as meticulous in her professional life as she was messy at home.

No point in panicking, he told himself. It might yet turn up at Jennifer's office. If it wasn't there and Orville hadn't kept notes, there might be a technician with a lab book that covered the period in question. But it was bound to slow things down just when time was of the essence. He decided that with a problem of this magnitude, Linstrum ought to know as soon as possible. At the very least he could put a rocket under Jennifer's staff and get them to search their offices from top to bottom.

Daniel had just reached for the phone when Alison buzzed through.

"I've got Bryony on the line – she's Jennifer Blunt's secretary. I think you'd better hear what she has to say."

There was a click and Bryony said, "Mr Marchmont? I've had an idea. She might have taken the lab book home – she did work at weekends sometimes if there was a real rush on. There are some other papers missing and I think that's where they might be."

Of course. Why hadn't he thought of that?

"You're going to go and look?" he asked.

"I've got a spare key – she kept one in the office. I could meet you there, if you like."

He hesitated. What if Nick was there?

As if she'd read his mind, she said, "I've checked with her husband and it's OK. Actually, he's not living there. They separated a month or two ago."

"Fine. I can meet you there in three-quarters of an hour." As Daniel put down the phone, he felt a surge of... what? Satisfaction? Pleasure, even? So it hadn't worked out. *Good! Serves him right.* Then it occurred to him that maybe this time it was Jennifer who had been dumped. Even better.

Somehow the house in Newnham – a modern one in a small development – wasn't what Daniel had expected. Of course, being Jennifer's, it wasn't just any modern house, but an interesting, even quirky one, probably designed by some well-known architect. There were six of them, all slightly different. In the middle of the day, the only sign of life in the cul-de-sac was a woman sweeping up leaves in the garden next door. She'd lifted her head to glance at them as they arrived.

Bryony let them in. He had picked her up on his way there. He had expected her to be young, maybe because of her name, but she was middle-aged, fifty at least. She was carefully made up, but that didn't disguise the fact that she had been crying. Yes, this was exactly the kind of secretary Jennifer would have picked. He remembered her ability to surround herself with reliable people who would support her and pick up the slack. He had been one of them once.

"The study's over there," Bryony said, gesturing to a room off the hall. "I came round and did some work here when she was on maternity leave."

They went in. Bryony made straight for a desk with papers stacked neatly on it.

"Ah," she said, picking something up.

Daniel followed her eagerly. "Is that the lab book?"

"Oh, sorry, no. It's something else that I've been looking for."

Together they examined everything on the desk and searched the drawers. Daniel found some notes that related to the case, but no lab book.

"It might be somewhere else in the house," he said.

It was one of those grey overcast November days. Bryony switched on the lights as they went into the kitchen.

The place was heroically messy. Daniel glanced at Bryony and saw from her face that she was not surprised. Neither was he. Jennifer had had a gift for ignoring the chaos around her and focusing on one thing at a time. The sink was full of soaking dishes and scummy water. The kitchen table was covered in crumbs and the half-cleared evidence of lunch. There were several half-drunk cups of tea and coffee. A bag of flour had been left open with a spoon stuck upright in it. He thought of Rachel and her orderly, methodical ways. However had he managed to live with this? Anyone else might think that Jennifer had been interrupted or had made a hurried departure, but Daniel knew otherwise. It was just that there was no one to clean up after her at weekends now that Nick wasn't there any more.

"The lab book won't be in here," Bryony said.

No, it wouldn't be; Jennifer wouldn't risk getting toast crumbs and tea stains on it. She shouldn't really have brought it home at all, particularly as she didn't seem to have left a copy in the office.

It wasn't in the living room either.

They went upstairs. Through an open door Daniel glimpsed a mobile of paper elephants hanging from the ceiling and a duvet cover with a dinosaur pattern.

They went into the next room: this was Jennifer's. The bed hadn't been made: the duvet was pushed back as if she had just climbed out, and the pillows were crooked. A familiar scent hung in the air and it was this that did for him. A picture flashed before his eyes. He saw Jennifer propped up with a duvet wrapped round her, shoulders bare. She never wore anything in bed. "Except Chanel No. 5, like Marilyn Monroe," she liked to say. She was reading a patent application, annotating it with a pencil. He had found that incredibly sexy...

The sense of her physical presence was so strong that for a moment it was as if she was standing beside him. He swayed and Bryony took his elbow.

"Are you alright?"

He nodded, not trusting himself to speak.

By the window was a piece of furniture that he recognized: a desk that had belonged to Jennifer's mother. A memory stirred, but he knew he didn't want to go there. To give himself time to compose himself, he went over and looked at the framed photos that were arranged on the surface. They were all of the same little boy, sitting on a swing, or dressed as a shepherd for a nativity play with a toy lamb under his arm, or hunkered down on the beach, gesturing with a spade. There was something familiar about the child and he wondered if he had seen him before. Perhaps it was just that he resembled Jennifer. He searched for her features and found them in the quirk of an eyebrow, the shape of the chin.

Bryony broke into his thoughts. "I'm really sorry, Mr Marchmont. It's not here, is it?"

"What?"

"The lab book. We've looked everywhere now."

***

Daniel waited, shivering, on the garden path, while Bryony locked the door.

There was the sound of a gate closing. They looked round. It was the woman who had been sweeping up leaves earlier. She had a little dog fussing at the end of a leash.

"You're Jennifer's secretary, aren't you? I've seen you here before." She looked from Bryony to Daniel, obviously hoping for an introduction. When none was forthcoming, she said, "I was wondering if you knew what had happened to Harry."

"Harry's with Mr Blunt," Bryony said stiffly.

"Poor little boy."

Daniel could tell from Bryony's expression that she found the avid expression on the woman's face repugnant. So did he, and yet...

"Do you live next door?" he said.

The woman snorted. "For my sins. What I used to overhear sometimes. I couldn't help it." The little dog was whining and pulling at his leash. "Stop it, Fred," she said sharply. "At it like hammer and tongs," she went on. "More than once I nearly called the police. Thought he might do her an injury. I was glad when he moved out, I can tell you."

"I need to get back to the office," Bryony said to Daniel. She turned away.

Daniel got out his car keys and bleeped the car open.

Bryony went round to the passenger's side and got in.

The woman was clearly affronted. She shrugged and allowed the dog to pull her away.

Daniel got into the car, started the engine and pulled away.

"Jennifer would hate this," Bryony said.

Daniel glanced sideways. Her face was set. "You got on with her alright?" he asked.

"She was good at her job, very good – and so am I. She respected that and we were a good team. So yes, I liked her and I liked working for her."

"How long had you been with her?"

"Seven years."

Daniel was silent. So Bryony had come on the scene shortly after their break-up. She couldn't help but know some of what had gone on.

Neither of them spoke for the rest of the journey.

Daniel pulled up outside Jennifer's office. Their arrival obviously reminded Bryony of the errand they had undertaken together.

"I really can't understand that lab book going missing." Her voice was troubled.

"Neither can I."

"It's not like her..."

"Maybe if she was upset, distracted..."

She shook her head. "No," she said flatly.

He saw from her face that she took this personally. Her boss didn't make that kind of mistake and that was an end of it.

"If her marriage was breaking up – "

"Even so."

Bryony had already turned to get out of the car when Daniel said, "Do you think it was permanent? The split, I mean."

Bryony looked back at him. At first he thought she wasn't going to answer. But perhaps she was sorry for him, or felt that he was owed something, given his history with Jennifer. She said, "Jennifer thought it was. She asked me to make an appointment with her solicitor. She was devoted to Harry. Nick wanted custody of him. She wasn't going to stand for that. She intended to fight him all the way."

Half way home it occurred to him that Jennifer's death had settled the question of custody for good. He found that tears were streaming down his face. He couldn't see the road and pulled over into a lay-by. He folded his arms on the steering wheel, buried his face in them and wept. Oh Jennifer, Jennifer... She had never been Jenny or Jen, even to him. He had once looked her up in a book of babies' names and found that Jennifer was a version of Guinevere, the name of King

Arthur's adulterous queen. He had not for a moment imagined how appropriate that would turn out to be... or that she would be dead by forty. It was as if he had lost her all over again.

Chapter Seven

Katie fiddled with her fork, took another mouthful of pasta.
They were in the staff canteen at the lab. Katie had had to dash back to the hospital, heart in mouth, to hunt for her lab book. To lose that would be a disaster. Everything was in it: every detail of what she'd been doing, every step, every formula, so that if she got knocked down by a bus, her experiments could be replicated. Luckily she'd left it on the table in the café at the hospital and it had been handed in to lost property. She only just got back in time to meet Rachel.

The lunch was turning out to be just as dire as Katie had feared. Maybe she'd just spent so much time with other scientists that she'd forgotten how to talk to normal people. They'd managed a bit of conversation about the DBA society and what it was like being on the board. They'd deplored the loss of Michael Goring and agreed that it was unfortunate that Katie had had to move labs. Then the talk had dried up.

Rachel poured out a glass of water. It was her third and Katie guessed that she felt just as awkward as she did. She didn't know what Rachel was normally like, but she seemed on edge; there wasn't much eye contact. They just didn't seem to have much in common. And she was dressed so formally it was a bit off-putting. She was Katie's idea of a middle-class mum up in London for a matinée. Cool scarf, though: gorgeous colours.

How soon could she decently draw things to a close? Could they skip dessert? Well, at least she hadn't asked how the research was going.

Rachel cleared her throat. "How's the research going?" she asked.

Katie sighed. "Oh, so-so. Fine really." She shrugged. "There are always setbacks."

Rachel's face fell. Katie knew what she hoped to hear: that an amazing breakthrough was imminent, that in a year or two there'd be a complete cure or, if not in a year or two, at least by the time her daughter was a teenager. One day she would have to manage those overnight infusions herself and that was a tough regime for a young person. Those who couldn't handle it risked dying of cardiac failure.

"There's still time," Katie hastened to add, "but, you know, even if I do make a breakthrough, we're still talking about years. Even if my research is successful, it'll only mean that it works in vitro – that means outside a human body. What works in a Petri dish might not work in a human being. There'd have to be more experiments using mice and then primates and then human trials..."

"But if you do crack it..."

Yes, if Katie – or someone else – did crack it, did manage to replace that faulty gene with a healthy one, or did what was equally miraculous, find a way to alter the gene so that it did its job and switched on the production of red blood cells, Chloe's condition wouldn't just be improved, she would be cured. It would almost be as if it had never happened. If a therapy was found before irreversible damage had been done, it would be like turning back time. How Rachel must yearn for that, and how far away from it they still were.

It struck Katie that this was the real reason she preferred to stay in the lab. It was better to keep the heartbreak at arm's length. After her degree in medicine, she had decided to switch to research and that had been the right decision.

"Would you like a pudding or coffee?" Katie asked.

Rachel shook her head.

"I probably ought to get back," Katie said. "I've got a cell-line waiting for me."

Rachel hesitated, and then she said, "I wonder – you'll say

if it's not convenient, but I'd really like to see where you work. I've never been in a lab before."

Katie's heart sank, and she hesitated in her turn. Then she remembered what Paul had said. She knew he was right. She ought to accommodate Rachel as far as she could.

"Here – best to wear one of these. It'll protect your clothes from toxins and radioactivity." Katie handed a white lab coat to Rachel.

"Oh, don't worry," she added hastily, seeing the look on Rachel's face, "there really isn't any danger. Work involving radioactive isotopes is tightly regulated."

"I remember reading a biography of Madame Curie once. Didn't she die from radiation poisoning?" Rachel said, shrugging on her coat.

"She died from radium-induced anaemia and her lab books are still so radioactive that they're kept in lead-lined boxes. People have to wear protective clothing to consult them. Even her cookbook is highly radioactive! They really didn't appreciate the dangers in those days. Nowadays we fall over backwards to be careful."

Rachel looked around. Katie followed her gaze. The lab was such a familiar place, but taking a visitor round, she saw it with fresh eyes. It wasn't as tidy as it ought to be. The benches running back to back down the room were crowded with notebooks, stray pieces of paper, plastic trays holding test tubes. The shelves above were full to overflowing with beakers, flasks, all sorts of glassware. The desk areas at the end of each bench bore more personal clutter: a copy of *Nature*, a row of miniature teddy bears, a box of tissues. The walls were covered with photos, calendars, posters of brightly coloured complicated diagrams, cartoons snipped out of newspapers.

Perhaps Rachel had expected something sleeker, something more high-tech?

"Not what you'd imagined?" Katie asked.

"I thought it would all be more..." Rachel said, obviously casting around for a polite way of putting it. "It's more... homely than I expected."

"More of a mess, you mean! Though come to think of it, homely is right in that I sometimes spend more time here than I actually do at home. I'm often in here late at night and at weekends. Sometimes I get so absorbed, I just forget about the time. I've got to move out of my place very soon and last week I was supposed to be viewing a flat. I thought I'd just got time to pop in to check on a culture and I was still here three hours later."

"That's how it used to be for me – before I had Chloe. I'm a restorer, I specialize in wood. When I'm working, time just seems to slip away. So which is your desk?"

"This is my desk and bench over here." They walked over together.

"It's tidier than the others."

"Give me time! I only moved in yesterday."

"So what are you actually doing? What's that?" Rachel pointed at a large flask.

"That's my E.coli culture. Oh no," Katie said, seeing Rachel's eyes widen, "these can't do anyone any harm. They're non-pathogenic. In the environment they are generally found in soil, but ours are entirely lab bred, descended from ones first used decades ago."

"They've been in captivity all these years?"

Katie laughed. "All these years... and you know what? They have a life cycle of only twenty minutes. That's a lot of generations."

"And what are you going to do with them?"

Katie hesitated.

"It doesn't matter if you haven't got time," Rachel said quickly.

"No, it's fine. I was just thinking about how to explain it. Look, sit down for a minute." Katie pulled up a stool. "You know broadly what I'm trying to do?"

"It's to do with a hormone, a growth factor that occurs naturally in the body, and you're trying to get it into the bone marrow cells and you're hoping that it'll stimulate the production of red blood cells."

"That's it. What I do is make a culture that's a kind of DNA factory. E.coli are reproducing in it and they are carrying the growth factor, so that's reproducing too. The next thing is to kill the E.coli and take the DNA out. OK, so then I've got the copies I need of my growth factor. This is where it all gets a bit complicated, but basically I have to get that DNA into my cell-line. So I insert the growth hormone into a virus. I have to do that very, very carefully, using one of these," she reached for a pipette, "a drop at a time. Then I harvest the virus in an ultracentrifuge – it looks a bit like a top-loading washing machine."

Rachel was frowning in concentration. "Then the virus can carry the DNA into the stem cell?"

"Yup. You've got it. Once it's inside, the virus inserts the engineered gene into the stem cell genome and the cell can now produce the missing protein."

"And that will switch on the red cell production?"

"That's the idea."

Rachel sat silently for a few moments. Then she said, "Your job, it must take a lot of manual dexterity."

Katie was surprised. "Yes, it does. Most people don't realize that. They think it's all computers and software."

"It's important in what I do, too. But the things you work with – can you even see them under a microscope?"

"Only just. And that's all you can see. You can't see inside them."

"Yet those tiny, tiny things make us what we are."

There was a thoughtful silence.

"I'd better let you get on," Rachel said. "Thanks for showing me round."

"It's a pleasure," Katie said, and realized that against all expectations that was the truth. "I'll see you out."

As they made their way down the corridor, Rachel said, "Are you still looking for somewhere to live?"

Katie groaned. "On top of everyone else. It's a nightmare. My landlord's daughter's coming back to live at home and he wants the flat. He gave me a month's notice and that was two weeks ago. Problem is, I only need somewhere for a few months."

"For a few months..." Rachel repeated. She seemed to be thinking something over. "I wonder... how would you feel about living on a boat?"

Chapter Eight

When Katie got back to the lab, Minnie was waiting for her. She had the bench next to Katie and was in her first year as a postdoc. To have a doctorate she had to be twenty-four at least, but she looked about eighteen and from the scraps of conversation that Katie overheard, she was still leading the life of a student; whereas Katie wouldn't see thirty again and was worrying about getting a permanent job and if she'd ever be able to afford a mortgage.

Minnie was looked flustered.

"What's up?" Katie asked.

"My radio-labelled methionine. I ordered it in last week and it arrived yesterday. It was in the fridge."

"And it isn't there now?"

Minnie shook her head.

"Someone must have taken it by mistake," Katie said. "Or maybe it got shoved to the back of the fridge. Let's double-check."

She followed Minnie back to the fridge. Together they moved everything, but Minnie was right. It wasn't there. Katie hadn't really thought it would be, because it wasn't something you could easily overlook. The glass vial containing the radio-labelled methionine was itself fairly small, but it would be in a lead container and that in turn would be in a plastic box. And the box would be bright yellow to indicate the presence of radioactive material.

They looked at each other.

Minnie said, "I don't see how someone could have taken it by accident. I checked the book. No one else has ordered one in the last week."

Katie looked at Minnie's anxious face. The isotopes weren't hugely radioactive, but they weren't something that you wanted to lose track of either. At the training sessions, you were always told that cabin crew get higher doses of radiation because of the height at which they travel, but all the same no one took any chances. People stuck to the rules. Perspex shields and lead-lined containers were used, and if you were working with a radio isotope, you had to wear a body badge on your lapel to tell you if radiation levels were too high.

"Look," Katie said, "most likely someone got muddled, thought they had ordered one, and that it was theirs when they spotted yours in the fridge. Have you asked around?"

"No..."

"OK. Well, that's the first thing to do. No, on second thoughts, why don't you ask Ian first?"

Ian was the head technician. Katie guessed that he would be the father of the lab, the old hand who knew the ropes, the one that everyone turned to for help.

Minnie brightened. "I don't know why I didn't think of that. He always knows what's going on – and he's the lab's radiation officer too. Hey, thanks, Katie."

"You are very welcome."

Minnie went off with a backward wave of the hand.

Katie turned her attention to her work. Sometime later, she heard the door of the lab swing open and looked up to see Professor Masterman come in. She crossed the lab, heading for Will Orville's bench. Will had his head down. Katie couldn't quite see what he was doing. He was a stocky, fair-haired guy, about Katie's age and at about the same point in his career. They had been introduced briefly, but she hadn't managed to have a chat with him yet.

As for Honor, she was quite a contrast to the male heads of labs that Katie had known, with their nylon shirts and awful haircuts. She was wearing narrow black trousers and a wool jacket in black and white with a small geometric pattern:

Jaeger or something like that. And you rarely saw lipstick in the lab. Her greying hair was cut into a sleek bob. She looked great for fifty. Actually she looked great, full stop.

Honor had reached Will's side, and he was turning to look at her. Honor put her hand on his shoulder. There was a gentleness in the gesture that made Katie wonder; of course, she was old enough to be his mother...

The two of them conferred, faces serious, Will frowning at whatever Honor was telling him.

There had been a profile of Honor in *The Guardian* not long ago. She was married to another academic – older, Katie seemed to remember – but she'd married late and didn't have any children. Had the chance just passed her by, Katie wondered, or had it been a deliberate decision? The life of a young scientist, in and out of the lab all hours of the day and night, wasn't easy to combine with children. Would Honor be running her own lab with a Nobel Prize in the offing if she had taken time out for babies? Katie wondered if further down the line she herself would end up in a Jaeger suit with research students as surrogate children.

She could almost hear what they were saying, but not quite. It was tantalizing.

Then she reminded herself that if she didn't complete this project successfully, she wouldn't have a scientific career next year, let alone in twenty years. She turned back to her lab book, determined to give it her full attention. But she'd no sooner picked up her pen than Minnie arrived, breathless, at her side.

"It's alright," she said.

"Ian sorted it?"

Minnie nodded. "It was in the fridge in the lab over the way – on the other side of the corridor."

"Panic over, then."

"Well, yes, but..."

Katie pushed back her chair. "Well?" she prompted.

"I know I didn't put it there. Why would I? I haven't set foot in that lab for weeks – " she broke off, gazing over Katie's head.

Katie spun her chair round to see what Minnie was looking at.

Will was on his feet. He was shaking his head, as though he couldn't believe what he'd just heard. Honor's lips were pressed into a thin line and she was nodding her head as if to confirm that yes, it really was that serious.

"Bad news," Minnie said in a low voice.

"Looks like it."

Chapter Nine

Katie parked where Rachel had suggested, on Ship Lane. It wasn't quite raining, but a fine drizzle was hanging in the air and forming haloes round the street lamps. As she got out of the car she felt the chill on her face and wrapped her scarf more closely round her neck. Half past six on a November evening, and it was so quiet that she could hear her own footsteps. She passed just one person walking a dog. She emerged on Quayside opposite the duck feeding station, where the sleeping geese were pale, grey shapes in the dark. She wondered if she'd feel comfortable living down here.

She found herself yawning. It had been a long day and it wasn't over yet. She had to go back to the lab to run her experiment again. If it didn't work this time... But it was no good thinking like that. It *would* work. Fingers crossed, the result would be unambiguous and it would be publishable. She had to have something to show for two years' work.

She found the house with no difficulty and saw that the brass door knocker was in the shape of an anchor. The whole area had a nautical, seaside flavour: higher up the hill she'd noticed a ship's chandler with a window full of barometers and clocks.

Katie rapped on the door and Rachel opened it immediately.

There was an impression of warmth and soft light and colour. The door opened straight into the living room, where a man was sitting on a sofa with a pile of papers on his lap.

"Come in, come in," Rachel said.

Katie closed the door behind her and stood with her back to it. "I won't come any further, my boots are dirty."

"I'll just get the keys from the kitchen." Rachel moved away, adding as an afterthought, "This is my husband, Daniel. Dan, this is Katie."

He looked about forty and had a kind, tired face. His white shirt was unbuttoned at the neck and his tie had been pulled loose. He gave her a brief smile and turned his attention back to his papers. Clearly Katie had interrupted him at work.

She glanced around, trying not to seem nosy, but curious to see where Rachel lived. This was the kind of place that she'd like to have – if she could ever afford it – a lovely red and blue rug on the floor, an entire wall covered in bookshelves, alcoves containing plants and pottery. Katie remembered that Rachel was a woodworker and wondered if she'd made the shelves herself.

Just as Rachel emerged from the kitchen at the back, a little girl appeared at the top of an open staircase on the right. She was wearing a fairy outfit complete with wings and a tiara trimmed with pink feathers.

"Are you Katie?" she asked, advancing down the stairs. "Are you going to live on our boat?"

"Well..." Katie wasn't sure how to answer. But an answer didn't seem to be required, because the next question came immediately.

"How old are you?"

"Chloe!" Rachel chided gently.

Katie laughed. "It's alright. I'm thirty-three. How old are you?"

"I'm four and I'm starting school next year. Are you married?"

Rachel said: "That really is enough, young lady. It's time you were getting your night things on."

The child's face crumpled. "But I want to come with you to the boat. Can I, Mummy?"

Rachel hesitated.

Daniel looked up from his work. He gave Chloe a wink. "Oh, let her go," he said to Rachel. "You're not going to be long, are you?"

"Well, if Katie doesn't mind…"

"Of course I don't mind," Katie said.

Chloe's face lit up.

Rachel laughed. "OK, quick then, wings off, coat and wellies on."

Katie was amused to see that both coat and wellies were pink too.

The three of them set off, Chloe skipping ahead. The old-fashioned cast-iron street lights shed a watery, yellow light. The pavement was black and slick with rain and reflections.

"The *Matilda Jane*'s moored down the other end near the railway bridge," Rachel explained.

"What sort of boat is it?" Katie asked.

"She's a Dutch barge, a Steilsteven, built around 1926. She was a total wreck when I bought her. I restored her myself."

They passed beneath two vast weeping willows whose leafless, dripping tendrils almost brushed their heads.

"You actually did all the work yourself?" Katie asked.

"Most of it, yes. Took me five years in my spare time. Couldn't afford to buy a house or a flat, though actually now that she's been restored, the barge is worth as much as a house. I'd always fancied living on a boat. And I loved it. It's a world all of its own – a real community."

They passed the Maltings, now a cinema and restaurant, and then an open grassy space with a bandstand. On the other side of the water, cabin cruisers rocked gently at their mooring and lights glowed on the jetties.

The floodlit cathedral came into view, floating above the town, blurred and hazy in the damp air.

They had just passed a pub called The Cutter when something moved in the shadows and a small ginger cat appeared.

Chloe gave a cry of delight. "Orlando!"

The cat wound himself around her legs. She bent down and with an effort picked him up and clutched him to her chest.

She staggered along for a few yards, he struggled, and she dropped him. He followed along behind them.

"Is that your cat?" Katie asked.

Rachel nodded. "He was a stray. Adopted me when I was living on the boat. Chloe adores him."

They reached a smart-looking restaurant called The Boathouse and a row of cottages. Then the street lights ended and Rachel produced a torch from her pocket. "Chloe, stick close now, please."

Chloe put her hand in Rachel's. She reached up and took Katie's too. The little gloved hand was warm in hers.

Orlando ran ahead of them and vanished into the gloom.

They moved out of the light into the dark. There was a smell of rotting leaves and the ground was slippery underfoot. The dark shapes of the willows that overhung the path were only just discernible against the night sky. The beam of Rachel's torch caught the white surface of a sign that warned of deep water and a strong current.

There was a rumbling and ahead of them the lights of a train crossing a bridge were briefly reflected in the water.

Rachel said, "There are plenty of people around during the day, even in the winter, but even at night it's not as lonely as it looks. The people on the next boat – Frank and Daisy – live there all the time and they keep an eye on things for me. I can introduce you to them."

The path continued under the railway bridge, then over a little bridge that spanned the entrance to a large boatyard. There weren't many boats moored along here, just a few long dark shapes.

Rachel stopped by one of them. She shone the torch along the side of the hull and picked out the words *Matilda Jane* in white cursive script. She led Katie along the length of the boat to the wheelhouse.

"Here – would you mind holding the torch?"

Rachel climbed aboard and Katie shone the beam on the door,

while Rachel unlocked it. The door swung open. Rachel reached in and switched on a light. Then she leaned forward, seized Chloe under the arms and swung her onto the boat. Katie followed them into the wheelhouse and down a flight of stairs. A short corridor opened into a room with wooden floorboards covered with brightly covered rugs. Katie saw an L-shaped kitchen and a scrubbed oak table at the near end, and at the other, a sitting area with a slim black leather sofa and easy chairs. A full-length mirror on one wall gave an illusion of depth and space. Between the oblong windows were built-in shelves and cupboards made of pale wood. Was that beech? Katie recognized the style that she'd seen in Rachel and Daniel's house.

"It's a bit chilly in here at the moment," Rachel said, "but there's a little wood-burning stove in the corner there, and it soon warms up. This is the main living area, and through here in the stern is the master bedroom."

Rachel led the way, explaining as they went. "There's an en suite bathroom... just a shower, of course, but it's a good one..."

The double bed with its blue and white checked cover, the two portholes on either side, and the white-painted wall: it was all so spic and span and yes, shipshape – that was surely the word.

Katie said, "It's bigger than I thought it would be."

"You were probably thinking of a narrow boat. They're only about seven foot in the beam. The *Matilda Jane*'s sixty-five feet long, about the same as a typical narrow boat, but she's fourteen foot in the beam."

"Where's Chloe?" Katie asked, looking round.

"Come and see," Rachel said, smiling. She led the way back through the living room to the corridor they had come in by. There was a door there that looked as if it ought to be a cupboard, but when Rachel opened it, Katie glimpsed bunk beds on the right and another door on the left. "This is the guest room, with its own en suite shower room," Rachel explained. "Chloe sleeps in here when we are on board."

They squeezed in. Chloe waved from the top bunk. The room had the charm of all small tightly organized spaces.

"It's all so compact," Katie marvelled.

"It's a bit like being in a submarine," Rachel said. "You have to have a place for everything and put things away as you go along." She ran a hand caressingly along a shelf.

You really love this place, Katie thought. *All the work you've done on it... you're the kind of person who gives 100 per cent. I like that – and I like you.*

Rachel said, "In the summer we spend as much time here as we can, cruising the river or just hanging out, sitting on deck with a glass of wine. There's nothing like it. But we usually shut it up for the winter and move back into Daniel's house. I don't really like it being empty, so if you're interested..."

"Interested? I love it! What would you want for rent?"

When Rachel hesitated, Katie said firmly, "I'd have to pay a proper rent."

"Of course," Rachel said hastily, "but you'll be a kind of caretaker, too, so I'll take that into account. So how about – " and she named a sum considerably lower than Katie was currently paying. "And if we say for three months? That'll take you just past the end of January."

"And the end of my contract. It's perfect." Katie looked at her watch. "And now I really ought to get going. I need to get back to the lab."

Chapter Ten

"Working late again, Dr Flanagan?" Malcolm said as he turned the signing-in book towards her. He was one of the night porters. "Ought to have better things to do at your age."

It could have sounded flirtatious, but Katie knew it wasn't intended that way. Malcolm was the fatherly type.

"What about you?" she said, as she picked up the pen.

"Oh, me? I'd just be watching the box at home. My wife works shifts, too. She's a nurse at Addenbrooke's. So I might as well be working. Then I get to go fishing during the day."

She glanced at her watch. Quarter to eight. She wrote it in the book.

"Is it just me in tonight?" she asked as she scribbled her name.

"Only Dr Orville's left in the lab."

So hopefully she'd have the darkroom to herself. The western blot that she was planning to run should prove that she'd succeeded in introducing the growth factor into her stem cell.

As she walked along the corridor to the lab, she saw that a door to one of the offices was ajar. She glanced in as she passed. She'd gone a few more yards down the corridor before she took in what she'd seen and came to a halt. Will was in there, lying back in an armchair with his eyes closed, his face so haggard that she wondered if he was ill.

She went back and knocked on the door.

He sat up and opened his eyes.

"Are you alright?" she asked, pushing the door further open.

"Oh yeah, I'm OK. Had a bad day, that's all. Just trying to make up my mind to go home. Come in, why don't you? How're you settling in?"

"Fine, thanks. What's gone wrong?"

"How long have you got?" he said.

"I saw Professor Masterman come into the lab earlier."

He gestured to a chair. Katie sat down.

"She'd just had a phone call from our lawyer – well, I say 'our lawyer'. He's working for Calliope Biotech. I don't know if you know anything about the work we've been doing...?"

She did know about it, but she let him tell her anyway: about the discovery, almost accidental, of a possible therapy for obesity, the shock of the death in the clinical trial that he and Honor could not have foreseen, the regrouping that took place afterwards. She guessed that it was an account he'd given many times before and the emotion had leached out of it. He knew the death was shocking, but at the same time he'd got used to it, and anyway, he'd been absolved of blame.

He grew more animated when it came to recent events and the claim from a rival team of researchers that they had got there first.

"I'm sure it was us, we were the first, but whether we'll be able to prove it... That woman who was killed in a car crash out towards Cambridge a couple of days ago. It's been on the local news? She was our lawyer."

"Oh!"

"It's awful," he said, "just awful. When it's someone you know – and then there's what this means for the project... We've been so unlucky – it's as if it's jinxed. And that's not all. There's a new hotshot lawyer on the case, Daniel Marchmont – "

"Marchmont?"

"Do you know him?"

"How funny – I've just been to his house. No, I don't know him, but his wife's renting out their barge to me. Sorry – go on."

"He rang Honor earlier today. That's what she was telling me about. Apparently one of our lab books – one of *my* lab books – has got lost. And would you believe it? Jennifer – that's the lawyer – didn't keep a copy." He shook his head. "I can't believe this is happening."

Katie groaned in sympathy. Only another scientist could fully enter into this. To be the first in the field with a dazzling new discovery – and not to be able to prove it...

"You don't keep a rough notebook, then?"

Lots of researchers did, though not Katie. She wrote everything in her lab book as she went along.

He grimaced. "I do now." He gestured to a notebook with a black cover lying open on the desk. "But I didn't then. I'm just hoping that the lab book's got mislaid somewhere in Jennifer's office."

Katie said, "Where else could it be? Surely it'll come to light?"

He rubbed his forehead and sighed. "Hope you're right. But in any case, I'm not doing any good here. Too tired. Oh well." As she watched, he sat up straight and seemed to shake off his despondency, like a dog throwing off water. "There's always tomorrow," he declared.

He closed the notebook, opened the drawer in his desk, and tossed it in. She glimpsed other notebooks in there. He closed the drawer and locked it, slipping the key in his pocket.

He smiled at her. There was something uncertain about that smile, a hint of shyness that was at odds with his confident demeanour. That was attractive.

"Don't fancy going for a drink, do you?" he said. "Could do with going out and sinking a few beers."

She shook her head regretfully. "Sorry, I've got a date with a western blot."

"Another time?"

"Another time."

Chapter Eleven

Katie went thoughtfully on down the corridor. Could she herself have gone on with the research after a death like that? She didn't know. It must have been devastating, but Will had the resilience of the true researcher, willing to go on and on, no matter what the setbacks. She guessed that he was good, very good; as Honor Masterman's postdoc, he'd have to be. He could still have a brilliant career ahead of him.

She let herself into the lab with her swipe card. The door closed behind her with a pneumatic sigh.

Katie had told Rachel that the lab was a home from home, and during the day that was true. But at night when the place lay still and silent under the sterile glow of the fluorescent lights, it was very different. Without the background noises – people coming and going, the whirring of extraction fans – she was very much aware of all the noises that she just ignored during the day, and it was surprising how many of them sounded like someone unlocking a door or trying a door handle. Working alone into the night, an uncomfortable feeling would come over her as if at any moment she might catch sight of someone – or something – out of the corner of her eye. She liked the quietness, but really it was better when there were one or two other people also working late.

She walked to the far end of the lab to where her gel dish swayed lazily with the circular motion of the orbital shaker. In it, floating in a buffer solution, was her western blot, a piece of nitrocellular membrane, looking like an ordinary scrap of paper about six centimetres by four. The orbital shaker should have washed off everything except the antibody that would bind to her particular protein and so reveal that it was present in her stem cell. Down the left-hand side ran a series of narrow blue lines, her baseline band of proteins, like the rungs of a ladder. When she'd developed the western blot, another line would appear on the right-hand side. And that would be proof that her experiment had worked. It was a bit like a pregnancy test.

She took the gel dish off the shaker and set it on the counter. She cut off a length of saran wrap cling film – but she was all fingers and thumbs this evening and it twisted back on itself. She threw it away, cut a second piece, and laid it on the counter. With a pair of tweezers she removed the western blot from the gel tray and laid it on the saran wrap. She mixed the reagents that would make her protein luminous. Using a pipette she spread the solution over the surface of the western blot and patted off the excess with a piece of kitchen roll. She wrapped the blot in the saran wrap and walked the length of the lab to the darkroom.

When she pressed the switch for the infrared light that would allow her to expose her film, nothing happened. Oh, hell, the bulb had gone again. She'd have to manage with the small light over the sink.

She bolted the door and switched the main light off. At first it was pitch black. Moving along the counter she stubbed her toe on a metal waste paper bin and let out a curse. Working mostly by feel, she got the photographic paper into the plate and waited for a few moments to let it dry. By now her eyes had adjusted and the faint red light was enough to allow her to slot the plate into the developer.

As she waited, her thoughts drifted to Will and his problems with the obesity project. So much of scientific discovery came down to luck. That was what no one told you when you were starting out. It was impossible to predict whether your project would be the one to make medical history, no way of knowing if the horse you were backing would be the one to win the race. But soon she would know if her own gamble had paid off...

She came to herself with a start. She had heard something so familiar that it hadn't registered at first: the hiss of the pneumatic door just outside the darkroom. Someone had come into the lab. They had probably just popped in to check on a culture – she did that often enough herself. But she didn't like not knowing who was there, and she found herself listening. Because if they *were* just checking something, it wouldn't take them long and she'd hear them leaving the lab.

But then time was up with the developer, it spewed out the photograph, and here it came, the moment of truth. She switched on the light and was dazzled. She seized the photograph. It took a few moments for her eyes to adjust. She could scarcely have been more anxious for the result if it *was* a pregnancy test. She held it up and couldn't immediately process what she was seeing. There was just a ghostly grey outline. As she went on staring at it, her hands began to tremble. Her protein hadn't appeared. This wasn't just a weak or ambiguous result. This was no result at all.

It seemed that she had completely failed to transfer the growth factor to her stem cells. Somewhere in the process she had made a catastrophic mistake. What could it be? Something wrong with the DNA cloning? Or had the cell-line somehow got contaminated? Or what if it was... Oh, it could be anything. What on earth was she going to say to Paul?

She bit her lip, but couldn't stop the tears welling up. She let herself give in to it, allowed them to roll down her cheeks, and mopped them up with a paper towel. *Come on*, she told herself; *it's not the end of the world, nobody's dead, it's only a job*. But she knew that wasn't true. She thought of Rachel and her little girl. In the end it really was a matter of life and death.

She left the lab and made her way down to the entrance. Tomorrow she would have to think hard about what had gone wrong. She tried to tell herself that the failed experiment was just a hiccup, that was all. She would test every link in the chain, find the problem, and fix it. She wouldn't let herself contemplate the heartbreaking truth that sometimes it was the successful experiment that was the hiccup and the failure was the one that counted.

There were always times like this, difficult stretches when you didn't seem to be making any progress, when things didn't turn out as you'd expected and you didn't know why. You started to get bogged down; worst of all, you started to doubt yourself as a scientist. You couldn't let that happen. What she needed was a good night's sleep and then she'd start all over again.

It wasn't until she signed herself out that she remembered that someone had come into the lab.

"Who else is working late tonight?" she asked Malcolm.

Malcolm shook his head. "I haven't seen a soul since Dr Orville clocked out not long after you came in."

"But I heard someone come in while I was in the darkroom."

He turned the signing-in book for her to see.

Hers was the last name to be entered.

Chapter Twelve

She had thought she'd be the first into the lab the next morning and was surprised to discover Ian already there, doing paperwork. He lifted his head when she came in. The smooth grey hair pulled into a ponytail, the goatee beard, and the earring had all said "aging hippy" when she'd met him on her first day in the lab. But she'd soon seen how competent he was, and she liked the fact that he was a fellow northerner.

"You're in early," she said.

He sighed. "Trying to catch up on some paperwork. One of the big freezers has gone on the blink. Full of frozen mice, thawing out. Who knows when it was last cleared out! They should have been incinerated yonks ago. You can imagine..."

"Nasty," she agreed.

"Funny thing. We're missing a mouse. I ask you! How can that have happened?"

Katie made a sympathetic noise. In her line of research she didn't use mice, thank goodness, but friends did and she knew the rules were strict. Every single mouse was recorded and ear-tagged, and all the numbers were returned to the Home Office, with details that included whether or not they had been used in an experiment, and the date of death.

Ian pushed his glasses up onto his head and massaged his eyes. "I might not have noticed if the freezer hadn't broken down and they'd defrosted. I was just about to sling the bag into the incinerator when it split and they came slithering out."

"Yuk!"

"It said ten on the bag and there were only nine."

"Ear-tags?"

"No. That is what's making them hard to trace. I'm going

through to see if the books balance. But what brings you here so bright and early?"

"Couldn't sleep. I've made a complete mess of my western blot and I've come in to try to sort it out."

"Come on, I'll make us a brew and you can tell me about it. Two heads are better than one."

"Well... OK, thanks... might help to talk it over."

He smiled and the lines around his eyes deepened. He looked as though he smiled a lot, and he was a good-looking guy – for his age. What was he? Fifty?

"Tell you what," he said in an Alan Bennett voice that was only a slight exaggeration of his normal voice, "I'll crack open a packet of custard creams."

One of her undergraduate lecturers had told her that the first rule of life in the lab was to make friends with the technicians and porters: they were the ones who really ran the place. It was advice she'd always followed.

They reached the common room. He opened the door and ushered her in.

She sat down and watched while he filled the kettle, noting the care he took to fill it to exactly the right level. When he reached up and opened the door of a cupboard above the sink, light glinted off the diamond stud in his ear.

He reached for a tea caddy. She saw a label: "Ian's tea. Don't even think about it."

"Real Yorkshire tea," he said, spooning the leaf tea into a small brown teapot. "Can't abide teabags."

He took two cups and saucers out of the cupboard. She was pleasantly surprised. A stained mug – often chipped into the bargain – tended to be what was usually on offer.

"How do you like it?" he asked.

"Nice and strong, please."

She took a sip and gave a sigh of appreciation.

Ian smiled. "Not much a good cup of tea can't put right. Now tell Uncle Ian all about it."

"Oh, heck," he said when she'd explained, and the homely northern expression made her smile. "Let's go through it stage by stage, shall we?"

She said, "I'll throw out the DNA, obviously."

"Yep. That's the first thing to do. And you'll check the cloning?"

"Of course."

He pondered, pushed his granny glasses up his nose with his forefinger. No doubt about it, Katie thought, he must have been pretty hot in his day, and even now... Good job he couldn't read her mind.

"You'll need to check that the cell-line hasn't been contaminated. It could have been infected with mycoplasma; that happened to Minnie a few weeks ago."

She sighed. "There are so many possibilities."

"Agreed. You could check the copy-number of the gene in your stem cells. You could also check that the cells were producing mRNA for your protein."

Katie groaned. Both would require techniques that were time-consuming and difficult.

"Yeah, yeah," he said. "It'd be a pain. It makes sense to start with the DNA – rule that out first."

"That was what I was thinking, too."

"If you'd like me to run something for you, you've only to say." He clapped her on the shoulder. "Come on, back to the drawing board. And I've got to get back to my mice."

What a lovely guy he was. Feeling much better, she went back to her bench to begin all over again culturing her E.coli from scratch. She started to assemble what she needed.

If that wasn't the problem and if it wasn't the cell-line, she'd really be in trouble. It wasn't just that she was running out of time, she was running out of money, too. Some of the chemicals she'd need for further tests were expensive.

It was at times like this that she missed Michael, her old supervisor. He wasn't one for ladling out easy sympathy, but he could always make her laugh. Once she'd been feeling sorry for herself and had complained to Michael: "Sometimes I feel like one of those people in Greek myth or fairy tales with an endless task that they have to keep repeating day after day without getting anywhere." He didn't say anything, just smiled and nodded, but the next day he emailed a quotation to her. "*La lutte elle-même vers les sommets suffit à remplir un cœur d'homme. Il faut imaginer Sisyphe heureux.' Albert Camus.*" He didn't translate it. She looked it up on the internet and it made her laugh. "The struggle itself towards the summit should be enough to satisfy the human heart. One can imagine Sisyphus happy."

Hah! She bent her head to her work and was soon absorbed. Hours passed. She was barely aware of people coming and going around her. At eleven everyone departed for the common room for morning coffee.

"Coming?" Minnie asked.

"In a bit."

The lab emptied and she was vaguely aware of Ian doing something in the background. Then he uttered a loud curse.

She was startled out of her reverie.

She turned to see him, a few metres away, bending over something on a bench.

He looked up and she registered the dismay on his face.

"What's up?" she said, moving towards him.

And then she didn't need to ask – she could hear for herself. Ian had his hand on a Geiger-Müller tube and it was clicking at a rate that meant it was registering high radiation.

"I'm radiation officer for the lab and I was just checking that this works," he said. "I can't believe it. Look at this reading! How did this bench get so hot?"

They stared at each other.

"Is that the only hot spot?" Katie said. "Here, try my bench."

He picked up the GM tube, and together they walked towards her bench. The clicking slowly subsided. Katie hadn't realized that she had been holding her breath. She slowly let it out now.

They looked round the lab. No one else had come back from coffee yet.

Ian moved on to Minnie's bench. The clicking increased with a sound like the fierce crackle of radio interference, then subsided as he moved on to the next.

He moved on round the lab. Half the benches were hot. This was a disaster. They'd all have to be decontaminated.

Ian's face was set. Something seemed to occur to him and he set off down the lab with long strides.

Katie followed him, half-running to keep up.

"What is it?" she asked.

He didn't reply. They reached the door. He held the GM tube against the handle. It went wild.

"Someone's been tracking radioactive material all over the lab."

Katie was aghast. She hadn't thought things could get any worse, but –

"There'll be hot spots everywhere," Ian said. "I've got no choice. I've got to close the lab and clear the building."

Chapter Thirteen

"**B**ut it has to be somewhere!" Honor said.

That was undoubtedly true, Daniel thought, but it wasn't very helpful. He had rung her to let her know that a thorough search of both Jennifer's office and her home had failed to turn up the missing lab book.

Honor continued. "I don't know how Jennifer could have been so careless – and so unprofessional! Why didn't she make a copy as soon as she got her hands on it?"

"I'm surprised too," Daniel said. "What has your postdoc got in the way of notes?"

"He hasn't got anything!" The pitch of her voice was rising. "It was all in the lab book!"

"Nothing? Nothing at all?" This was worse than he had thought; much worse.

"I don't want to be hard on Jennifer after this terrible thing's happened to her and she isn't here to defend herself, but I wish now that I'd asked Lyle to take her off the case. I never dreamt she could drop the ball as seriously as this..."

"You weren't happy with her work?"

"I was impressed by her at first, and Lyle thought so highly of her, but as time went on... It was clear her mind wasn't totally on her job. She was late for an appointment with me, failed to return a phone call..."

Daniel was taken aback. This didn't sound like the Jennifer he knew.

"Where do we go from here?" There was an edge to her voice that made him wonder if she was losing it. He couldn't blame her. For a lab book to go missing, and such a vital one, too... Well, at least no blame could be attached to him.

"We haven't reached the end of the road yet," he said. "We've still got some options. I'll look at the technicians' lab books – see if I can find any confirming details – maybe look at the order books for materials. And I'd better talk to Will Orville. The sooner the better."

"I could meet you in the lab in an hour."

"Fine. I'll have to let Lyle know the situation."

"Of course."

They hung up.

He was beginning to think that Rachel was right and he should never have taken on this case. Even if everything had gone according to plan, time would have been very tight. And now this! He'd taken a gamble on his knowledge of Jennifer. He'd thought he could trust her as a lawyer even though he hadn't been able to trust her as a woman. Was she going to let him down yet again? Was this her final legacy to him? A case so screwed up that he wouldn't be able to salvage it? Everything depended on what he could scrape together as evidence.

He wondered if Bryony had realized how flaky Jennifer was getting. Surely she must have done, or – more likely – was she too loyal to admit that Jennifer was going off the rails?

Of course it was still possible that the lab book would come to light – it had to be *somewhere.* Honor was right about that. But as he punched in Lyle's number, he had to admit to himself that it wasn't looking good.

When Daniel turned into the car park, he saw straightaway that something was amiss. A throng of people was milling about outside the entrance to the lab. He got out of his car and made his way towards them. As he approached the fringes of the crowd, he saw a woman that he guessed must be Honor. She was older than almost everyone there and she wasn't wearing a lab coat. She was conferring with a man with a grey ponytail.

Someone said hello to him, a young woman, and he realized it was the girl that Rachel was renting the boat to. What was her name? Katie – yes. Her hands were thrust into her pockets of her lab coat and she was shivering.

"What's going on?" he asked her. "Fire alarm?"

"Worse. Radioactive hot spots. I wasn't even allowed to go up to my office and get my coat. They're checking the rest of the building before they let us back in."

A stocky blond young man was standing next to her.

Katie noticed Daniel looking at him and said, "Sorry, this is Will, and Will, this is – umm – Mr Marchmont – it's his boat that I'll be staying on."

Will? This must be Honor's postdoc. He looked pale and drawn – and no wonder – the loss of the lab book must be a bitter blow for him, too.

Honor had spotted Daniel and was making her way towards him followed by the man with the ponytail.

"It is Daniel?" she said, holding out her hand. They shook hands. "You've found us at a bad moment –"

She didn't get a chance to say more. There was a screeching of tyres as a red Audi swung into the car park and came to a halt. Lyle Linstrum got out, leaving the car askew across two parking bays.

"What the hell is going on here, Honor?" He gave off waves of energy. Daniel remembered one profile of the man that described him as sucking the oxygen out of the room. More than that, he seemed about to combust. Daniel resisted the urge to step back.

"Lower your voice, Lyle," Honor said, raising a hand, and such was her natural authority that he did restrain himself – at least for a few moments. "We have a problem with the lab. Probably it'll turn out to be a storm in a teacup."

"Exactly what sort of problem?"

She told him. He stared at her in disbelief.

"Just what kind of outfit are you running here? Do you realize what's resting on this?"

Honor's face was grim. "All too well," she said.

Lyle told her anyway. "Billions of dollars. I've staked everything on this."

"And I haven't?" Honor said.

Daniel thought of the rumours going around and the gossip in the scientific press. There were some who thought that a Nobel Prize was long overdue and next year it could be Honor's turn.

As if she hadn't spoken, Lyle went on, "What am I going to tell the investors?"

Daniel glanced at Will. He hadn't said a word yet.

"Something you seem to be forgetting, Lyle," Honor said. "This is no fault of mine or Will's."

"Oh no?" he said. "Didn't it occur to anyone to make a copy of the lab books?"

Will spoke at last. "Jennifer said she'd make a copy and return it to us."

"But she didn't! Unbelievable! You guys are really something!" He was shouting now. "Are you telling me there isn't anything – no rough notes – no nothing?"

Daniel was uncomfortably aware that everyone in the car park could hear what Lyle was saying.

"Lyle, lower your voice," Honor said.

"I will not!" But he had, if only by a fraction.

"This isn't getting us anywhere," Daniel said firmly. "I'll begin by talking things through with Will. See if he can reconstruct what he did. The lab's order books will tell us what materials were bought and when, and that will give us some idea of a timeline."

"Ian can help you with that," Honor said. She gestured to the ponytailed man who was hovering behind her. "Ian Gladwill is our head technician. What he doesn't know about what goes on in the lab isn't worth knowing."

"OK," Lyle said. "It's a start. But don't think I'm leaving it at that. I'm going to get to the bottom of what happened to that lab book if it's the last thing I do."

Chapter Fourteen

"This kind of thing gives a lab a bad reputation," Daniel told Rachel. "The Health and Safety people will be all over the place like a rash."

Chloe was in bed and asleep at the proper time for once, and they were having a late supper together.

"What'll happen if the lab book doesn't come to light?" Rachel asked.

"I put the best gloss I could on it, but it's not looking good. I'm going to have my work cut out finding evidence that they really did make the discovery first."

The phone rang and Daniel got up from the table to answer it.

"Hi Dan, it's Julia."

"Julia! How are you? And Toby and the girls?"

Julia was an old friend from university days. They met now and then for lunch when Daniel was in London on business, though it occurred to Daniel now that it had been a while since the last time.

"We're all fine. And you and Rachel? And Chloe?"

"We're OK, thanks."

There was a pause, then Julia said, "It's terrible about Jennifer." She sounded awkward, and Daniel understood why. Just what was the right level of condolence in a situation like this?

"I hadn't seen her since the divorce. But yeah, it is."

"Look, Dan, I didn't ring about that – at least, not exactly. Thing is, I hear you've taken over from her on the Calliope patent case. You're working for Lyle Linstrum, yes?"

Alarm bells were ringing. Julia was a financial journalist, and a very good one.

"What have you heard?" Daniel asked.

"Nothing I'd go public on," she warned, "but one of my sources informs me that Lyle might be on the way out."

"Really?"

"You know how these things go. There've been a lot of problems with Calliope. First that disaster with the clinical trial, now the problem with the patent. Of course it won't make that much difference to you, you're working for the company rather than Lyle personally, but I thought you should know. Like I say, there might be nothing in it – "

"But you think there is."

"That's my instinct. Of course if you hear anything your end..." Julia said, hopefully.

Daniel laughed. "Come off it, Julia. You know me better than that."

"Yeah," she sighed. "Always worth a try, though."

"But tell you what, lunch is on me next time."

As he went back to the table, he thought about what Julia had said. That instinct of hers... A few years ago she had broken a story that had got her a Press Association award. And this time she didn't know the half of it. When news got out about the missing lab book, the balloon would really go up. It wasn't Lyle's fault, but that didn't matter. He was developing a reputation for being unlucky.

"Shall I heat that up?" Rachel asked, pointing at his plate of risotto.

"No, it's fine," he said, picking up his fork. He told her what Julia had said.

Rachel stared at him, her glass of wine half way to her lips. "How do you mean, on the way out?"

"He might be fired."

"But how can that happen? It's his own company, isn't it?"

"But it's not his money. At least, not all of it. It's kept afloat by venture capital. If they want to get rid of Lyle, they can.

People are ousted from companies they've founded all the time. Look at Steve Jobs."

"It seems so unfair!" She thought for a few moments. "How will this affect you?"

"It won't. At least, not personally. None of what's happened is down to me. But it means the stakes are that much higher for Lyle. No wonder he lost his temper this morning." Daniel looked at his watch. "Is that the time? I've got stuff I've got to finish."

He pushed back his chair and began stacking the plates.

"Leave them," Rachel said. "I'll do them after the news. You get on with what you've got to do." She hesitated. "There's something in the *Ely Standard* about Jennifer. I thought you'd want to see it. I've left it on your desk."

He'd only opened the door to his study when she called him. "Dan, Dan, come quickly!"

He got there in time to see a policeman talking to the camera. "... and so we would be grateful if anyone who saw Jennifer Blunt that evening would come forward."

"What was that about?" he asked Rachel.

"The police don't think she was alone in the car."

He stared at her. "You mean, when she crashed it?"

"They didn't say that. All they said was that someone had reported seeing the car before it happened and there was a passenger. They're asking whoever it was to come forward."

He sat at his desk, turning it over in his mind. Had someone left the scene of the accident without alerting the emergency services? He wondered how long Jennifer had been lying there – but it was better not to think about that.

He turned his attention to the newspaper, lying open at the page with the piece about her. They had managed to find a photo from their archives. Jennifer's company had sponsored the restoration of a local children's playground and she had represented the firm at the opening. The photo showed her with Nick and their son. Again he had the feeling that there was something familiar about that child. When you are a parent, you see a lot of small children, but where could he have seen Harry without seeing Jennifer or Nick too?

He gazed at the three faces. What *was* it? He thought of the way he had scrutinized the photographs on Jennifer's desk looking for her likeness in Harry. It hadn't occurred to him to look for Nick's. Now he did look and he couldn't see it. Of course, that didn't necessarily mean anything.

And yet, and yet... A memory that he could no longer keep at bay came sidling into the front of his mind and suddenly it was as if it were yesterday, that July afternoon in the house in Chesterton. The removal men had been and gone. Dust moats danced in the shafts of light that came through curtainless windows. His footsteps echoed on the floorboards as he roamed the empty house, waiting for Jennifer to come and collect the desk that had belonged to her mother, the only piece of furniture that she wanted to keep. She arrived and he helped her carry the desk out. It was a baking hot day and she came into the house to get a drink of water. There weren't any glasses, and she drank from the tap. When she straightened up, her chin was wet. He saw the tiny blonde down at the corner of her lips and something inside him shifted. The outline of her legs through the thin summer dress, the swell of her breasts, the freckles on her chest: he had never desired her more.

Afterwards he felt that it couldn't have happened any other way. It was as if the heat and the light, that specific time of day, had somehow brought it about.

"I've got to have you. Now," he heard himself say.

"Yes," she said.

Those were the last words they had ever spoken to each other.

There was no furniture in the room except the large sofa that the next inhabitants had agreed to have. Without a word they moved towards it.

It was a coupling like nothing in their married life, and thinking of it now, he was aroused. It wasn't about love. It was about taking back what had been stolen from him, getting his own back on Nick.

When it was over, he went out into the garden and watched the river flowing past. Standing there, he understood that until that day there'd been a part of him that did not believe his marriage was over – a part that even today had hoped that when she walked into the house she'd say that it had all been a mistake and it wasn't too late to cancel the divorce and pull out of the house sale. Now he saw that for the fantasy it was.

When he went back into the house, Jennifer had gone.

The next day the decree nisi had come through, and two months later the marriage was officially over.

From that day onwards they had managed to avoid each other. They had contrived things so that their paths would not cross. They were strangers to one another. How else could it be when your wife ran off with your best friend? Just that once he had seen her in the distance at Cambridge station and his heart had lurched.

He knew that he didn't love, had never loved, Rachel in the way that he had once loved Jennifer. Perhaps it just wasn't possible to fall in love at thirty-five in the way that you can at twenty. Or perhaps that kind of love only comes once –

"Dan," Rachel said. She was standing in the doorway.

He gave a start.

"I'm off to bed," she said. "I need an early night. Don't stay up too long, will you, love?"

"No, no, I won't. I'll be up soon."

He waited until he had heard her go upstairs into the bedroom, then he examined the photo again.

"With her son, aged five," he read. A year older than Chloe. But was he only just five or was he nearly six? Could it be...? He stared at the photo, looking now for his own features. He knew it wasn't easy to see your own face in another's. People told him that Chloe took after him, but he couldn't see it himself. Of course, likeness wasn't just a matter of physical resemblance: it was also a fleeting expression, a smile, the tilt of the head. And those were things that Harry would have picked up from Nick, just from being around him.

He counted forward from July. When had Harry been born? If it was April, or perhaps May... It shouldn't be difficult to find out. It was a matter of public record, after all. After prowling around the internet for a while, he realized that it wasn't as straightforward as he had hoped. There were records, but he would have to consult them in person. Was there maybe another way? Jennifer's parents were both dead, but what about Nick's parents? His father was retired from the army, his mother was a local conservative councillor, both of them inveterate *Daily Telegraph* readers. Nick was an only child and, OK, they certainly wouldn't have approved of his running off with his best friend's wife, but on the other hand, Harry *was* their grandson. He typed "Daily Telegraph" and "Birth Announcements" into Google. Seconds later he was looking at an online entry: "On 30th April to Jennifer (née Ewing) and Nick, a son Harry David Francis."

He told himself to get a grip. Yes, the timing was right, but that still didn't mean he was Harry's father. Jennifer and Nick were in the full flush of their affair and would have been at it like rabbits. And come to think of it, wouldn't she have been using some sort of contraception? Otherwise she wouldn't have risked having sex with Daniel. Would she?

An idea came to him. He looked at his watch. Eleven o'clock. Dad would still be up.

He punched in the number. Sure enough, his father answered on the third ring.

"Hi, Dad."

"What's up, son?" He sounded anxious.

When there is a sick child in the family, an unexpected phone call always rings alarm bells.

Daniel hastened to reassure him. "Chloe's fine. I was just wondering if you could lay your hands on a photo of me, aged five or six." What reason could he give? "Chloe needs one for a project at her nursery."

"Your mother never did get round to putting the photos in albums, but she wrote names and dates on them all. I've got them all in a box somewhere. I'll see what I can do."

They chatted for a bit, and the call ended with loving messages for Chloe and Rachel. In his father's eyes, Rachel, the mother of his only grandchild, could do no wrong. Rachel loved the old man and was an attentive daughter-in-law. Her own father had died young.

When Daniel went up to bed, Rachel was asleep.

He lay awake for a long time beside her, his thoughts churning.

What if Jennifer *had* risked it? What if Harry had inherited half his chromosomes from Daniel and was Chloe's half-brother? What were the odds that Harry would be a match for Chloe? It wasn't straightforward, because he would need to have the same rare tissue type that Chloe had inherited from Daniel *and* a more common one that belonged to one in five of the population. So this meant that if Harry was Daniel's child, there was a one in ten chance that his bone marrow could rescue Chloe from a lifetime of blood transfusions and the spectre of an early death. A one in ten chance... not great, but far, far better than anything else that was on offer.

A photo of Daniel as a child would only tell so much. Even if Harry turned out to be a dead ringer for the six-year-old Daniel, it wouldn't be actual proof. If he'd only realized earlier, he could have taken something of Harry's – a hairbrush or, better, a toothbrush – when he had been at Jennifer's house. But at the time he hadn't suspected, and now there was no way he could get back in.

Or was there?

Chapter Fifteen

Katie dumped her suitcase and her rucksack in the saloon. It was blissfully warm. Rachel must have come over and lit the fire, bless her. When Katie had realized that she wasn't going to get back into the lab that day, she'd rung Rachel and asked if she could move into the boat right away. Rachel had said it was fine, so Katie had popped over to pick up a key and had spent the afternoon packing up at her flat. It meant that the day hadn't been completely wasted, and also she'd save travelling time when she was allowed back into the lab. It was only a few minutes' drive away.

Coming along the tow path she'd bumped into Frank from the next-door boat. He was a burly bloke with a beard who'd introduced himself and hoicked her case onto the boat for her. Daisy had come out to say hello and to tell her not to hesitate if she needed anything. They seemed a lovely couple. Rachel was right: there was a real sense of community here.

She went up to the wheelhouse and, sighing with relief, locked the door. Talk about "battening down the hatches"; after the day she'd had, that was what she longed to do.

There was a note from Rachel in the galley. "Help yourself to anything that needs eating up. And there's pasta and so on: just replace anything that you finish."

As she took her coat off she caught sight of the letters that she'd stuffed in her pocket when she left the flat. She looked at them. Junk mail, except for an envelope with a Glasgow postmark. She ripped it open and found a letter informing her that she hadn't got the principal scientific officer job that she'd applied for. The end of a perfect day.

She opened her iPad to check her emails. There was one

from her mum. A picture of the Shanghai skyline against an improbably blue sky came up. She was out there visiting Katie's brother and his family, and having the holiday of a lifetime. Australia was next on the itinerary. Well, at least the sun was shining somewhere.

She opened an email from Becky, her best friend from school days. It was to tell Katie that she was pregnant and the baby was due in May. Before she could stop herself, she felt a pang of envy, and how mean was that? She was thrilled for Becky, of course she was, but taken unawares, she'd been ambushed by a feeling that Becky had somehow stolen a march on her. And not only Becky. In the last year, two other friends had had babies. But it was Becky who really brought it home.

Katie's last relationship had been one of those long-distance ones that are so often the lot of ambitious young scientists. When one of you is in Cambridge and the other is in Durham, you have to be really committed to make it work, and it turned out that they weren't. Joe had met someone else up there and she discovered that she didn't really mind. Was even a bit relieved. That had been six months ago, and however was she going to meet someone new, if she went on staying late in the lab before going home to slump on the sofa with a pizza and a box set?

She went into the bedroom, sat down on the bed and kicked off her shoes. She lay back on the pillows, too tired to do anything but gaze at the ceiling. After a while she realized she was hungry. She padded into the galley and looked in the fridge. There was a can of lager, a packet of ground coffee, half a bottle of milk, a lemon, a tub of black cherry yoghurt, and a small piece of cheddar. She opened some cupboards and found teabags, pasta, rice, olive oil, tins of tomatoes and tuna and dried herbs. She could put together a meal of sorts and that was what she'd do, because no way was she going out again tonight. She'd rather expected that she might have a visitor, but it didn't look as if that was going to happen. She'd got her laptop and *Breaking Bad* DVDs and that was all the entertainment she needed.

She reached for the can of lager and was just about to snap the ring pull, when there was a knocking upstairs on the wheelhouse door.

"Who is it?" she called, as she went up the stairs.

"It's Lyle."

"Hang on." She unlocked the door.

Lyle's long, lean face peered in.

"I wondered when you'd show up," she said.

Lyle stepped in and they went down to the galley together. He put two white plastic bags on the table and the enticing aroma of Chinese food made Katie's mouth water.

He opened his arms and enveloped her in his usual bear hug. She only went up to his shoulder. Some of the tension left her.

He released her and looked into her face. "You look tired," he decided, "and I'm guessing you haven't eaten. No? Good. I bought enough for two."

He began taking foil cartons out of one of the bags. "Prawn in black bean sauce, beef with ginger and spring onions, plus egg-fried rice, and spring rolls and prawn crackers, and this here is a vegetable dish – I forget what."

She gave a sigh. "Bliss. But why didn't you let me know you were coming?"

"Didn't I reply to your text?"

"You did not."

"Ah, well."

Typical Lyle, taking it for granted that everyone was at his beck and call, but there was no point in remonstrating, especially as pretty much everyone *was* at his beck and call.

He opened the second bag and brought out two bottles of Tsingtao beer.

She found a bottle-opener. He opened both bottles. They took one each and clinked them together.

"Let's get this food on the table," Lyle said. "We can talk while we're eating. Got any chopsticks?"

"What if I'd already eaten? Would you have scoffed the lot?"

"I'd have had a damn good try, but you can save me from myself."

It was three weeks since at Lyle's suggestion they had met at Kettle's Yard in Cambridge.

"Have you been here before?" he'd asked her as they went in through the front door.

She shook her head. "No, never."

"There's a gallery, but it's the house that's the gem. It was the home of Jim and Helen Ede. There's a fine collection of twentieth-century British art, but the whole place is a work of art. It's almost as if they're still living here."

Katie saw what he meant. There were pebbles arranged in a spiral, a lemon in a pewter dish, bowls of flowers.

"We're not likely to meet anyone we know, or maybe anyone at all," Lyle said. "And besides, I've been wanting to have another look at those Gaudier-Brzeskas." It was an unexpected side to Lyle: he was a keen collector of early twentieth-century prints and drawings.

And sure enough, on this grey October day they had the place pretty much to themselves.

The house was all lightness and white walls and wood. Lyle was different here, less in-your-face, less hyperactive. As they moved through the house, he stopped here and there to point out a Ben Nicholson painting or a David Jones drawing.

Katie had known Lyle since she was eighteen and he had arrived at Imperial College to deliver his daughter, Juliet, for her first term. Katie and Juliet had become best friends and Katie had spent fantastic working holidays out at the ranch in Texas.

Lyle was one of the first people she'd contacted when Michael died. He'd known Michael too and understood what a fix she was in. By the time they met at Kettle's Yard it was looking likely that Paul would take over as her supervisor, but she didn't know what she was going to do for lab space.

They climbed up to the first floor and stood by a little geranium-filled conservatory that overlooked a patch of lawn rimmed by trees that were shedding their leaves.

"I'm sure I can pull a few strings, Katie," Lyle said, "and get you a bench in Honor Masterman's lab. I happen to know they've got some spare capacity. It's over near Ely, but you won't mind that."

"Oh, Lyle, could you? That'd be great!"

"Sure."

Lyle tucked her arm into his and pressed it to his side. There was something of the courtly Southern gentleman about him.

"You're doing good work, important work. I can't see you stymied at this point in your career for want of lab space."

They made their way through the library and down the stairs into a large white space, top lit with diffused light.

"Let's sit down here, shall we?" Lyle gestured to a white sofa that ran almost the entire length of a wall. "It's my favourite part of the museum."

They sank down into it.

"I want to put something to you," Lyle said. "Whatever you say, makes no difference. That bench in the lab is yours – as long as I can swing it. So, no strings, OK? At the same time, there are reasons why it would suit me just fine to have you in that lab."

Katie was intrigued. "What's this about, Lyle?"

"Honor Masterman. That's mostly what it's about. Look, when the chance of investing in this gene therapy for obesity came along, I won't say I didn't jump at the chance. The good it could do – and yes, it's true I stand to make a bundle – "

"Not to mention being the guy who goes down in history for making it happen." Lyle had an ego the size of... well, Texas. A little gentle teasing didn't go amiss.

"Well, yeah, that as well," he acknowledged with a wry smile. "Thing is, I had mixed feelings about getting into bed with Honor – in a manner of speaking." He sighed. "Let me tell you a little story, Katie. Long ago when I was a postdoc, when I was just a working scientist slogging it out in the lab, I knew Honor – "

"You once actually worked in a lab?"

"Yeah, I've served my time at the coalface. In those days Honor and I were both young, very young."

There were footsteps on the stairs and a middle-aged woman came into view. Lyle fell silent. She drifted round the room, looking at the paintings and sculptures, and then left the way she had come.

Lyle went on.

"We were working on different projects. For her there was a rush to get to the Patent Office – just as there was with the obesity therapy – and one of the team cut a corner or two to get there first. When it came out, she categorically denied knowing about it. I happened to know that she did. So one thing I learned about Honor: she's the kind of person who wouldn't think twice about lying to get out of a hole. So, yeah, she's brilliant, but is she 100 per cent reliable? I guess I managed to put that incident to the back of my mind. It was a long time ago, and like I said, we were very young, but then… the death of that young man in the clinical trial…"

"That wasn't their fault, though, was it?"

"No way they could have foreseen it, I admit that. She and Will Orville, her postdoc, were exonerated. But it's niggled away at me. And now we've got this interference case coming up – well, I don't want it all to blow up in my face in court. We've got one of the best patent lawyers in the UK going through the lab books. We should be just fine, but…"

"But that's where I come in?"

"Truth to tell, I hardly know what it is I'm asking you to do. Maybe just keep your eyes open, get a feel for what's going on…"

"Hey, this is exciting. You want me to go undercover," she joked.

He acknowledged the absurdity of the idea. "Hardly. But see if you can get the measure of Will Orville. He'd talk to you in a way that he wouldn't to me."

That was how it had begun. Sure, it felt a bit underhand and grubby, poking about in the lab and pumping people for information, but it was interesting, too. It was almost like a game, but not just a game. The integrity of the scientific process: that wasn't just part of her job, it was something that really mattered to her. The idea of someone cutting corners didn't sit well with her. For all his flamboyance and his financial risk-taking, she knew that Lyle felt the same.

"Things aren't looking good," Lyle said now, as he picked up a prawn with his chopsticks.

The lines in his long, leathery face looked deeper, as if he hadn't been getting enough sleep.

"You've heard about our lady lawyer?" he went on.

Ordinarily she'd have teased him about the "lady" bit, but she just nodded sombrely. "Will told me. And about the lab book."

He looked at her keenly. "So he *has* been talking to you?"

She nodded. "He's pretty upset about it all."

"What a mess. Turns out I was right to have my suspicions about Honor. That woman is not running a tight ship. Take that radiation leak. How could that have happened?"

"I've been wondering about that. Either someone was very careless, or..."

"Honor's lab seems to be – well, shall we say, unusually accident-prone?"

She and Lyle looked at each other. She didn't want to put it into words. The thought that someone might have tracked that radioactivity around the lab on purpose made her go cold.

Another idea occurred to her – triggered by that term

"accident-prone". She too had been "unusually accident-prone" lately: the disaster of her western blot, the way her E.coli culture had failed. She put down her chopsticks. What if they weren't accidents?

"You've thought of something?" Lyle said.

"You don't know the half of it, Lyle."

She told him what had happened to the E.coli culture and the western blot. "I don't like to think that someone could have messed things up deliberately. Labs operate on a basis of trust, but..." Her voice trailed off and Lyle finished the sentence.

"But maybe there's someone who's not playing by the rules."

"It's easy to get paranoid. Most likely they were just mistakes on my part. These things happen." She toyed with her mixed vegetables. "I wonder, though..."

"Yes?"

"About the lab book. It'll be good news for the other firm – the one that's claiming they got there first – if you don't manage to find it. You don't suppose they..."

He shook his head. "I can see why you might think that, but no, it wouldn't occur to those guys. It wouldn't be worth their while to take that kind of risk. Their dirty work is reserved for high-class lawyers. They'll bend the law as far as they can, but they can't afford to be caught breaking it."

When they'd finished eating, she made him an espresso – he seemed to live on the stuff – and herself a cup of tea.

"Got to be off soon." He drained his coffee. "Driving to London tonight." He hesitated, then said, "Katie – I don't want you to put yourself at risk in any way."

She stared at him. "How do you mean?"

"I'm not easy in my mind. Two people are dead. The guy in the clinical trial and our lady lawyer."

"But they were both accidents, surely?"

"I guess so. But there's something I haven't told you. Jennifer was concerned about something – something that she didn't want to talk about in the office. That's why we agreed to meet at her house. That was the day of the accident. I waited there, but she never showed."

"But... did she say what was wrong?"

"Nope. I have a bad feeling, a very bad feeling about this project. Wish I'd paid more attention to my intuition at the start."

She couldn't help laughing. "Intuition! You're supposed to be a hard-headed scientist, Lyle. Don't tell me you believe in intuition."

His expression was serious. "Sure I do. Now, mind you keep in touch – and watch your step. I don't want to end up regretting that I placed you in Honor's lab."

As she unlocked the wheelhouse door, he said, "You know, I wish you'd think again about coming over to our side, Katie."

It wasn't the first time Lyle had said this. But she'd always thought of it as gamekeeper turned poacher. The bigger world of patents and drug development and money had never appealed.

"I'm a lab rat, through and through," she said.

"A lot of good work goes on in companies like mine, and we're always looking for talented folk."

"I know that, Lyle. And thanks, but no thanks."

"Come here." He hugged her.

Then he raised a hand in farewell and walked off down the tow path. She watched for a few moments as the bobbing light of his torch grew smaller.

She locked up, went down into the galley and picked up her cup of tea. She sat down on the black leather sofa in the saloon. She'd switched off her phone while they ate. She switched it on to check for messages and almost immediately it began to ring.

It was Will.

"Hi there, I've got a message from Honor. It's not as bad as it might have been. It's only a soft shutdown and it's just our room. They might be able to squeeze some of us in elsewhere. You're to come in first thing."

"That'd be great. Thanks for letting me know."

"OK then, see you tomorrow. Maybe we can fit in that drink sometime soon?"

"Yeah, cool."

Will reminded her a little of Lyle. They weren't similar to look at, but there was something of Lyle about his energy and his confidence. You knew that he was setting out to charm, but it still worked.

She didn't think of Lyle's warning until she'd hung up. She shrugged. There could surely be no danger in just going out for a drink.

Chapter Sixteen

Daniel was in his car outside Jennifer's house waiting for Bryony to arrive. Daniel had dressed it up as conscientiousness, arguing that he needed to be absolutely sure the lab book wasn't there. And actually there was some truth in that. Bryony had rung that morning to let him know she had searched Jennifer's office again and she was 100 per cent sure that it wasn't there.

As for Harry, Daniel veered between thinking he was crazy for even entertaining the idea that Harry might be his son and being convinced that he was.

His mobile rang and it was Alison.

"An Ian Gladwill rang," she told him. "He wants you to ring him back."

The lab technician? What did he want? Daniel took the number and was about to ring him when there was a tap on the car window.

It was Bryony.

He got out of the car.

"Let's get this over with," she said.

They walked up the path and she let him into the house.

Things seemed different somehow. Last time it had been as if Jennifer had just left and might be back at any moment. But now there was a brooding quality to the silence. It was as if someone was there waiting for them.

Perhaps Bryony felt it too. She gave a little shiver. "It's cold in here," she said. "Shall we start with the study again?"

"OK."

They went in and Daniel checked again, but it was just a matter of form. He knew the lab book wouldn't be there.

"I was wondering," he said. "What about the little boy's bedroom? We didn't really look there."

Bryony frowned. "How would it have got in there?"

"Well, what if he took it and hid it? You know what kids are like. Or Jennifer might have hidden it."

"Why on earth would she have done that?"

"We were burgled once, money and passports pinched, so she took to squirrelling things away, hiding them in unlikely places. The lab book – she'd have known that she shouldn't have taken it home, not without making a copy and leaving it in the office. She wouldn't have left it lying around."

"OK, then."

She headed for the stairs and he followed her.

They stood for a few moments in Harry's room, looking around. Daniel began to look through the books in Harry's bookcase, checking that the lab book wasn't wedged behind them. Harry had some of the same books as Chloe: *Dear Zoo*, *Where's Spot?*, *Each Peach Pear Plum* – Daniel could recite that one off by heart. The bed with its dinosaur-patterned cover was just as Harry had left it, the cover trailing on the floor. Daniel wondered if he and Nick would come back to live here. But he didn't want to dwell on that. More to the point was finding a way to get rid of Bryony for long enough to take something with Harry's DNA on it.

The doorbell rang. He and Bryony exchanged glances. It rang again.

"Oh, hell," she said, making for the door. "You go on looking."

He heard her go down the stairs and open the door, then voices.

He slipped out onto the landing and into the bathroom. He snapped on the light. There were toothbrushes in a glass on the shelf above the basin. The small one must be Harry's. He snatched it up, switched off the light, and was back in Harry's room just in time to hear the front door shutting. He wrapped the toothbrush in the plastic bag that he'd brought and slipped it into his inside breast pocket.

His heart was thumping. He tried to steady his breathing.

"Just that awful next-door neighbour," Bryony said as she came into the room. "She was with her husband this time; said she saw the light on and thought she'd better check. I think she's just nosy."

She looked around the room. "How are you getting on?"

"No luck, I'm afraid."

He had got what he wanted and his instinct was telling him to get out while the going was good. Yet, perversely, he felt inclined to linger, to play for time. And after all, he *did* want the lab book, too. *What have you done with it, Jennifer?* he silently asked her. *Give me a clue.*

The silence of the house settled round them. It was disturbed by a small sound downstairs.

"Probably the heating system," Bryony said.

He nodded.

"This must be hard on you," she said.

"It's been quite a while since the divorce... but yes... Can we just check the bedroom?"

"Of course we can."

They went into Jennifer's room.

"I'll check the drawers," she said.

"Fine." He went over to a wardrobe with sliding doors that took up the whole of one wall. He opened one of the doors. The business suits and shirts were all lined up at one side. They were part of Jennifer's working life and they had been organized as meticulously as the rest of it. How strange it was, the way inanimate things outlasted their owners. The scent of Chanel No. 5 still clung to them.

And then it hit him: a wave of longing and desire. He had an almost irresistible urge to step in among the clothes, to grab them and press them to his face, holding his lost wife close in the only way he could. Only the presence of Bryony stopped him. He heard her come up behind him, but he didn't turn round. He needed a few moments to say goodbye to Jennifer, goodbye to his younger self. He let himself think about the times they had been so close that they had finished each other's sentences, had laughed without having to explain what was funny; the times they woke up to find they were holding hands.

Yes, it was all over, the love and hope and pain, the tenderness and the anger. Jennifer had gone.

"We'd better go," he said, turning to Bryony.

But she wasn't there. She was on the other side of the room, coming out of the bathroom.

His scalp crawled. Who had come up behind him? *No one,* he thought; *just my imagination. I'm losing it.*

Bryony came over and looked in the wardrobe. "She had some lovely things."

"She always looked great."

"I suppose all this'll go to the Oxfam shop."

They were silent.

"Well, I think we're about finished here, aren't we?" Bryony said.

He nodded. They made their way downstairs.

They were about to step out of the front door, and Bryony was reaching to switch the hall light off, when he said, "Just a minute."

She waited with her hand on the switch.

Something was tugging at him. What was it? Something he'd seen. Something to do with those immaculate white shirts. Or was it something he hadn't seen?

"Where's the ironing board?" he said.

"What?"

"It was the way we divided things up. I did the supermarket shop. Jennifer always did the ironing, always – my shirts as well."

It was how Daniel had found out that she was having an

affair. Jennifer had gone away for the weekend to a reunion of old university friends – or so she'd told him. He never did find out if that was true or not. Daniel had decided to get ahead with things and do the ironing for once. He got out the ironing board and he had felt something crackling under his fingers as he opened it out. He slipped his fingers under the cover and pulled out a piece of folded paper. Curious, not suspecting for a moment what he was about to discover, he unfolded it and read it.

A love letter – an old-fashioned love letter in these days of mobile phones and texts and emails. But then, Nick always had been the literary type. He was an English teacher and a published poet. The letter was explicit about what they had been up to. Daniel had to read it twice before he could take it in, and even then his mind offered him a variety of explanations. It was just a literary exercise, unrelated to real life; no, it was real but Nick's feelings were unreciprocated; OK, maybe they were having a flirtation, but... Even as he ran through these alternatives, he knew that he was just buying time, bracing himself for the awful truth. His wife and his best friend were having a full-blown affair and they were at it every chance they got.

"So where's the ironing board?" he said now. "Did you see one?"

She thought about it. "No, but then I wasn't looking for one. But so what?"

"I've just had an idea. Something I've remembered about Jennifer. A hiding place... Bear with me. Please? Just five minutes."

"Oh, alright. You take downstairs and I'll take upstairs."

Five minutes later they met back in the hall. He hadn't found it and he could tell from the look on her face that she hadn't found it either.

"There has to be one," he said.

"Professional woman with a busy life, perhaps she sent her stuff out to be ironed."

"Maybe." He was unconvinced. "But there *is* an iron. I found it in a cupboard in the kitchen."

She shrugged and turned to the door. Then she paused, seemingly struck by a thought. She turned back and went into the kitchen. Daniel followed her. She opened a drawer. It was full of cutlery. Next to it was what looked like a solid piece of wood.

"We're planning to have our kitchen redone," she said. "They're awkward things to store, ironing boards. I'm thinking of having one built in."

She curled her fingers under the bottom edge of the wooden panel and pulled. The wood slid out and tilted forwards to reveal an ironing board. She pulled it out and felt along it into the recess. She drew out an A4-sized notebook.

Once again Rachel had gone to bed, leaving Daniel working in his study. This time he really was working, going through the lab book just to check that it was complete, no pages missing. And it was fine. There was still a lot to do before the deadline, but he had everything he needed now. *Thank you, Jennifer,* he said silently.

He'd emailed Honor to let her know the good news.

It was midnight now. He was absolutely shattered, but there was still a decision to be made. He opened his desk drawer and took out Harry's toothbrush. It was green, and the handle was shaped like a dinosaur. Chloe had one similar, but the handle on hers was shaped like a seahorse.

He went online and typed "DNA tests" into Google. There was no shortage of private labs carrying out this kind of work. He was offered a range of options. It would take around a week. He hesitated. He had thought he'd made his mind up – why else risk stealing this from Jennifer's house? Because he was under no illusion. It *was* stealing. Even if the DNA proved that he was Harry's father, he wouldn't be able to explain how he knew. He'd have to find another way of bringing it to light. If he *was* going to bring it to light. Because first he would have to confess to Rachel that he had a child by Jennifer.

"Daddy?"

He gave a start. He looked round to see Chloe standing in the doorway.

"I want a drink."

He got up and went over to her.

"Come on, little chick. Let's get you back upstairs."

He hoisted her up and she put her arms round his neck.

The plastic mug by her bed was still full of water. He was touched by the obviousness of her subterfuge. He sat down on the bed with her on his knee.

"Did you have a bad dream again?" he asked.

She nodded. "Daddy, I don't want to go to the hospital again."

A cold hand closed round his heart.

"I know," he said. "I wish you didn't have to. But you have to go so that you'll stay well and be able to do all the things you like doing. Do you understand?"

She nodded and the resignation, the acceptance, made her seem much older than four, and pained him even more than her reluctance to go to the hospital. There were things small children shouldn't have to understand.

"Shall I tell you a story?" he asked.

Her face brightened. "Yes, please. Rumpytiltskin."

As he tucked her into bed, he reminded himself that she lived very much in the present. Already she had moved on. For her the disease wasn't the constant burden that it was for him and Rachel.

She snuggled down with the rabbit in the crook of her arm and put her thumb in her mouth. He lay down beside her and began for what seemed the hundredth time. "There was once a..."

Sometime later, his eyelids jerked open. Chloe was fast asleep beside him. He looked at his watch. He must have slept for at least an hour. There was a sour, metallic taste in his mouth. He got up and looked down at Chloe. He removed her thumb from her mouth and tucked her hand under the duvet. She sighed in her sleep.

He got up and went into the bathroom. He opened the bathroom cabinet where sensible, well-organized Rachel kept the spare toothbrushes. He got out one for Chloe, took off the packaging and substituted it for the one currently in use. Luckily it was the same colour and shape, so hopefully no one would notice. He took the old toothbrush down to his study. He put each toothbrush in a separate plastic bag, taking care to keep them well apart, labelled the bags, and found a padded envelope. He called up the page of DNA testing companies. He noted with a grimace that most of the websites emphasized the potential of the test to settle questions of paternity quickly and reliably, and he had a vision of hundreds, even thousands, of men up and down the country looking at their children and harbouring suspicions that they weren't really the father. If it hadn't been for Chloe, his instinctive distaste would have got the better of him. But he was doing it for her, so he pressed on. He found one website that was relatively sober in its claims and presentation. That would do.

The odds were against Harry being a match, but he had to know one way or the other, simple as that. He told himself that it was more a matter of elimination than anything else. The test would come back negative – or even if Harry was his, he wouldn't be a match for Chloe – and Daniel could put the possibility out of his mind once and for all. And no one need be any the wiser.

Chapter Seventeen

The garlic hit the hot oil with a sizzle.

"When you said you were going to throw a meal together, I didn't realize you meant it literally," Katie said.

Will laughed. "I spent two summers working in the kitchen of a vegetarian restaurant. Learned how to do it properly. And we can't hang about, can we?"

He was dealing with the onions now, chopping them in a series of rapid movements – so rapid that she feared for his fingers. Into the pan went the onions, releasing a scent that made Katie's mouth water. She'd skipped lunch and she was ravenously hungry.

Earlier that evening she had managed to time things so that she left the lab at the same time as Will. "Off home?" he'd asked. "Yes," she'd said, "but I've got to come back later." Turned out it was the same for him. They were both scrambling to catch up after their enforced break from the lab. She'd been going to suggest having a drink together, but he'd invited her to join him for something to eat. She'd readily agreed, curious to see where he lived.

She had followed Will's car to a Victorian house on the side of Ely furthest from the river and the quay. His flat was in the attic, a big room with a sleeping area divided off at one end and a bathroom and kitchen at the other. Tidy it wasn't. There were piles of DVDs and books everywhere, and on the sofa a towering pile of clean clothes, folded but not put away.

She watched him work. He was wearing a pale blue cotton shirt and had turned up the sleeves to reveal lightly tanned forearms covered in fine blond hair. Now that he wasn't wearing a lab coat, it was more obvious how solidly built he was, how muscular his shoulders were.

He said, "Some good news: Honor rang just before I left the lab. They've found the lab book."

"That's great," she said, thinking how relieved Lyle would be. "Can I do anything to help?"

"You could make a dressing for the salad."

He opened a cupboard, passed her the olive oil and vinegar.

She made the dressing and then went off to the bathroom.

It was clean, thank goodness, a point in Will's favour. She looked around for signs that he had regular female company, even sneaked a look in the bathroom cabinet. There was a box of tampons, so it looked as though there was someone.

As she went back to the kitchen, she stopped to examine a framed photo. Will was standing on a beach, wearing a wetsuit and holding a surfboard. One arm was draped around the shoulders of an attractive blonde woman, also in surfing gear.

Will saw her looking. "Lennox Head, New South Wales," he said. "I caught the biggest waves of my life there."

"You're a keen surfer?"

"Love it. Spend all my spare time on it. Well, that and skiing."

"Off-piste, of course?" she said, tongue in cheek.

He smiled, acknowledging the tease. "Naturally. Right old adrenalin junkie, that's me. I need something to counteract all those hours sitting around in the lab. I'm a rower as well."

A glorious smell of tomato and olive oil and garlic and oregano filled the air.

As they sat down to eat, Will said, "You didn't choose a great week for starting in a new lab, did you? Is the new bench OK?"

"Fine, thanks. Ian helped me move my stuff. He's a sweetie."

"Did you know he used to be a roadie for one of those heavy metal bands, Metal Bodice? I'm surprised he hasn't bent your ear about it. They were a bit of a one-hit wonder, but I think Ian misses the glory days."

That explained a lot – the earring, the ponytail – and she could just imagine him humping speakers about, soothing a temperamental bass guitarist, rustling up food at two in the morning.

They went on chatting over the meal. Before she'd started at the lab, Lyle had emailed her a whole load of information about Will, and about Honor. She took care not to show that she knew far more about Will than he knew about her.

Katie had gone to a comprehensive and had been the first in her family to go to university. Will's background couldn't have been more different. He came from a family of scientists and high achievers. After public school, he'd come to Cambridge as an undergraduate and had never left.

"What's Honor like as a supervisor?" Katie asked.

Will twirled spaghetti round his fork as he considered. "Well, she's the only supervisor I've ever had..."

"Really?" That was unusual. Katie wondered what it was like being with the same supervisor all the way through your career, instead of leading a nomadic life, following the grant money from lab to lab.

"She's brilliant, of course – that goes without saying. When I run into problems, she's able to stand back and see every angle. She's got the best scientific mind of anyone I've ever come across."

"And as a person?"

"As a person..." he mused. "She can be sharp, doesn't suffer fools gladly; her own mind works so fast, she can get a bit impatient if people can't keep up."

"But you can?"

He grinned. "Usually. I've always found her very supportive. Very..." he cast around for the right word – "loyal," he finally came out with.

"Loyal," Katie said. It was an interesting word to choose. Had Michael been loyal? Well, loyal to the work, maybe. She hadn't thought of their relationship in quite those terms.

The food was delicious, the sauce rich, sweet, and oily. She took a piece of bread and mopped her plate.

"So, what's next for you, Katie?"

She sighed. "Just been turned down for a job in Glasgow."

They were at much the same point in their careers, had both reached the stage where they could start applying for grants on their own account. The next year or two would be crucial for both of them.

"How about you?" she asked.

"One or two possibilities."

The alarm on Katie's phone went off. She had to get back to the lab.

Will stacked the plates in the sink and they went out into the night. They agreed that she'd drive them both in and bring Will back later.

They didn't talk much on the way to the lab. Katie concentrated on driving. The temperature was dropping and the roads would be icy later. The car park was empty except for Malcolm's Ford Fiesta.

They signed themselves in.

"Just us tonight," Will said, scanning the book.

"Just you," Malcolm agreed.

The lift had been switched off for the night. They went up the stairs to the fourth floor and Katie swiped her card to let them into the lab. She and Will had been moved into the same one.

Will clicked on the lights and the room lit up section by section. Katie was glad that she wasn't alone. Even with Will there it felt as if the lab had a secret life of its own and they had interrupted something.

She worked away at her bench while Will was busy at his own on the other side of the lab. The room was cooling down. The heating went off at night. Her fingers got cold and clumsy.

Will finished before she did. She was conscious of him in the background, flicking through a copy of *Nature*, yawning and fidgeting.

She'd already cultured her E.coli and she'd be able to

check that in the morning. Her current task was to find out whether her cell-line had been contaminated. That meant testing the culture medium the cells were growing in. She set to work using a pipette to pick up tiny amounts and mix them with reagents. Then the little plastic tubes went into the PCR machine, which would amplify the DNA overnight.

In the morning she'd find out if her cell-line had been infected with mycoplasma or some other organism. And in a way she hoped it had, because at least she'd know. The worst scenario was that she'd go on testing every link in the chain and not be able to pinpoint what had gone wrong. That could and did happen. *But you're a long way from that point*, she told herself as she at last loaded up the PCR machine. She set it to run for thirty cycles and pressed the button.

Katie grabbed her bag, and they headed for the door. Will turned out the lights, and section by section the lab disappeared into darkness. They went out, allowing the door to swing shut behind them and lock itself.

They'd reached the half-landing between the second and third floor, when Will paused and touched her arm. Katie turned and saw him pointing out of the window. This was the back of the building and there was a tangle of bushes beyond the tarmacked area. A fox had emerged. No, two foxes.

As they watched, the animals began to chase one another, batting each other with their paws, tumbling over and over, playful as kittens. Afterwards, Katie couldn't have said how long they stood there mesmerized by the sinuous movements, the speed, and the elegance. Then the foxes must have been spooked by something, because one moment they were there and the next they were gone.

Somewhere above them, Katie heard a sound. Will had heard it too; he gripped her arm and they stared at each other.

"What was that?" she whispered.

"I'm not sure."

They stood listening in the silence. It came again: footsteps overhead. Someone was moving around, very quietly, very surreptitiously.

"There's someone up there – and look – " Will hissed. He gestured to the window. She turned and looked. Except for the pattern of light thrown out by the windows in the stairwell, it was dark.

"No lights on up there." He spoke close to her ear and she felt the damp heat of his breath.

Someone must have heard them leave the lab and set off down the stairs. Someone who thought they had the building to themselves again. They weren't to know that she and Will had stopped to watch the foxes.

Will moved away from her. He sat down on the stairs and started unlacing his shoes. He gestured to her to come close. She bent down to listen.

"You go for Malcolm," he whispered. "I'll make sure they don't get away."

She hesitated. She didn't like this. Those other things that had happened in the lab... if this was someone crazy enough to leave a radioactive trail, what else might they be capable of?

"Go on," he breathed. "I won't confront them. I'll wait for Malcolm."

She nodded and slipped off her shoes. Will started off up the stairs, moving slowly and silently. She set off the other way, tiptoeing, one hand holding her shoes and the other touching the wall. After a few metres she looked back. Will had reached the corner. He nodded to her and went on.

She tiptoed down the stairs, concentrating on not making a sound, her mouth dry and her heart racing.

At last she rounded the final corner and Malcolm came into view. He was a peaceful sight – a newspaper spread out in front of him and his hand reaching into a lunchbox for a sandwich. Never had he seemed more solid and reassuring.

Surely she was out of earshot of the upper floors by now.

She put on her shoes and ran down the last flight of stairs. Malcolm looked up, and when he saw her expression he got to his feet.

"No one signed in after us, did they?" she asked.

He shook his head.

"Well, there's someone up there on the third floor in the dark. Will's making sure they don't get away."

Malcolm's mouth set in a grim line. He pulled the phone towards him and dialled 999. Katie listened in an agony of impatience as he reported an intruder.

As soon as he'd hung up she said, "Come on, come on, they might get away – and Will's on his own up there – "

"Hold your horses, hold your horses," he muttered.

He looked around as if searching for a weapon of some kind. He reached behind the desk and grabbed a large torch.

"You stay here," he said.

"Oh, no, no!"

"Yes." He was adamant. "Someone needs to let the police in. Come round here. This button opens the door."

Reluctantly she went round the desk and sat in Malcolm's chair. She watched him head up the stairs and disappear from view.

There was a large clock on the wall by the desk. She watched the second hand jerk round. A minute passed, then another. She couldn't help listening for the police to arrive, straining to hear sirens, though she knew they couldn't possibly be there yet.

As it came up to the four-minute mark, something happened. There was a vibration that she felt to her core, as if something had seized her and shaken her. Afterwards she recalled that time seemed to be suspended and that she had to wait for the sound of the explosion to reach her, but in reality it could only have been a split second. The silence that followed rang in her ears. Then the fire alarm went off and the air was full of its clanging racket.

She got to her feet as calmly as if she had all the time in

the world. Her thought processes had slowed almost to a standstill. She was half way to the stairs before she thought, *No*. She went back to the phone. She noted with interest that her fingers trembled as she pushed in the numbers. She told the operator to send an ambulance and alert the fire brigade. She hung up and pressed the button that released the door and propped it open with a waste paper basket.

She sprinted up the stairs. As she reached the first floor, a billowing cloud of plaster dust came tumbling down the stairs towards her. She pushed on, gasping and coughing.

At the top of the stairs to the third floor she found Will lying on the floor, struggling to raise himself on one elbow. He was coated in plaster dust. When she bent down to ask him if he was alright, he looked at her as if he didn't understand. She asked again, but he shook his head. She realized that he had been deafened by the blast.

The corridor was in darkness, and automatically she put up her hand to switch on the light. Will grabbed her leg and she looked down to see him frantically shaking his head.

"Gas!" he shouted.

He was on his knees now and she helped him stagger to his feet.

"Where's Malcolm?" she shouted, forgetting that he couldn't hear. But he understood anyway. He shook his head and pointed down the corridor. It wasn't just dark, it was opaque with dust. He went groping into it, coughing and spluttering, and she followed him.

At the door of the lab Katie fell over Malcolm, landing heavily on her knees. She could hear him groaning – he was alive at least, thank God. She groped around, found his hand and squeezed it. He squeezed back.

Cold night air flowed over her. Will must have gone into the lab and opened a window.

Behind her came the sound of boots thudding up the stairs. A powerful flashlight raked the darkness in which dust was slowly settling. Then strong arms were round her. She wanted to protest, to say that she couldn't leave Malcolm, but it was no good, the virtue was draining out of her. Her legs were trembling. She was weak now, too weak to resist, and she let herself be lifted to her feet and led away.

Chapter Eighteen

"Have you heard the news?"

With an effort Daniel tore his attention away from the lab book. Alison was standing in the doorway. She was still wearing her outdoor clothes, including a bobble hat, at odds with the rest of her svelte appearance.

He glanced at his watch. Half past eight. He'd arrived in the office at seven. He'd got up without waking Rachel and left her a note. He sometimes did this when he was really up against it at work, and she wouldn't think anything of it.

On the way in, he had posted the toothbrushes to the DNA testing lab.

"What's the matter?" he asked.

"There's been an explosion at Calliope Biotech. I heard on my car radio on the way in."

"No!"

"It'll be on the BBC News website."

She came and stood behind him while he called it up. Under "Breaking News" he read: "Explosion at biotech lab near Ely late last night – reports of casualties."

He opened his inbox to see if there was anything from Honor. He hadn't looked at his emails yet, preferring to make the most of the quiet time before everyone else arrived in the office. But there was nothing – not even an answer to the email he had sent her the night before.

"Can you get me Honor on the phone, Alison?"

She came back a few minutes later to say that she couldn't get through.

"Go on trying, and keep an eye on the website, would you, and let me know if there are any developments?"

She nodded. "Coffee?"

"Please. And don't put any calls through unless it's Honor. I've got to get on with this."

He focused on the lab book and put everything else out of his mind. He was working on the one that came chronologically before the one that had been missing. He grew more and more absorbed, following the ups and downs of the research project, making notes as he went. He could enter into Will's frustration and impatience when things seemed to reach a dead end, and the hope when a way round was discovered, or a flaw in an experiment detected. He reached the end of the lab book. There was important work in it, but he would have to work his way through the next one – the one he'd found at Jennifer's – and the one after it before he could be certain of their case.

Around ten o'clock, Alison brought in another cup of coffee and a croissant.

"I still haven't managed to get hold of Honor," she said. "But there's more news on the website. Two men were injured and one of them's in a critical condition. It didn't give their names."

"Keep trying Honor," he said.

She nodded and went out and he turned his attention to the lab book, the one that they had found at Jennifer's house.

Half an hour later he pushed his chair back, frowning. Was there something not quite right here? On the face of it, the lab book was perfectly OK. The writing was Will's alright, and the whole style of record-keeping was what he'd expect from the earlier lab books, right down to the scribbles in the margin. Perhaps it wasn't the actual book that was bothering him but the circumstances in which he'd found it. He had been so preoccupied with Harry and the DNA testing that he hadn't really thought that through. In spite of what he'd said to Bryony, was there something odd about Jennifer going to such lengths to conceal the lab book? Something even a little bit paranoid? OK, so she had taken it home to work on it over the weekend – which she absolutely should not have done without making a copy – and she had decided to put it somewhere safe. Why wasn't it safe enough in her study, locked away in a drawer? It was hardly likely that anyone would break in and steal it. It was only valuable to Calliope Biotech – or maybe to the opposing firm in the suit. It wasn't the kind of thing that an ordinary burglar would take. He remembered what Honor had said about a missed appointment and that she wished she'd asked Lyle to take Jennifer off the case. And Jennifer must have been under a lot of pressure, if she was planning to fight Nick for custody of Harry. He couldn't imagine the Jennifer he had known letting things slide. But then the Jennifer he'd thought he knew wouldn't have committed adultery either.

He rubbed his forehead. There was a tightness around his eyes and he had a headache coming on. Too little sleep, too much coffee. He drank some of the mineral water that Alison kept him supplied with and ate the croissant.

The effect on his blood sugar was almost instant. His mind cleared and he felt a surge of energy. He saw that he'd overreacted. Understandably; there was a lot of stuff muddying the waters, the involvement of Jennifer, the mishaps at the lab, and all this with Harry. But once you looked beyond that, was there really a problem? He had the lab book – that was the main thing – and now that he looked at it again, it was really no different from all the others that he'd seen over the years. He riffled through it. No pages missing. They had all been signed off by Honor, who would surely have spotted anything amiss.

As for Jennifer, he shrugged, no way now of knowing what she'd been thinking. It was simply that he had been spooked by the trip to her house and his sense of her presence there. Rachel had been right. It had been a mistake to take the case. And yet, and yet, if he hadn't, he wouldn't have realized about Harry, and if Harry did turn out to be his son...

He shook his head, annoyed with himself. He was doing it again – letting his mind wander.

He bent his head over the book.

Ten minutes later, Alison buzzed through to say that she had Honor on the line.

Daniel picked up the phone.

"Daniel?" she said.

"What's happened, Honor? Who's been hurt?"

"One of my security staff was injured, but not too badly, he'll be OK. But my chief technician is in the head injuries unit at Addenbrooke's. He's in a critical condition."

She sounded exhausted and he guessed that she hadn't had much sleep last night. A thought struck him.

"Your chief technician? Is that the guy I met yesterday in the car park?"

"That's him, Ian Gladwill."

Ian Gladwill! The guy had rung him yesterday and it had gone clean out of his mind. He had meant to ring him back, but he hadn't.

"How did it happen?"

"It was gas. But we don't quite know what happened yet. The police are looking into it."

He sensed that she was holding something back.

She went on. "I need to go over to the hospital. I only just read your email a few minutes ago. It's good news. You've got everything you need now, haven't you?"

"The lab book – the one that was missing – is open in front of me as we speak."

"Ah good, that's fine then. I'll let you get on."

They hung up.

Poor guy. Daniel wondered what Ian had wanted to tell him. Probably something to do with the orders for materials which he said he would look out for Daniel. Those could have filled in some of the gaps if he hadn't found Will's lab book.

It wasn't anything that could matter now.

Katie was trying to load up the PCR machine, but she was all fingers and thumbs. She kept dropping the pipette or sucking up too much. And now she was running out of time. And the awful thing, the dreadful thing, was that a child was going to die if she couldn't get this done tonight. And now someone was knocking at the door of the lab. Why couldn't they leave her to get on with it?

She broke the surface of her dream. She was in bed. The sense of relief was exquisite. The knocking began again. So that bit had been real. She groaned and groped for her watch. Half past eleven! How had that happened? And then she remembered. Last night – the explosion...

She struggled out of bed and pulled a big, warm woolly over her pyjamas.

The knocking had ceased, but now it began again. "Alright, alright," she muttered. She went through the saloon and up into the wheelhouse. There was someone standing outside the rain-streaked door. It was Will.

She unlocked the door, aware as she did so that she hadn't even brushed her hair.

"Are you alright?" he asked.

A gust of damp, cold air came in and she shuddered.

"Come in."

He came, moving slowly. "You weren't answering your phone – I just wanted to be sure you were alright. After last night – "

She raked her fingers through her hair. "Must have switched it off. I'm fine. I think."

"I'm sorry – "

"No, no, come through, sit down."

He followed her down into the saloon and lowered himself onto the black leather sofa.

"Are *you* alright?" she asked.

"Some nasty bruises – I went down heavily on my backside – and I've still got some ringing in my ears."

She shivered. "Just let me go and put something on my feet. I'll be back in a minute."

She went back into the bedroom and worked her feet into the thick hiking socks that she wore instead of slippers. She gave herself a few moments to orientate herself and brush her hair. Her memories of the night before, after the police had arrived, were just a jumble of snapshots... Malcolm on a stretcher being loaded into an ambulance; the horror on Honor's face when she'd arrived on the scene. The paramedics had checked Katie over and she'd been taken home in a police car. She'd thought she would be too wired for sleep, but she had gone out like a light.

She went back to the saloon. Will was sitting back with his eyes closed.

"I'll light the fire," she said, and he opened his eyes and smiled.

She assembled logs and screwed-up paper, and struck a match. When the paper had caught, she closed the door and opened the vents. The flames roared as they took hold.

"Is there any news?" she asked. "Will Malcolm be alright?"

"Honor rang me earlier. She says he'll be OK."

Katie sat back on her haunches, warming her hands. "And what about the other person? Who was it?" The last thing she'd seen as the police car drew away was someone else being loaded into the ambulance.

"Katie." He reached out to put a hand on her arm. "Come and sit down for a minute."

She got up and sat beside him on the sofa, wondering what was coming.

"There was another person in the lab," Will said. "Ian was there and he was badly hurt. He was thrown back against a bench and hit his head."

Katie stared at him. "Ian? But..."

"There was no one else in the building. They're saying that he was the intruder."

Intruder! The word conjured up a faceless and shadowy figure dressed in black, wearing a balaclava. She laughed out loud. "Don't be silly. Ian *belonged* in the lab. He must have had a reason for being there."

"I can't get my head round it either."

"But isn't it obvious? He must have been working late and heard what we heard. He came to investigate."

Above their heads, rain pattered on the roof of the boat.

"He hadn't signed the late book," Will said. "Don't you remember, we were the only ones in?"

"Well, people don't always, do they? Or he might have signed out, then remembered something he'd meant to do and popped back upstairs, thinking he'd just be a few minutes. I've done that before. Haven't you?" Katie shrugged. "And then, you know how it is, one thing leads to another..."

"It's easy to lose track of time," he agreed. "And his office is on the other side of the corridor so we wouldn't have seen the light on."

She could see that he wanted to be convinced.

Then his face clouded over. "But it doesn't stack up. Think about it, Katie. What was he doing there in the dark? And why didn't they find anyone else in the building?"

"Oh, that's nothing," she said stoutly. "There was plenty of time between me leaving Malcolm's desk and the police arriving for someone to escape."

He thought about that.

A cabin cruiser chugged past, leaving a wake that rocked the boat. It was raining harder now, streaking the windows, blurring the view.

"You're right," Will said. "We should keep an open mind. At least until we see what the police come up with." He winced and shifted his position.

"Let's have some coffee," Katie said.

"Good idea."

She went over to the galley, and put the kettle on. She needed the loo and went into her bedroom to visit the en suite bathroom. As she washed her hands, she brooded over the fate of her PCR.

Would the vibrations from the explosion have damaged the calibration? It was awful to be worrying about her work when people were lying injured in hospital, but she couldn't help it. Maybe the whole building was unsafe and they'd have to close the lab completely. She'd already lost so much time.

She came out of the bathroom. The day had a time-out convalescent feel to it, something to do with still being in pyjamas. The paramedics had warned her that she was probably suffering from shock, and the after-effects could be unpredictable. She felt sleepy, disinclined to make an effort, and a bit chilly. She pulled open one of the drawers under the bed to see if there was a blanket she could wrap herself in.

The bedroom door was open into the saloon and she heard the theme tune from *The Wire*. It was the ringtone on Will's phone. She smiled and shook her head.

"Oh, hi," she heard him say, and then, "What?"

She paused in what she was doing, struck by the concern in his voice. He lowered his voice to a murmur and she didn't catch what he said next.

She went on with what she was doing, found a fine wool plaid blanket, more like a shawl, really, and draped it round her shoulders.

By the time she went into the saloon, he had ended the call and was putting the phone back in his pocket.

"Everything alright?" she asked.

"Yeah, fine, thanks; that was Honor." His tone was casual. "She wants to see me. Logistical problems of how we're going to keep the work going while the lab – or some of it – is out of commission."

"No news about Malcolm or Ian?"

"Nope. I said I'd go round to her house."

He had recovered himself well and if she hadn't overheard his initial response, she might not have known anything was wrong. Even so, the signs of strain were evident. He couldn't conceal the tension in his body and he was distracted, not quite there with her.

He drank his coffee so quickly that he must surely have burned his mouth, and then he said he had to be off.

She watched through the glass window of the wheelhouse as he limped down the tow path in the rain.

She went thoughtfully back to the saloon. Maybe it *had* been Honor on the phone, but she wouldn't mind betting her next research grant – always supposing there was one – that there was more to it than he had let on.

She was about to go and get dressed when there was a knock on the glass doors. Rachel and Chloe were standing outside.

She hurried to let them in.

"Katie, are you alright?" Rachel said. "I heard on the news about the lab."

"Come in, come in."

Rachel ushered Chloe in. The little girl was wearing a pink sou'wester as well as her pink wellies and raincoat.

"Hello, Katie," she said, beaming up at her. "I do hope you are well," she added with quaint formality.

"Hello, sweetie. Rachel – I've just made some coffee. It'll still be hot. Come through to the galley. What would you like, Chloe?"

"Well, if you're sure. Chloe's just had some hot chocolate at home, but I'd love some coffee." She unwound the scarf from round her neck and plucked Chloe's hat off her head. "Take your wellies off, love."

The wellies were kicked off with a clatter. Just the presence of Chloe, her guileless face and her overflowing energy, had changed the feel of the day. It was as though a fresh spring breeze was wafting through the boat. Katie couldn't help smiling.

Chloe took a small stuffed duck out of Rachel's bag. "I'm going to put Quack-Quack to bed," she announced, and skipped off down the corridor to her old bedroom.

Katie and Rachel exchanged a glance of woman-to-woman complicity.

"She really is gorgeous," Katie said. "I could eat her up."

Rachel's face brightened. "She's wonderful. I didn't know I'd enjoy being a mother so much. But Katie, tell me what's going on. What's going to happen about your work?"

Katie poured out a mug of coffee for Rachel. "Yeah, that's the question. Or one of them." She didn't want to tell Rachel about Ian. After all, they hadn't got to the bottom of it yet and she was still hoping it would somehow turn out that he wasn't to blame. "It was the lab next to ours – I don't know how much can be rescued from what I was doing. I'm fine myself, thank goodness. Malcolm insisted that I stayed downstairs – "

Rachel's eyes widened. Her hand shot to her mouth. "You mean, you were actually there? Oh my goodness! And here's me worrying about the research!"

"Don't give it a second thought. I've been worried about it too – even before the explosion."

They went back into the saloon and sat down. Katie told Rachel about the problems with the western blot. Rachel listened intently. It was a relief to talk about it, Katie realized.

When Katie had finished, Rachel said, "It's funny. I'd imagined things would be, I don't know, more clear-cut than that. That once something has worked, it'll always work."

"I wish," Katie sighed. "You have to be able to replicate your results, show that it wasn't a one-off, a fluke. And I haven't been able to do that. Sometimes, like now, experiments that should work, don't, and you don't know why. You can start to doubt yourself, even though you know it happens to everybody."

"Stick with it. It's worth it, it really is. I've got to take Chloe for her blood transfusion in a couple of days. I can't tell you how wonderful it would be if one day I didn't have to do that. And that reminds me, I'd better go and see what she's up to."

While she was gone, Katie wondered why Rachel hadn't had

127

another baby, who might have been a match for Chloe. They could have gone for embryo selection. But she didn't know Rachel well enough to ask.

Rachel came back with Chloe dancing along behind her.

"I've put Quack-Quack to bed now, so we can go home and have lunch," she told Katie. She turned to Rachel. "But can Katie come too, please? Is she allowed?"

"Of course she is. We really ought to be getting home," said Rachel. "But Katie, you're very welcome to come for lunch."

"I can't, I'm afraid. I'm expecting the police to come round and interview me about last night."

Chloe's face fell and she made a moue of disappointment.

Rachel was looking around for Chloe's wellies. As she picked them up, she said, "I don't like the idea of you being here on your own after a shock like that. Is there anywhere you could go for a day or two – your parents', maybe?"

Katie laughed. "It's just my mum and she's visiting my brother and his family in Shanghai. I'm not telling her until she gets back. The police offered to ring her but I wouldn't let them. She'd be on the next flight home."

"But still... I know: why don't you come for supper? Just pot luck..."

"Yes!" shouted Chloe. "Katie's coming for supper!"

Katie hesitated, but Rachel's "Yes, do come, we'd love it" seemed warm and genuine. Perhaps it *would* be nice to be looked after a little bit. Then Chloe laced her fingers round Katie's arm and, looking down at her imploring face, Katie was lost.

"Well, if you're sure," she said.

"We'll see you at six thirty," Rachel said, planting the pink sou'wester on Chloe's head.

Chapter Nineteen

Daniel arrived home to find Rachel standing with her back to him at the kitchen sink, her shoulders shaking with sobs.

Oh no, she had somehow found out about Harry. But how? No, that surely wasn't possible. So what...

"Rachel?"

She turned and he saw that actually she was laughing.

"Oh, hi," she said. "How was your day?"

"I'll tell you in a minute. What's going on?"

"It's Chloe. She's just told me what she wants for Christmas."

He put his briefcase down on a chair. "And?"

"She wants a pair of wings."

"But she's got a pair of wings."

"No, *real* wings. She wants a pair of real wings. And a magic wand that works."

Their eyes met and they burst out laughing.

"Well, who wouldn't?" Daniel said. "What's she doing now?"

"Watching *Waybuloo* on CBeebies. It finishes at twenty past. Cup of tea? Or..." She raised her eyebrows in enquiry.

"Or, please."

"Gin it is, then. Bad day?" She opened a cupboard and got out a bottle of gin.

He took a couple of tins of tonic out of the fridge. Rachel sliced a lemon, and its sharp perfume made his mouth water.

"Actually, a pretty good day on the face of it. It's beginning to look as if the lab book bears out Calliope's claims. I'm hopeful we'll find that Will and Honor were first in the field. And that reminds me – I'll be flying over to the States next week to disclose the documents to the other side."

"But? I'm hearing a 'but'."

"Yeah, there is, but I can't quite put my finger on it."

"All the same, something's bothering you." She passed him the drink.

He took a sip and sighed with pleasure. "Oh, it's probably nothing."

"Something about the lab book?"

He shrugged. "Not really. It seems absolutely fine." He hesitated, reluctant to mention Jennifer and the way he had found the book. He hadn't told her that he had been to the house. She might not like it, and what was the point of upsetting her needlessly? He'd let her think the lab book had come to light in Jennifer's office, though he hadn't actually said so. And he didn't want to spoil her good mood now. "Maybe it's all this other stuff that's been going on in the lab."

Rachel cradled her glass. "Katie was actually there when there was that explosion. She could have been badly hurt. You didn't mind me inviting her over?"

"No, of course I don't mind."

"Have you brought the lab book home? Can I see?"

They went through into the sitting room. He got the lab book out of his briefcase and handed it to her. "Needless to say, the first thing I did when I got into the office was to make several copies."

They sat down together on the sofa. Rachel turned over the pages.

"Where did you say you found it at last?"

He hesitated. "I didn't, but her secretary found it stuffed behind the ironing board at Jennifer's house."

He saw a question forming in her eyes. If she asked him whether he'd been to the house, he wouldn't lie. But all she said was, "How funny. I wonder why she put it there. I'd better get on with the dinner."

She got up and went back to the kitchen. He went on sitting there, idly turning over the pages of the lab book. He wondered why he had felt uneasy. There really wasn't anything wrong, so why was he worrying?

Rachel called from the kitchen. "Katie'll be here soon and Chloe needs her bath."

"OK, I'm on the case."

He closed the lab book, resolving to put his doubts behind him.

Katie made her way along Quayside past the Maltings.

A movement in the shadows made her jump. Orlando appeared and ran towards her with a little chirrup. He twined himself around her legs. She bent down and picked him up. He didn't struggle, but reared up against her chest and pushed his face against her chin. Even through her coat she felt the vibration of his purr.

"Who's a gorgeous boy?" she asked him, and the purr picked up speed.

She stroked his head and gently put him down. She walked on and he trotted at her side.

She reached Rachel's door. As soon as it opened, Orlando slipped inside.

Rachel smiled. "Did he come along with you? He's a soppy old thing. Here, let me take your coat. Dan's upstairs bathing Chloe – I'm letting her stay up for supper with us – and I'm busy with the veg, so can I get you a gin and tonic and settle you here in the sitting room?"

"You certainly can," Katie said, sinking gratefully onto the sofa.

Rachel brought her the drink and a little dish of olives.

Katie settled back with a sigh. A weight slid off her shoulders. It was such a luxury to be sitting here in the warm with a drink and the prospect of a meal that had been cooked by someone else. She was glad not to be alone this evening. Half the time she felt like curling into a ball and falling asleep; the rest of the time she felt super-sensitive: sounds were louder than usual, colours brighter. She must still be suffering from shock.

A copy of the *Cambridge Evening News* lay on the coffee table in front of her, but for now she was happy just to sit there admiring the taste which had produced this room with its terracotta tiles, its blue and red kilim, and the wood-burning stove that was a larger version of the one on the boat.

After a few minutes she did reach for the newspaper – and there, underneath it, was a lab book with Will's name on it. Was this the one that had been missing? She looked at the date. Around two years ago; yes, that seemed about right. Daniel must have brought it home to work on.

She looked around and listened. Rachel was still busy in the kitchen. Katie could hear her humming to herself. From upstairs came sounds of laughter and splashing. She pulled the lab book to her and began to leaf through it. She read the odd page here and there, and began to get a sense of Will's style. Everyone had a slightly different way of going about things. Will's handwriting was flamboyant, there were lots of scribbled calculations. Of course, there was no way she would be able to tell if the claim to be first with the discovery was valid. That would be for Daniel to establish. She reached the end. Something had snagged her attention, but she wasn't sure what. Slowly she turned back the pages.

The sounds from upstairs grew louder – the bathroom door must have been opened. She slipped the lab book back onto the table. She half-covered it with the newspaper, so that it would look as if it hadn't been disturbed.

She picked up her drink, stood up, and sauntered into the kitchen.

"Can I do anything to help?" she asked.

Rachel looked up from chopping parsley. "Not really – but you can keep me company."

"What a glorious smell!"

"Beef casserole. The recipe's from Elizabeth David." She

gestured towards a book lying on the counter beside her. "It was my mother's cookbook, and it's still one of the first places I look when I'm craving a bit of comfort food."

Katie pulled the book towards her and turned the pages of the battered volume. In the margins were scribbled notes about substitute ingredients or simply recommendations: "v. good", "excellent". It was a book that had been worked hard over the years. Little greasy circles of fat, wine stains, spots of tomato sauce that had faded to orange bore testimony to that...

At that moment she realized what was odd about that lab book.

"Katie! Katie!"

Chloe, dressed in pink pyjamas, was heading for her. Katie put the book aside just in time, and held out her arms for Chloe to run into them.

Chapter Twenty

Rachel wouldn't have dreamed of opening something addressed just to Daniel, even if it was her father-in-law's handwriting. But the letter was addressed to her as well.

It was Monday morning and she was in her studio. In a hurry to get out with Chloe that morning, she'd stuffed the letter in her pocket. She used a putty knife to open the envelope, and a photograph slid out. It was a picture of a small boy on a beach, bucket in one hand, spade in the other. She could tell by the colour register and the way that it had faded that it dated from the seventies or earlier. She turned it over. "Daniel. Cromer. 1975" was written on the back in pencil.

There was a letter in the envelope and a £20 note folded inside it. The letter read, "Dear Dan and Rachel, hope this is what you need for Chloe's project. Use the money to buy something for my lovely granddaughter. Give her a hug and a kiss from me. Looking forward to seeing you all at Christmas. Love, Ron."

She smiled. There couldn't be a better father-in-law. She was lucky there, and Chloe was the apple of his eye. But what was this about Chloe's project? Ron must have misunderstood something she'd said. Or something Dan had said. He did get the wrong end of the stick sometimes.

She looked at the photo again. The shape of the face, the set of the eyes: yes, she could see the adult Dan in this little boy. And though Chloe was so much like Rachel – had her colouring and Rachel's blue eyes – she could see Chloe here, too. Something about the expression, so single-minded and serious... Was it something she had inherited from Dan, or did it come simply from imitating him? Or a bit of both? How mysterious it was, this mingling of chromosomes, and that familiar thought led to another: how easily Chloe could have received a different genetic inheritance, one that didn't contain DBA. But then she wouldn't be Chloe.

She ought to get to work on the angels. She slid the photo and the letter back into the envelope and put them in her bag. She could ask Daniel about it later.

She switched on Radio 3 and straightaway recognized Bach's first Brandenburg Concerto, the second movement. There was a plaintive air to it, yet there was an assurance too, a confidence in a divine order that was expressed in the entwined harmonies of the music. It was one of her favourite pieces of music, dating from around the same time as her baroque angels. They could be playing it on those trumpets of theirs.

She had finished making the missing trumpet during her last session in the studio. She examined it now, comparing it to the one she had copied. Yes, it was fine; more than fine – it was one of the best things she'd ever done. She got out her book of gold leaf and her gilder's tip, the brush that she used to lay the leaves on the wood. She settled down to gild the trumpet and time disappeared. The music flowed on and it was as if her own thoughts were reordering themselves, growing calmer and more composed. The trouble over Jennifer would pass as all things passed. In a week or two, Daniel's work on Jennifer's case would be over and they could begin to put it behind them.

She finished at twelve. Chloe stayed for lunch at nursery on Mondays, and Rachel treated herself to lunch out. Sometimes Daniel got away from work to join her, but usually not, and that was fine. She had lived alone for a long time before she became a wife and mother. She wouldn't want to return to her single life, but still she relished these little islands of solitude.

She walked over to the cathedral. The rain had cleared away and it was a bright, invigorating autumn day. The leaves of the lime trees that fringed the cathedral green were golden in the sunlight.

In the cathedral café it was warm and steamy. She got her soup and settled herself down at a table. Someone had left a newspaper there – a tabloid – not the kind she'd buy herself. There was a headline: "Husband arrested for leaving death car". She had to look twice before she realized that it was about Jennifer. She pushed her soup to one side and read the article. Jennifer's husband, Nick Blunt, was suspected of being in the car at the time of the accident and of leaving the scene. How terrible...

Underneath was a photograph of a grim-faced man holding a little boy by the hand. They were facing the camera but seemed unaware that they were being photographed. The definition was poor too. A telephoto lens, no doubt. It was outrageous that they were allowed to do this, to exploit the suffering of a child. She put the newspaper in her bag. Dan would want to see this.

Back at home, she went into his study to put the newspaper on his desk. She looked at the photo of Harry again. The little face was serious and dignified. She wondered if there was something familiar about that expression.

She fumbled in her bag for the letter from Ron and got out the photograph of Daniel. She laid it next to the newspaper photo.

Her heart skipped a beat.

She knew now why Daniel had asked Ron to send him the photo, and it had nothing to do with a project at Chloe's nursery.

Chapter Twenty-One

Amazingly the PCR had worked in spite of the explosion. Maybe things were taking a turn for the better. There had been some minor damage to their lab that needed sorting, so Katie was now working at her third bench in little over a week, but at least she *had* a bench. It was in the other wing of the lab and its usual occupant was away on holiday for a fortnight. She was impressed by the speed and efficiency with which Honor – or Honor's secretary – had managed to sort out temporary berths.

She was feeling better for having had a break. She'd woken up on Sunday morning knowing that she had to get away from Ely, away from botched experiments, away from a lab where she didn't know who to trust, away from everything. She rang Becky and half an hour later she was on the train to London. She'd met Becky and her husband at the Tate Modern and once they'd hooked up, Katie had switched off her phone. They had lunch, took in an exhibition. Later they walked along the South Bank to the National Film Theatre where they saw a fabulous new Argentinean film and had supper.

Now she'd had her head down for two solid hours and she knew for sure. Her cell-line was infected with mycoplasma. It was a relief in a way, because that meant it wasn't a mistake on her part. It could happen to anyone. She'd have to throw it away and start again with fresh stem cells. And with any luck she'd have a decent western blot by the end of the week. Paul would be irritated by the delay, but he couldn't blame her for it.

Better record her work on the cell-line, while it was fresh in her mind. She wrote it up and sat back. Her lab book was

137

very nearly full and represented six months of effort and solid hard work. She thought about Will's lab book, the one that she'd seen at Rachel's. Compared with hers, it had looked clean, or fairly clean. Lab books inevitably got a bit battered, kicking around the lab. Her own was creased and dog-eared, with ethanol stains on the cover. Of course, some people were more careful than others, but she distinctly remembered Will saying that he hadn't used a private notebook in those days. Shouldn't his lab book show more signs of wear and tear? She shrugged. Probably nothing in it. Some people were just neater than others.

She looked at her watch. There was just time before lunch to get a new lab book. They were kept in a room next to the administrator's office. Katie put the old lab book in her bag and went down the corridor to the office. When she tried the handle, the door was locked. Polly, the young administrative assistant who dealt with the lab books must already have gone for lunch.

Katie's eye was caught by Ian's name on a noticeboard just outside the office. There was a bulletin about both Malcolm and Ian. The news about Malcolm was that he was doing well and would be out of hospital soon. Anyone who wanted to contribute to a collection for him and to sign a card could do so at the entrance desk. About Ian the notice said simply that he was holding his own. There was no mention of a collection.

Katie made her way over to the canteen.

Going in through the swing doors she was met by a buzz of conversation. She looked around and spotted Will at a table on the other side of the room. He hadn't noticed her come in and she had time to think how tired he looked before he glanced up and saw her. He gestured to an empty seat opposite. She nodded, hung her coat on the coat rack, and went to get her food.

As she returned she saw Polly at the next table, deep in conversation with another girl.

"Any news?" she asked Will as she took her seat.

He gestured for her to come closer and she leaned across the table.

"I've just been with Honor," he said in a low voice. "She's convinced that Ian is responsible for the explosion – and maybe some of the other things that have been going wrong in the lab lately. When he recovers – if he recovers – she thinks the police will charge him. She *wants* them to charge him."

Katie gave a little yelp of disbelief. "They really do think it was him? But why would he do something like that?"

"I know he'd put in for a pay rise that he didn't get. He was sore about that."

"Sore enough to blow up the lab? Oh, come on! I hardly know the guy, but..."

She thought of his open face, the smile that never seemed far away, the sense of reassurance that he exuded, his readiness to find a solution for every problem. She shook her head. She didn't want to believe that someone she'd known and liked, however briefly, could do something like that.

"I've known him for years," Will said bleakly. "And I can't believe it either. Honor seems pretty sure, though. Look, I'd better get on. See you later."

She stayed, finishing her tuna sandwich, mulling things over.

At the next table, Polly got to her feet. Katie remembered about the lab book. She leaned over and said, "Are you going back to your office?"

Polly nodded. She couldn't be more than twenty, with long blonde hair that she was constantly tucking behind her ears, and was always immaculately made up.

"But not for long," she said. "I've got to help with a stationery inventory."

"I'll be along in a minute, then."

Katie caught up with Polly just as she was taking her key out of her pocket and unlocking her office door. Polly hung up her coat and sat down behind her desk. The lab books were on a table behind her in an unsealed box, on top of which was a folder labelled "lab book signing out forms". Katie handed over her old lab book so that Polly could see it was full. It was like being at school. You weren't allowed to get a new one until you'd shown that you'd finished the old one.

Polly flipped through to the back of the book, nodded, and gave it back. She turned and took a new lab book out of the box. She took a form out of the folder and handed it to Katie. As Katie filled in the form, she saw that the lab book only got a number once it was registered to someone.

"Have you worked here long, Polly?" she asked, handing her the form.

"Oh, about five years. Why do you ask?" She seized a hole-punch and slipped the form in.

"You must get to know everyone, working in this office. I was thinking of Ian..."

Polly's face clouded over and she stopped what she was doing. "Isn't it awful? You know what I call him? The lab's go-to guy. If anyone'd be a have-a-go hero, it'd be him."

So she hadn't heard yet. Katie wasn't going to be the one to tell her.

Polly went on, "I had a flat tyre here in the car park last week and Ian changed the wheel for me. That's him all over. I love him to bits. Reminds me of my dad. Do anything for anybody."

She squeezed the hole-punch until there was a click.

She said solemnly, "After work I'm going to go to the cathedral to light a candle. He'll be alright. I know he will."

She reached for the file where the forms were stored.

How very young she seemed; too young to have learned that bad things really do happen, even to the good guys. Or that the good guys aren't always what they seem.

Katie's phone rang. She fished it out of her bag and answered it.

It was Paul's secretary, letting her know that he wanted to see her the next day after his clinic, and she made it clear that Katie didn't have any choice in the matter.

Chapter Twenty-Two

"It wasn't about love. It was... I don't know what it was about," Daniel said.

He was facing Rachel across the kitchen table. The photograph that his father had sent was lying between them, along with the newspaper.

Rachel had rung him at the office and told him that she had to speak to him right away. He was still trawling through the lab book that had been missing, and asked if it could wait until later. "I know about Harry," she'd replied. He'd told Alison that he was going out for lunch and had gone straight home.

"When did it happen?" Rachel said.

He hesitated, but nothing less than the truth would do. She would be able to work it out for herself anyway. He told her and she looked incredulous.

"But that was just... it must have been... that was around the time we met?"

"It was a couple of weeks before."

"You told me you'd been separated for a year!"

"That was true."

"You were sleeping together! You were separated, but you were still having sex?"

"It was just once."

"Just once," she said in wonderment.

Daniel was silent. Then he said, "I'll try to explain. At least, I don't know that I *can* explain. I – that is, we... it just happened. I knew it was all over – "

How could he explain what had overtaken them, the ferocity of his desire for Jennifer, her frenzied response? No caresses, no endearments, it had been over almost before it began.

142

Afterwards there had been an aura of inevitability about it, as if it were something that had to be done, something necessary, a purging of his love for her.

"It was crazy," he said.

He saw the pain in Rachel's eyes and his own stomach clenched in sympathy. He guessed what she was thinking. Her Daniel, always so calm and rational and civilized...

"It wasn't about love," he said again. But he didn't know if that were true or not, and even if it were, did it make things any better?

He reached over and took her hand. She snatched it away.

"So what *was* it about? Getting your own back on Nick?"

He had never heard her speak like this; the bitterness in her voice...

"Well," she went on, "you succeeded beyond your wildest dreams."

"What do you mean?"

"Presumably Nick has absolutely no idea that he is bringing up another man's child! When did you find out? Or have you known all along?"

He stared at her. "Of course not – it never occurred to me. If I'd thought about it at all, I'd have assumed – when we were together – she had a contraceptive implant. It was only last week that I... You can't think I knew before that!"

"I don't know what to think."

"It was when I went to her house to look for the lab book. I saw a photograph of Harry. He looked older than I expected, and... Rachel, darling, I'm so sorry. The last thing I've ever wanted was to hurt you – and look, you asked when I knew, but actually, I don't know anything – not for sure."

"But you think he's yours, don't you?"

"The dates stack up," he admitted. "But she must have been sleeping with Nick as well."

"Dan, he looks like you!" Rachel gestured to the photographs.

143

"I'm not sure." Daniel looked again at them. "I'm really not sure. It's easy to find a resemblance if you're looking for one."

"But I saw it and I wasn't even looking!"

"And anyway, aren't we missing the point here? If Harry is mine, have you thought what that might mean for Chloe?"

She shook her head, and he wasn't sure if she meant that she hadn't thought about it – or whether she didn't want to talk about it.

"There'd be a chance that he was a match for Chloe. And if he is – "

"But he'd only be a half-brother."

So she *had* thought of it. Of course she had.

"Even so, there'd be a one in ten chance. It could mean," he spread his hands, "oh, it could mean just everything – a whole new life for Chloe – no more transfusions, and think of it, no more overnight infusions. When the DNA results come back – "

Rachel's mouth fell open. "DNA results? What DNA results?"

"I went to Jennifer's house to look for the lab book and that was when I saw photos of Harry and he looked older than I expected. When I went back the second time, I took Harry's toothbrush and..." He hesitated, but it was too late to stop now and he plunged on. "I took Chloe's toothbrush and I sent them both off to a lab to be tested."

"You did all this without telling me?"

"I didn't want to raise your hopes."

"My hopes?" She seemed lost for words.

"Rachel, can't you see? I didn't want to upset you when it might all be for nothing. What if Harry doesn't turn out to be mine? I wanted to be sure before I said anything."

She got to her feet. He got up, too, went around the table and put his hand on her shoulder. She pulled away. Her stricken face wrung his heart.

"Oh, Rachel..."

She took her glasses off, stared at them, and put them back

on. "I can't believe this is happening. That you'd go behind my back like this."

"Darling, I'm so sorry."

"I've got to have some time."

"Of course. Look, I'll make some tea."

"No." She looked at her watch. "I asked the nursery to keep Chloe for an extra hour, but I've got to go and get her now. Why don't you go back to work?"

"I don't have to."

"Just go!"

Chapter Twenty-Three

There was no answer when Katie knocked on Will's office door. It was just after six and most people had gone home. Maybe Will had, too. He wasn't in the lab either. She tried the door. It wasn't locked and she eased it open. She peeped inside. She'd been in there once before, that evening when she'd glimpsed Will looking so miserable and had come in to ask if he was alright, but she hadn't had a proper look. It was untidy, but there was no personal clutter, no postcards or cartoons cut from newspapers and stuck up with Blu-Tack. Will's real life went on mostly in the lab, she guessed.

She looked up and down the corridor. There was no one in sight. She stepped into the room. If Will came, she'd say that she'd come to see if he'd like to go out for a drink.

A lab book lay open on the desk as if he'd been interrupted while writing it up.

She went back to the door and looked down the corridor again. No one about. She left the door ajar so that she could hear if anyone came.

She went and picked up the lab book, noticing that there were watermarks on the cover and one corner was torn. She turned the pages. He was even sloppier than she was. There was a brown ring from a coffee cup on one page. She shouldn't be surprised, remembering the way he had splashed olive oil and tomato sauce around when he was cooking dinner.

The lab book she had seen in Rachel's house was different. There had been the odd small stain, but no wavy pages. It hadn't felt soft and worn in the hand like this one. The paper had been crisp and new.

The thought which had been lurking in the back of her mind came into focus.

That wasn't the original lab book.

She heard footsteps in the corridor. Hurriedly she put the lab book back on the desk. She stepped away and pretended to be looking at something on the noticeboard. Her heart was thumping.

Will appeared in the doorway.

"Oh, hi," she said. "The door was open, so I thought I'd wait. Hope you don't mind?"

He frowned and she could see that he was puzzled. He obviously didn't remember leaving it open.

She went on, "Was wondering if you'd like to go out for a drink?"

"I've got to see Honor, I'm afraid. Been waiting long?"

"Just got here."

His eyes went to the lab book. Her face grew warm. Had she left it as it was? Was it open at the same page as before?

He smiled at her. "Another time, yeah?"

"Of course. Another time, then."

Thank goodness he'd said no, Katie thought, as she walked along the tow path. She needed time to think.

Her torch on her mobile phone went out just as she was walking along the darkest part of the tow path.

"Oh, hell," she muttered. She realized that she had forgotten to charge it.

She walked on cautiously. She wasn't in any real danger of falling into the river as long as she could feel the pavement beneath her feet. The silence was broken only by the boats creaking at their moorings. Someone loomed out of the dark and she gasped. It was just a man with a dog, and he murmured an apology.

She walked on, her heart beating fast.

She regretted even more that she'd forgotten to charge her

phone when she got to the boat and had to fumble with the lock in the dark.

It was lonely here. She wanted more than anything to ring her mother, but it was the middle of the night in Shanghai. Once her phone had charged, she tried to ring Becky instead, but got her voicemail.

She made herself a big plate of pasta and drank a large glass of wine. Then she got into bed with her laptop and watched two episodes of *Breaking Bad*. She turned off the light at ten o'clock, but at midnight she was still awake, her thoughts churning, caught in a loop.

That lab book she had seen at Rachel's – was it a fake? According to Will, that earlier lab book had been written without the back-up of a notebook, so it had lived with him in the lab with all the spills and splashes that entailed. But the book she had seen and handled didn't look like that. It was clean, way too clean, though not completely clean. Didn't it look as it would if someone had had to fake up a lab book in a hurry? They'd add a stain or two here and there, but they wouldn't be able to make it look as used as it really would have been.

Why would someone do that? The answer was all too obvious. The original lab book must show that Will and Honor hadn't been first with the discovery. Even a few days could make all the difference. A fake lab book could have been concocted to bring the date forward.

When Lyle had spoken of Honor perhaps cutting corners and had asked Katie to sniff around, it hadn't occurred to her that she might find something like this. If she was right and this came out, it would be the end for Will – and for Honor, too. Her long and brilliant career would be in ruins. There would be no Nobel Prize, that was for sure. And what about Katie herself? She would have struck a blow for the integrity of science, but her fellow scientists wouldn't be sympathetic. She would have broken ranks and she'd probably never get another scientific job again.

And did it really matter who had discovered the obesity therapy first? Let the thuggish pharmaceutical companies slug it out between them. Well, OK, so maybe it wasn't Big Pharma versus Big Pharma. Maybe Lyle was the little guy here. And he was her friend – but she shouldn't be thinking about that.

And anyway, she had no actual proof, none at all, that the lab book she had seen wasn't the original. She hadn't had long to look at it. She might have made a mistake. And was it even possible to get hold of a substitute lab book? They were supposed to be tightly controlled.

This was no good. She sat up in bed, turned the pillow over, and laid down again, her cheek to the cool side. She did what she always did when she couldn't sleep. She let her mind drift back and tried to focus on a special memory, something to distract her from the present. That time on holiday on the Peloponnese when she and a boyfriend had found a deserted bay, a huge sweep of sandy beach, and had stripped off and run naked into the sea... The Christmas before last with her brother and his little boys, the feeling of one on each side snuggling up to her on the sofa. A warm drowsiness crept over her. Her body gave a little jerk and then relaxed. She was slipping away.

Abruptly she was wide awake again, knowing that she'd heard something. There was a creaking overhead. It came again. Then again, exactly as if someone was walking along the roof of the boat. Afterwards she wondered why she hadn't switched the light on right away, but her first instinct was not to show herself. She picked up a torch from the shelf by the bed and switched it on. Training the beam of light on the floor, she moved silently on her bare feet into the saloon. She could still hear the creaking sound, moving ahead of her towards the wheelhouse.

She felt for the light switch and flooded the room with light. The ordinariness of the scene gave her courage. There was a scuffling overhead. She jumped onto a chair, banged on the roof, and yelled, "Go away!"

In the silence that followed she sensed the shock and fear of the creature on the other side. A pattering, a skittering, and then nothing. She guessed it had jumped off the boat. She ran up the steps to the wheelhouse and shone the torch out of the window. She glimpsed a long low shape moving fast along the tow path. A cat? A dog, maybe? But no, more likely to be a fox.

She sat down on the bench and waited for her heart rate to settle. It was only a harmless animal that was just as frightened of her as she was of it. Why had she assumed that it was a person creeping about overhead? She thought of the past week and all that had happened. It wasn't surprising that she was so easily rattled, and that she had been so ready to think that someone was trying to get into the boat. Maybe her suspicions about Will were just as ill-founded.

There was a scrabbling at the window. She saw Orlando looking in and heard a plaintive mewing.

When Katie opened the door, he dashed past her and disappeared down the stairs. She followed him and found him on her bed, purring loudly.

"Was it you all along?" she asked him. "You naughty boy! I ought to put you straight back out."

He blinked at her benignly.

"Oh, alright," Katie said. "I could do with the company, come to think of it. Budge up."

She pushed him to one side and got into bed. Orlando arranged himself so that he was curled against her. The warmth of his body against her hip was comforting.

Living on the boat had seemed such a great idea. And probably in the summer, when it was light in the evenings and there were plenty of people around, it was lovely. But in the middle of winter – in the dark – on her own...

She wished she'd never agreed to move in.

Chapter Twenty-Four

A unit of blood is about 250ml and it takes about four hours to get that much blood into a four-year-old child.

Rachel and Chloe had been at the hospital since half past eight.

Today, Rachel welcomed the visit. She wouldn't have got up that morning if she hadn't had to take Chloe for her transfusion. And now, sitting in the ward, she understood for the first time that the necessity to go on with Chloe's life wasn't just a burden, but was a structure that could support her.

As always, the first hour or so had been exhausting. After the nurse had smoothed anesthetic cream on Chloe's hand and inserted the cannula, the blood was hooked up to a drip on a stand. Chloe liked to pretend that the stand was a scooter and Rachel struggled to stop her whizzing up and down the ward. Now there was only an hour to go and they were playing snakes and ladders. Chloe's eyelids were beginning to droop. She often did sleep for a while towards the end. Her energy was getting low by the time the transfusion came round, and she wouldn't feel the full effect until the next day.

They had both reached the top of the board. A six would take Rachel to the end of the game. Instead she threw a two and landed on a long winding snake that took her back to the bottom.

"Oh, Mummy," Chloe said, looking anxiously into Rachel's face to gauge how upset she was. "That's awful."

"Yes, it's terrible!" Rachel said, smiling to show that she didn't really mind. "Your turn."

Chloe threw a four and that took her to the last square. She laughed with delight and then looked serious.

She patted Rachel's arm. "Never mind, Mummy," she soothed. "There's always a next time."

Which was what Rachel always said. She wanted to cry when she heard her own consoling words spoken back to her, but she managed to hold in the tears.

She smiled. "That's right, there's always a next time. Now, how about a little nap?"

Chloe nodded. Her thumb went into her mouth. They would have to discourage that soon or she'd end up with braces, but Rachel didn't have the heart just yet.

They went back to Chloe's bed. Rachel propped herself up on the pillows and positioned Chloe in the crook of her arm. A few sighs and snuffles, and Chloe was asleep.

Rachel had brought a book with her, Molly Hughes's *A London Child of the 1870s*, an old favourite, comfort reading of the highest order, but today the magic didn't work. She couldn't involve herself in Molly's world when her own was so tumultuous.

Daniel had been sorry, she knew, that they couldn't have another child, but largely because of Chloe and the possibility of a match for her. Rachel's pain was different. Yes, it gave her own sorrow a sharper edge, knowing that a second child might have been the means of curing Chloe. But she yearned for another child for its own sake, and sometimes her longing had been hard to reconcile with the fullness of her love for Chloe.

The thought of another woman bearing Daniel's child made her want to double over in pain. Until now, Rachel had consoled herself with the thought that OK, she was the second wife, but hers was the real marriage: she had given Daniel a child. Could it be that even here Jennifer had stolen a march on her? What if Daniel had found out that Jennifer was carrying his baby? Would Rachel have stood a chance?

Daniel had made a point of getting home early so that they could all eat together, but they hadn't talked any more about

Harry. They went through the routine of Chloe's bedtime and infusion – Daniel's turn this time – then Daniel had gone into his study to work and Rachel had gone to bed. When Daniel came up, he touched her tentatively on the shoulder, hoping, she knew, that she would turn to him, but she had pretended to be asleep. He settled down on his own side of the bed and they lay there separately in the dark. At last she had drifted off. When she woke in the early hours, Daniel was muttering something in his sleep.

She leaned over and heard him whisper, "Jennifer..." It was a lover's sigh.

It was as if she'd been slapped in the face. She wanted to shake him awake, shout at him, demand an explanation – but what was the point? He hadn't done it on purpose; in the morning he might not even remember, and that was what made it so devastating.

She got out of bed, went into Chloe's room, and squeezed into bed with her. In the morning Daniel left a cup of tea on Chloe's bedside table and went off to work while Rachel pretended to be still asleep.

In some deep recess of her mind she had always known that Daniel had loved Jennifer more than he loved her. What she hadn't known was that he still did. It was a terrible irony that in Harry Jennifer might have given them the means to cure Chloe, and –

"Mrs Marchmont?" A nurse was bending over her. "Mrs Marchmont, the transfusion's finished. I need to take out the cannula now."

This was sometimes the worst bit, but today the nurse eased it out with no difficulty.

"Mummy, I'm hungry," Chloe declared. "Chicken nuggets and chips."

They always had lunch at the hospital and Chloe always had the same thing. It was part of the routine, a little treat to look forward to.

In the café she found a table that she could keep an eye on, and settled Chloe with paper and crayons.

As she waited in the queue, she was hit by a wave of longing, she scarcely knew for what. For her mother, dead now for fifteen years? For refuge, for somewhere to go that wasn't Dan's house? If only she hadn't suggested that Katie move onto the boat, because that was it – that was where she wanted to be, back in her own place.

"Mummy, Mummy, it's Katie!"

Chloe was waving and pointing. Rachel had the disconcerting sensation of having someone she had just thought of pop up in front of her. Because, standing just inside the café door, there indeed was Katie.

Katie's meeting with Paul had gone surprisingly well. He had been unexpectedly sympathetic.

He gave her his full attention as she told him about how she had witnessed the explosion in the lab and how Ian had come under suspicion. Ian's condition was unchanged and he was still lying unconscious only a few floors away from where they were sitting.

"A bad business," he said. "It's bound to have knocked you back a bit. I've known things like this happen before, though not on this scale. My wife once worked in a lab where there was a spate of malicious damage. They never managed to nail anyone for it, but it all stopped after a particular individual left the lab."

Katie sighed. "And then there's the cell-line getting infected. Can't blame Ian for that."

Paul pursed his lips. "Can't you?"

She stared at him. "You don't think – "

"Who knows? Maybe not, but that's the trouble, isn't it? A lab operates on the basis of trust, and when that trust breaks down..." He shrugged.

Katie considered this. "Maybe, but either way, I've got to the bottom of it now."

"Let me know what happens when you run it again," he said.

"Of course."

"We know it works, don't we? It's a matter of getting enough evidence. I'm putting another research proposal together, based on this work. I'd like you on board."

This was excellent news, better than she could have hoped for.

"With a grant in the offing I need to know which way the wind's blowing as soon as possible," he said, and this time he did look her in the eye. "The deadline for the research proposal is next week, so I'll need to see the new, improved western blot in time to incorporate the results." He flicked through his diary. "Let's say Friday afternoon."

"I'll do my best."

"Friday afternoon," he said firmly.

And that was that.

Out in the corridor, she stood irresolute. It was one o'clock. Should she head straight back to the lab, or grab a bite to eat? A wave of fatigue swept over her. Her bad night was catching up with her. Better to at least have a cup of coffee. And if she had lunch in the lab, she ran the risk of running into Will. The morning light had put her suspicions into perspective. It could all too easily be a product of her overheated imagination. But still she wasn't in the mood for chatting with Will over lunch. She needed a bit of distance.

She yawned and pushed open the door to the café.

She wondered if Rachel would mind if she found someone to share the barge with her. There was a spare room, after all, and it had its own bathroom.

Above the buzz of conversation she heard her own name. She scanned the room and there, sitting at a table and waving frantically, was Chloe.

"I've been for my blood fusion," Chloe announced. She showed off her hand with the plaster on it.

Katie tried to emulate Chloe's matter-of-factness. "How long does it take?"

Chloe didn't know. She looked to Rachel for help.

"Around four hours," Rachel said, putting her soup spoon down.

She wasn't eating much and it was clear from her pale face and red-rimmed eyes that something was wrong. It couldn't just be the strain of the blood transfusion, could it? She must surely be used to it by now.

Chloe turned her attention to her chips and the conversation lagged.

With an obvious effort, Rachel said, "How's the research going?"

Katie gave a grimace. "Not great." She told Rachel about the trouble with the cell-line, without explaining that it might have been sabotaged by Ian. She didn't want to wash the lab's dirty laundry in public.

Rachel listened sympathetically.

"It's so easy for things to go wrong," Katie continued, "and that's one of the frustrations of the job. You do everything right – or you think you do – in a long preparation, and then it fails and you have no idea why. That's what happened to me with my western blot." She saw that she was holding Rachel's attention, distracting her from whatever was bothering her. She went on, "And some procedures are just downright difficult. You need a lot of experience to pull them off and you have to have really good fine motor skills. A friend of mine says of one procedure that you should only do it wearing purple on a Wednesday."

Rachel smiled. "Before you showed me round the lab, I imagined it would all be much more high-tech. Untouched by human hand. All done by computers."

Katie laughed. "Oh, no, no. They play their part, of course, but in the end it's all down to faulty human beings. You get tired and then you get clumsy and you fumble things or drop them and your confidence starts to slip. You start to think that it's your fault. That you're no good. The success or failure of something might hang on the fact that you had a row with your boyfriend before you came into work – or had a bad night's sleep – and that reminds me."

She told them the story of Orlando, making it funny and playing up her surprise for Chloe's sake. Chloe listened open-mouthed, her fork in mid-air, her chicken nuggets forgotten.

Rachel laughed too, and some of the strain left her face.

She said, "I should have warned you about him – actually, you must have got quite a shock."

Now was the time, if ever, for Katie to mention that she had made a mistake moving onto the boat by herself. She was still wondering how to put it when Rachel got there first.

"Are you finding it difficult being there on your own?" she asked.

"Well, I had been wondering... I know there isn't much room, but it might be better if I was sharing – "

Chloe dropped her fork with a clatter. "Mummy, Mummy, I want to share with Katie! Can I? Oh, please!"

Katie smiled at her eager face. "I'd love that, but there wouldn't be room for us all, would there – not if your daddy came too."

"Well, actually..." Rachel said.

Chapter Twenty-Five

The book was *Clever Polly and the Stupid Wolf* by Catherine Storr, a favourite from Katie's own childhood.

It was early evening, and Katie and Chloe were sitting together on the sofa in the saloon, Chloe in her pyjamas. Chloe was leaning on Katie's shoulder with her arm tucked under Katie's. She knew the stories off by heart. If Katie got the wording even slightly wrong, she was pulled up straightaway. And yet, when Polly got the better of the wolf, Chloe laughed as heartily as if she was enjoying the joke for the first time.

From the galley came the clatter of pans. Rachel had offered to cook and Katie had been happy to let her.

Rachel had explained that there was a problem with the heating at their house and it was freezing cold. It would suit her to move into the boat for a few days while it was being fixed. Chloe could have her own bed and Rachel could sleep in the other bunk bed. Maybe it was true about the heating, maybe it wasn't, but Katie was certain there was more to it than that.

When the story was over, Chloe asked to have it all over again and Katie turned back to the beginning. The comments and the laughter became less frequent. Chloe snuggled up closer. Katie looked down at her. Chloe's thumb was in her mouth and her eyes were vague.

Suppose this was my daughter, Katie thought, *and that was my husband in the kitchen cooking supper. How would that be? It could be good, it could be very good...*

"Dinner's ready," Rachel said.

Chloe roused herself to eat a little risotto, then Rachel took her off to clean her teeth and be tucked up in bed.

When Rachel came back to the table an awkward silence fell. The very fact that Katie didn't feel she could ask Rachel what had upset her made it difficult to think of something to say.

Maybe Rachel felt the same. She toyed with her food and said, "We won't stay more than a night or two."

Katie hastened to reassure her. "I meant what I said. I'm glad of the company. And it's lovely, spending time with Chloe."

Another silence.

Katie said, "How long did you live here on your own?"

"Four years."

"And it was fine – "

"Oh, yes, I never minded that. I always felt safe here."

And that's why you've come back here now, Katie thought, *to your refuge.* She reached for the bottle of wine and gestured towards Rachel's glass.

Rachel hesitated. "I don't usually drink much – oh, go on."

Katie filled up her glass, and then her own. There were times when it was a good idea to have a little too much to drink and she thought this was probably one of them.

"Did you get back on track in the lab this afternoon?" Rachel asked.

"I hope so," Katie said. "Sometimes I wonder if I'm really cut out for this. I wonder if I've got the right temperament. It's like I told you earlier. You can work all hours – you can spend evening and weekends in the lab, but you still might not pull it off. You can be the most brilliant researcher that ever lived, but it's not enough. You have to be lucky too."

"Napoleon thought that," Rachel said.

"What?"

"That's what Napoleon used to ask when he was thinking of making someone a general. 'Is he lucky?'"

Katie gave a grin of recognition. "Good question. For us scientists everything depends on choosing the right research project. That's where the luck comes in. There's really no way of knowing in advance if you've picked a winner."

"Even so, it's worth it, isn't it?" Rachel said. "The difference you can make to people's lives..."

"Or maybe you are on the right track, but someone else gets there first. You can spend years of your life working on something and then be pipped to the post by another researcher."

"Like the case Daniel's working on."

"That's what I was thinking of."

Rachel was silent. Then she said, "Maybe I shouldn't say this – "

"Go on."

"I can't help thinking, all that money, billions are being spent on this drug to combat obesity, when all the time children in the third world are dying of starvation."

"Or of malaria. I know. But this will save lives too."

"Wouldn't it be better if people just didn't eat as much and took more exercise?"

"Well, yeah, of course it would, but they're not going to, are they? At least an awful lot of them aren't. And meanwhile it's costing billions to treat them for diseases linked to obesity. The therapy will save lives *and* money in the end."

"Isn't there a danger that people will think they can eat as much as they like as long as they keep taking the drug?"

That gave Katie pause for thought. "That could happen," she conceded. "The law of unintended consequences. But that's not the scientists' fault, is it?"

"Do you really think that? That scientists don't have any responsibility for their discoveries?"

"Not that exactly, but it's difficult..."

"Well, you're in the clear, anyway," Rachel pointed out. "There can't be any question that your research is a good thing."

"Oh yeah, I'm one of the good guys, sure enough." Katie laughed, but it was nice to be appreciated. "But you know, it's hard. There's so much pressure to come up with results.

It's not just the kudos of being first in the field. You have to get results to get further grants. You *have* to publish. Let's open that second bottle of wine." She reached for it, adding, "Sometimes I can almost understand people taking shortcuts."

"How do you mean, shortcuts? You mean people cheat, or what?"

"There was a case, not so long ago. That doctor in South Korea... the one who claimed to have cloned a human embryo?"

Katie fumbled with the corkscrew.

"Here, let me," Rachel said. "I read about that in the paper."

"What was he thinking of?" Katie said, handing over the bottle. "He was bound to be exposed when people realized that the experiment couldn't be repeated. And using eggs from his female researchers. How unethical is that! And the strange thing is that he wasn't a maverick or some struggling second-rater. He was a leading international scientist, and now his career is in ruins."

Rachel drew the cork out of the bottle. "What I didn't understand – and what I still don't understand – is how he could have thought he'd get away with it." She filled their glasses.

"It's a world of its own," Katie said. She propped her chin in her cupped hands. Her head was beginning to swim. "Very successful scientists – they're very driven – they spend virtually their whole life in the lab – they lose touch with the world outside."

"I need something else to eat," Rachel said.

She went to the fridge, rummaged around and brought out some cheese.

"Like I said," Katie went on, "they lose touch with reality. Nothing matters except the science." She straightened up and gestured with her glass. The wine slopped from side to side. She looked at it, focusing with an effort. She put the glass to her lips and drained it. She poured herself another glass.

"That's OK," she went on, "because it *is* the science that

matters. The problem comes when the results matter more than the science. These are hugely smart people with hugely inflated egos and they've been right so many times. Maybe they start to take it for granted that they're *always* right. They start to see the actual experiments as just a formality. There was a case a few years ago, an article published in *Nature*, three lots of stem cell experiments that showed the same results. Unfortunately there was a reason for that: they were actually the same experiment – they hadn't been repeated."

"What happened to the researcher?"

Rachel's cheeks were flushed, Katie noticed. Probably hers were, too. She laughed shortly. "What do they say in Hollywood? You'll never eat lunch in this town again? That's about it. You'd be blacklisted. You'd never get another job. And you know what? The ones who are found out – I bet they're just the tip of the iceberg."

Rachel was staring at her, surprised by her vehemence.

"Are we talking theoretically here?" Rachel asked. "Or do you have something specific in mind?"

Katie hesitated. "If I tell you something, can it be just between us? Promise?"

Rachel nodded.

It struck Katie that Rachel wasn't entirely sober. But then neither was Katie. Very, very far from it. Oh, what the hell.

"When I was round at your house the other night, I saw that lab book, Will's lab book, the one that got mislaid."

Rachel shook her head. "It didn't get mislaid. It was hidden. Deliberately hidden. Jennifer had stuffed it away behind a built-in ironing board in her kitchen."

Katie stared at her. "Why would she do that?"

"That's what Dan wondered too, but he couldn't see anything wrong with the lab book."

"Well, I think it's a fake. I think Will didn't make the discovery first. What if he somehow got hold of another lab book, and faked it to look as if he did?"

Rachel said, "And Jennifer was on to it? That's why she hid it?"

"We'll never know now, will we?"

"No," Rachel said slowly. "We'll never know. Because Jennifer's dead."

They looked at each other.

Katie said, "No, no. Will couldn't have had anything to do with that. That's just silly. It was an accident. But the lab book – that I can believe, because so much rests on it."

Rachel's face slipped out of focus, but Katie squinted and got her back.

"These lab books," Rachel said. "How easy would it be to get hold of a blank one?"

"You have hit the nail on the head, Rachel. You have indeed. Not easy. Oh, no, no, no. Not easy at all. Tightly controlled. As least they're supposed to be." Katie put her glass down too heavily.

She explained the process of getting a new lab book. She had to explain twice. Either Rachel was being a bit thick, or Katie was.

Rachel questioned her. Did Polly keep her office locked absolutely all the time? What about when she popped out to the loo? And if someone did manage to swipe a lab book, would Polly notice? Would she realize when she got to the bottom of the box that there'd been, say, thirty books and she'd only given out twenty-nine numbers?

Katie considered this. "Maybe, maybe not. She's a sweet girl, but not the sharpest knife in the box."

"Know what I'd do?" Rachel said. There was just the suggestion of a slur.

Katie shook her head very slowly. "I do not. I do not know what you would do."

Rachel downed the rest of her wine. She thumped her fist on the table.

"I'd steal one myself, just to see if it could be done."

For a moment, Katie was taken aback, but then she saw that Rachel had indeed got to the heart of it. Clever Rachel. What a brilliant idea.

Chapter Twenty-Six

On the rare occasions when Katie had a hangover, she always felt better for eating, but maybe the macaroni cheese she had chosen for lunch hadn't been such a good idea. As Katie picked at it and wondered whether to take some more painkillers, her gaze kept straying to Polly on the other side of the canteen. She was chatting animatedly, unaware of Katie's attention.

Katie had noticed that Polly usually went for lunch about twelve and today she had timed it so that she was passing the office when Polly came out. Before Polly closed the door, Katie glimpsed the box of lab books on the table. Polly locked up and put the key in the pocket of her jeans. They walked together to the canteen, chatting, and queued together at the counter. Then Polly went to join her friends.

In the cold light of day, the idea of stealing a lab book seemed crazy, not something Katie would ever dream of doing. But there was no harm at all in mulling over the question of whether it was possible. The question was this: did Polly always lock the door, even when she went to the loo? If she was just popping out for a few minutes, surely she wouldn't bother? After all, the lab books weren't valuable in themselves. It was simply a matter of keeping track of them.

Katie's train of thought was broken by someone sitting down opposite her.

It was Honor.

Katie's heart seemed to flip over. A tête-à-tête with Honor would have been daunting at the best of times, but right now... There was no way Honor could know what she was thinking about, or her suspicions about Will, but all the same, Katie felt as if guilt was written all over her face.

Honor's bob cut wasn't as sleek as usual. Katie guessed she hadn't had time to blow-dry it. And she wasn't wearing lipstick. She looked tired, but her voice when she spoke was firm enough. "How are you, Katie? Fully recovered, I hope. That was a nasty experience."

Katie hastened to reassure her. "I'm fine. Will was much closer to the explosion than I was."

Katie caught a fleeting expression on Honor's face. For a moment she looked vulnerable, as though it were painful to contemplate what might have happened to Will.

"How's Malcolm?" Katie asked.

"I've just been visiting him in Addenbrooke's," Honor said, crumbling her bread roll. "He'll be out of hospital in a couple of days, but it'll be a few weeks before he's back at work."

"And Ian?" Katie hardly dared to ask.

"Not good, but it's looking as though he'll pull through. Of course, there's no question of him coming back to the lab."

"You really think he…"

Honor nodded and took a mouthful of soup.

"But why?" Katie said. "I just can't understand it."

"That's what I've been asking myself."

"Will told me Ian hadn't got a pay rise he'd put in for."

"He really wasn't that good – at least not as good as he thought he was." Honor's voice was cool. Katie caught a glimpse of the steeliness that had got her where she was. She was flattered that Honor was talking to her as an equal, but she was conscious of the need to tread carefully. She remembered that Honor had a reputation for not suffering fools gladly.

"He might have been sore about it, all the same," Katie remarked.

Honor put down her spoon. "If everyone who was passed over for promotion reacted that way, there wouldn't be a lab left standing. There must be more to it than that, maybe some kind of psychiatric problem. I had a word with a friend in the Psychology department. There's a recognized syndrome: people who yearn for praise and attention and manufacture crises so that they can step in and save the day."

Katie thought of the way Ian had comforted her over her failed E.coli culture and offered to redo it for her. She thought of what Polly had said about his being the department's "go-to guy", and the obvious pride that he took in it. But had he really been so needy that he would risk blowing up the lab?

"The gas taps – that was so dangerous!"

"He's admitted that he was sleeping in his office. No doubt he was going to pretend to come in first thing in the morning and discover the lab full of gas so that he could demonstrate his presence of mind. I suppose he wasn't to know that Malcolm would charge in and switch on the light."

So that explained why Ian hadn't needed to sign in at night. He'd never left. Katie understood now why he was always in the lab so early – and it was probably him who had come into the lab that time when she was in the darkroom and she'd thought she was alone in the building.

Honor sighed. "I'm seeing Ian's wife this afternoon. Poor woman. There are two children. Pretty much grown up, thank goodness."

"I didn't know he was married."

"Apparently they'd separated. Very likely that also had a bearing on the situation. We'll know more when Ian comes round. There are signs of improvement."

No wonder she looked tired, Katie thought. What must it be like to be in charge of a lab? To have all that responsibility, not just for your own work, but for other people, too. She couldn't imagine it, but perhaps it was something you grew into.

She glanced over at Polly, who was sharing a joke with her friend. They were giggling like schoolgirls.

And that was when it struck her. Honor was Will's principal investigator and they worked closely together. She would have scrutinized his lab books and signed them off – week by week, probably. Wouldn't she have noticed if there was something wrong? Katie felt a chill. What if Honor had not only noticed? What if she'd condoned it? Because with all Katie's preoccupation with whether Will had been able to steal a lab book, there was one thing she had been forgetting. This was Honor's lab. She was the boss and she could do as she damn well pleased. There was no way someone as far down the pecking order as Polly would query anything she did, and in any case, there was bound to be a set of master keys somewhere. Probably Honor could come and go as she liked.

If Honor wanted to get hold of a substitute lab book, there'd be no problem.

Chapter Twenty-Seven

By six o'clock Katie had transfected her new stem cells and now she had to wait for them to start producing whole virus. It would be another twelve hours before she could harvest them, so she packed up for the day.

The supermarket near the station was open late, so she stopped off on the way home. She was walking along the displays of vegetables, uncertain what to cook – did there really have to be so much choice? – when her attention was caught by an elderly woman standing further down the aisle. One leg seemed strangely straight and stiff: it was encased in a metal caliper. Katie didn't think she'd ever seen an adult wearing one.

The woman slipped her hand into the pocket of her coat and pulled out a mobile phone, and not just any mobile phone, but an iPhone – much sleeker and cooler than Katie's own smartphone. How incongruous was that, the juxtaposition of the phone and the caliper!

Katie was close enough to hear her say, "Was it Cox's you wanted? Or Golden Delicious?"

How old was she? Seventy maybe? And vaccination had begun in the early 1960s, so yes, she could have had childhood polio. Katie's mother had been born in the late forties and one of her childhood memories was of the polio epidemic of 1956 and her terror of catching it and ending up in an iron lung. It was amazing. In just a generation, polio had been eradicated in Europe and there was a prospect of eradicating it worldwide.

Katie thought of that later as she sat with Chloe on her knee, trying to distract her. The child knew too well what was coming and pushed the book of fairy stories aside. She wasn't going to be fobbed of with Rumpelstiltskin. In the end, Katie just clasped Chloe to her and felt the little arms clamp Katie's waist as the needle went in. She flinched herself in sympathy.

As soon as it was over, Chloe brightened up. She clamoured for a goodnight kiss. Katie left Rachel to settle her down and went into the galley to start cooking dinner. She felt wrung out. As she unwrapped the chicken breasts, she thought about the day-to-day effort that Rachel put into managing Chloe's disease. Working in the lab, you could lose sight of the reality of the disease you were studying. You could forget that it was not just cells in a Petri dish, not just an intellectual puzzle, but real children suffering in real life. Sometimes the goal of finding a cure for DBA seemed very far off, but that was what they must have thought about polio once.

Rachel came in and heaved a sigh.

"Are you alright?" Katie asked.

There was no reply. Katie turned and saw tears were welling up in Rachel's eyes.

"Hey…" Katie put down the chicken. "What is it?"

Rachel dashed a tear off her cheek.

"Do you want to tell me all about it?" Katie asked.

The tears were overflowing. Rachel gave a helpless little gesture, buried her face in her hands and wept.

Katie grabbed the kitchen roll, and tore off a couple of pieces. She pressed them into Rachel's hands and put a gentle hand on her shaking shoulders. She guided her to a seat.

"What is it? What's the matter?"

Rachel waved a hand as if to say, "Wait a minute."

Katie sat down and waited.

After a while, Rachel sat up straight and blew her nose.

"The thing is – it's just – giving Chloe her infusion – if only I could have had another baby, one who might have been a match for Chloe."

"And that hasn't been on the cards?"

"Not really. I nearly died giving birth to Chloe."

"That's tough," Katie said. "I'm sorry."

"Though of course, even if we'd had another baby, they might not have been a match for Chloe."

"Well – but IVF? Embryo selection?"

"That's what Dan would have wanted, I'm sure."

"And you wouldn't?" Katie asked. Surely it was the obvious solution. How could there be any question?

"I don't know, that's the thing. Sometimes I think I would have done *anything* to find a cure for Chloe. But that doesn't mean it would have been right."

"Why wouldn't it have been right?"

"Don't you see the irony of it – that we love Chloe so much that we'd be prepared to destroy other potential children for her? And think about this: if we'd known we were carrying this gene before Chloe was conceived, we might have been offered embryo selection and she might never have been born."

"But Rachel," Katie said, "at that stage Chloe would have been just a ball of cells."

"But a ball of cells with the potential to be Chloe."

"Surely, though," Katie sought for the words, "if you could have made Chloe without DBA – "

"Then she wouldn't have been Chloe. She is as she is. We're all children of God."

Katie felt a flash of annoyance. If Rachel was going to fall back on that, if she wasn't going to engage in rational debate, then it was pointless arguing with her. And yet, Katie couldn't help saying, "You know, there are an awful lot of spontaneous abortions anyway. Nature is very wasteful."

"That's different. But to choose to end a life – OK, a potential life – or to choose one over another... Who are we to do that?"

"Some forms of contraception – the coil, for example, that aborts a fertilized egg – "

"That's different, too."

"I don't see how."

"You're not choosing that one will live and one will die –

you're not choosing to give life to someone not for their own sake, but because you want to use their bone marrow. You're not – " She broke off.

Katie too had heard the pattering of bare feet. Chloe appeared, blinking in the light, clutching her bunny to her chest. Her face was anxious.

"Mummy, I can't sleep. I'm frightened. There's a monster in the bathroom."

Rachel got to her feet. "OK, let's go and see, and if there *is* a monster, what will Mummy do?"

Chloe smiled. "Chase that old monster away!"

"Come on, then."

Katie watched as Rachel took Chloe by the hand and led her back to her room. She saw what Rachel meant. She thought of how it had felt to have Chloe tucked into her arm. There was so much of her, the shiny hair, the unblemished skin, the dense compact heft of her. How could it be that she was at once so perfect and yet so terribly flawed? The answer was that she was just Chloe, simple as that. Rachel had said, "We're all children of God." Was there after all a kind of truth in that, a truth that didn't necessarily have to do with superstition and old-man-in-the-sky thinking, a truth that even an atheist could comprehend?

Katie's stomach rumbled. Food was needed, and fast. She reached for the jar of rice. That could be cooking while she was frying the chicken.

The cooking was well under way when Rachel came back.

She said in that tone of voice that indicates a definite change of subject, "So, you've decided that it's possible to steal a lab book. Now what?"

"I've been thinking about that," Katie said. "There could be a relatively innocent explanation. What if Will lost the original? We're not supposed to take them out of the lab, but people do and there are stories about lab books being left in trains or pubs or taxis or in briefcases that get stolen. If that happened to Will, he might not have wanted to own up. Instead he might have got hold of a blank lab book and tried to reconstruct the original." She decided not to say anything about Honor. It seemed so unlikely that someone with so much at stake could be involved in anything so unethical.

"How could you find that out?"

"I think there's a notebook somewhere, recording the same information that's in the lab book. Will told me that he's only recently started keeping one as a back-up, but I don't think that's true. I caught a glimpse of a lot of them in the drawer of the desk in his office."

"And you think that what's in the notebook won't be the same as what's in the lab book and you'll be able to see where he faked it?"

Katie nodded. "That's it."

"Could you get a look at those notebooks?" Rachel asked. She got cutlery out of a drawer and began to set the table. She paused in what she was doing. "Perhaps he's got rid of it! Perhaps he's destroyed the evidence!"

"I don't think so," Katie said.

That was one thing Katie couldn't see him doing. She wouldn't do it herself. It would go against her whole training and instinct as a scientist.

"He'd need that notebook," she explained. "He'd need to be able to go back and check the details of what he's done. No, it'll be somewhere where he can consult it if necessary. If I were him, I'd take it home."

"So what are you going to do? You can hardly go breaking and entering."

"I don't know. I had supper at his flat the other day. Maybe he'll invite me round again." Katie eased the chicken breasts onto plates. "But for now, I'd better concentrate on my own work. I've got enough problems of my own. Tomorrow I'll do the western blot again. If I don't get a positive result, I'll be in deep trouble."

Chapter Twenty-Eight

Daniel pushed his chair back from his desk. He was tempted to pour himself a brandy, but alcohol was always a mistake when you were potentially pulling an all-nighter. He'd better have some coffee instead.

He went into the kitchen and put the kettle on. The place had an uncared-for feel. It wasn't exactly untidy – he was good at putting things in the dishwasher – but there were toast crumbs on the counter and a gritty trail of sugar. The dishcloth needed chucking out or washing – there was a whiff of something unpleasant. In his marriage to Jennifer, he had been the domestic one, but the roles had been reversed with Rachel. Was it something to do with having a child?

He'd been shocked when he'd arrived home to find the note from Rachel. But he told himself now that she was only on the boat, hardly any distance away. Of course she was hurt, he understood that. She needed time to absorb the shock. She'd soon realize that if Harry turned out to be a match, they *had* to pursue the possibility of a cure for Chloe, and then she would be back, bringing Chloe with her.

At the thought of Chloe, he felt a pang. This was the second night that he'd been alone in the house. How strange it was sleeping alone and waking up alone, realizing that Chloe was not there in the next room. Family life had been like a garment so familiar that he was scarcely conscious of wearing it. Now that it was gone, he felt cold, exposed, no longer at home here. There was too much empty space, too much silence. He found himself switching on the radio and leaving it on even when he'd stopped listening, just to have some noise somewhere in the house.

That was what he did now. He switched on the TV in the sitting room. The national news was just ending and he caught the beginning of the regional news: "The police are still questioning Nicholas Blunt, who has been arrested on suspicion of failing to report an accident."

So they were still holding Nick. It was beginning to sound as if there might be more to it than leaving the scene of the accident. Surely he couldn't somehow have been involved in her death? No, unthinkable. But leaving the scene – that was bad enough. How could he have left Jennifer dead or dying in a wrecked car?

Time seemed to be doing strange things. Just for a few moments, the years of marriage to Jennifer and the even longer years of friendship with Nick – they had known each other since primary school – seemed more recent than his marriage to Rachel.

There was an interview with Nick's lawyer on the steps of the police station: "Mr Blunt is cooperating with the police to the fullest possible extent. He is confident – "

"What about the little boy?" a journalist demanded.

"Mr Blunt's son is at present being cared for by his family," the solicitor answered stiffly.

His son... Ha! Dan felt a flash of savage satisfaction at the prospect of disabusing Nick, if and when the time came. If Harry turned out to be Daniel's, he'd like to see the look on Nick's face when he realized that he had been harbouring a cuckoo in the nest. It was as if providence in one fell swoop had intervened to punish Nick and provide a cure for Chloe. He wondered who was looking after Harry; presumably Nick's parents, or maybe his sister.

Daniel wasn't sure exactly what rights he had – but he must have some if he turned out to be Harry's genetic father. Harry would have been conceived before the divorce had come through, which would make him a legitimate child of their marriage. Daniel had been able to discover that much. But if

175

Jennifer had been married to Nick by the time Harry was born, and Nick was named as Harry's father on the birth certificate...

The smell of percolating coffee reached him and he came to himself. He could do nothing until the DNA results arrived. And in the meantime, he had a deadline to meet. Tomorrow he was booked onto a night flight to the States. By then he had to have a clear idea of the case to be made for his client and the lab books had to be ready for inspection. The other side had asked to see the originals, and that was their right.

He brought the pot of coffee back to his desk and focused on the lab book. Billions of dollars rested on who had won the race. And the work itself, a treatment for obesity – he reminded himself that it was still only in the development stage – if it really did prove to be effective and safe, millions of people would be saved from years of poor health and premature death: the statistics for Type 2 diabetes, heart disease, cancer even, would be slashed. Daniel was present at what might prove to be one of the greatest discoveries of modern science.

Everything else slipped away, even the pain of missing Chloe and Rachel, as he worked on into the night. Finally he closed the last lab book and sat back, satisfied that everything was in order. They had a good case. But he wouldn't tell Lyle until he'd had time to go through it again tomorrow and double-check. There was still a hell of a lot to do before he had to leave for the States, but he was too tired to do any more tonight. He shut down his computer. He could let himself have that brandy.

Now that he was no longer focused on his work, the silence of the empty house closed in around him. If only he could look in on Chloe and watch her sleeping, before slipping into bed next to Rachel. He got up and went over to the cabinet where the glasses and the drinks were kept.

He poured himself a small brandy – more than that and he wouldn't sleep well. He swirled the viscous fluid in the glass, and inhaled the heady fumes. He went over to the window, pulled back the curtain and looked out. The quayside was deserted and the houses were dark. He could see the white shapes of sleeping ducks.

Then – afterwards he wasn't sure how – he knew he wasn't alone in the house. A footfall, a stirring of the air? The warmth of another human being? He turned, expecting to see Rachel, his face already breaking out into a smile.

The room was empty.

The sense of someone's presence had been so strong that the hairs went up on the back of his neck. He went into the sitting room to check that the front door was still locked. It was.

He went back into his study and looked around as if after all there might be someone there. He went over to his desk, where the lab book lay open in the pool of light from his desk lamp. Had he left it like that? He must have. He stared down at it, vaguely troubled. His eyes were sore and itchy. He rubbed them and glanced at his watch. Three o'clock. No wonder he was beginning to lose it.

He finished the brandy and went upstairs to bed.

That night he dreamt about Jennifer. He was searching for her at a party, going through room after room. How was it that he had managed to lose her? He thought he saw her, but when he touched her shoulder and she turned, he saw a stranger's face. Then in the way of dreams, everything changed and he found himself in the house they used to share, waiting for her to come to bed. She came in from the bathroom without turning the light on. He didn't see her face. She was simply a beloved presence in the dark. The mattress gave as she sat down, and he turned to take her in his arms. Another moment and his lips would find hers in the darkness. He felt a surge of love and desire. But then something was happening. He was beginning to wake up. With a supreme effort he succeeded in slipping back into the darkness and this time their lips met and she clung to him, but for the briefest of moments. Something was dragging her down into the dark, and then she was gone.

Chapter Twenty-Nine

It was certain to work this time, Katie told herself, as she waited in the red-tinged darkness. She'd done this dozens of times before. If it hadn't been for the failure last time, she wouldn't be giving it a second thought. The only thing really in doubt was whether it would be good enough for publication.

The western blot came out of the machine and she snatched it up. She turned on the light, narrowing her eyes against the sudden glare. She stared at the western blot, not quite understanding – or not allowing herself to understand. No ladder of protein bands, no baseline bands. Just a greyish ghostly outline. Exactly like last time. It couldn't be – it just couldn't. She'd done everything right: new culture of E.coli, new cell-line. It *had* to have worked. A sudden hope sprang up – there was something wrong with the machine! – only to be dashed the next moment. She was just kidding herself. There was nothing wrong with the machine; it was her. She'd screwed up and the worst of it was, she didn't know how. She was running out of time, she was running out of money, and worst of all, she was running out of ideas. She had reached a dead end and didn't know what to do next. The thought of her forthcoming meeting with Paul made her want to crawl under a stone and stay there.

She left the darkroom in a daze and, scarcely knowing what she was doing, headed for the common room, making instinctively for caffeine and sugar.

Only two people were in there. Minnie was at the sink, filling the kettle. Will was in an armchair, reading a newspaper. He looked up. His expression was guarded, but it soon dissolved into a look of concern.

"What's happened?" he asked. "What's the matter?"

Minnie looked round in alarm. "It's not Ian, is it? He's not –"

Katie burst into tears. She just couldn't help it. Her hands went up to her face. She didn't realize that Will had come over until she felt his hands on her shoulders.

"What is it? What is it?" he demanded.

She just managed to get it out. "Western blot – nothing, absolutely nothing – two years' work down the drain."

"Oh, what!" Will said.

Minnie didn't speak, but her face said everything.

They'd comprehended the scale of the disaster immediately.

Will pulled her into a hug and she rested her head briefly on his shoulder. Minnie came over and thrust a paper tissue into her hand.

"Tea," she said solemnly. "Strong tea with lots of sugar, and a biscuit. That's what you need. The kettle's on."

Will guided Katie solicitously to a chair. She sat down and dabbed at her face.

Millie said, "Oh no, we're out of teabags." She hesitated. "Well, there's this..." Her hand hovered over Ian's tea caddy.

"Go on," said Will, "you might as well. He's not going to be wanting it, is he?"

"Will!" Minnie looked shocked.

"Well, he's not. Oh, I didn't mean that he isn't going to recover. But he won't be coming back here, will he, whatever happens?"

It was all over the lab now that Ian was responsible for the explosion, and Katie saw that Will was coming to terms with it.

"True," Minnie agreed. She brightened up. "And while we're at it, there's these custard creams."

She bustled about, and when they were settled with their tea, she said, "Come on, Katie, let's hear all about it."

Katie went through it stage by stage. Minnie and Will listened intently. When she'd finished, they didn't rush in with their comments, but took time to think it over. Watching their faces as they pondered, Katie thought, *This is what I like about my fellow scientists: their quiet confidence that where there is a problem, there will also be a solution.* This kinship and camaraderie was part of what made the job worthwhile.

Will was the first to speak. "Just when did your work start to hit the skids? Was it before or after you got here?"

"It was when the E.coli culture failed – and that was on my first day in the lab." Hard to believe that it was less than a fortnight ago. "I can't believe I could be so careless," she added.

"Perhaps you weren't," Will said. "Tell me, was Ian full of sympathy; did he wade in and sort it all out for you?"

"Well, yes, but... you don't think..."

"It'd fit a pattern. If Ian was needy, desperate for attention – Honor and I have been talking it over."

Katie said slowly, "She said something similar to me. It's easy enough to kill E.coli."

"Piece of cake. You'd just tip in some antibiotic," Minnie said, dunking her biscuit in her tea. Struck by a sudden thought, she sat up straight. "What about the isotope – "

Katie remembered how impressed she'd been by the way Ian had taken control and cleared the lab. And yes, he *had* been the one to discover it, as if by chance. "You mean – he tracked it over the lab himself – "

"Well, yeah, maybe, but actually I meant my radio-labelled methionine," Minnie said. "Remember when it went missing and Ian found it for me? I *know* I didn't put it in that other fridge. I bet it was him. *And* he could have infected your cell-line."

"Oh, I don't know, Minnie," Katie shook her head. "That could happen to anyone. We can't pin *everything* on Ian. That's just paranoia."

"That's the trouble," Will said sombrely. "When something like this happens, it throws everything into doubt. But don't forget this is a guy who blew up our lab. I'd say a bit of paranoia is justified. Let's go with the idea that your western blot was deliberately sabotaged and see where it takes us."

Minnie nodded. "Because it's still not working, is it? We know that for sure. So there's something else wrong. Something that isn't the E.coli or the cell-line."

"If I wanted to play mind games," Will said, "I wouldn't just go for the things you'd test first, the DNA cloning, the cell-line. I'd choose something that it'd take you ages to tumble to."

Katie thought about that. "Maybe I've been asking myself the wrong question. Not what's the most likely thing to go wrong, but what's the most unlikely?"

For a few moments no one spoke, then Minnie said, "I know what I'd do – I'd pour out one of the antibodies that you added to the western blot and I'd replace it with water."

"You've got a nasty, devious mind, young Minnie," Will said appreciatively. "That's about the last thing anyone would think of. No antibody to bind to the protein, no result."

Katie said, "That would be a rotten thing to do. That antibody – it cost a couple of thousand quid – and I had to have it especially made. It took months – I haven't got the time or the money to replace it. If it *is* that, I'm royally screwed."

"That's not all," Will said. "It would mean that the experiment might have worked, you might have got it right, but you wouldn't *know* you'd got it right. As an act of sabotage, it's elegant; warped, mind you, but elegant. There's only one way to find out. Have you got archived samples which you know have got the protein?"

"I have."

"Try your antibody – or what you think is your antibody – on one of them and you'll soon know if it's been tampered with."

Chapter Thirty

Rachel put down her burnisher. It was hopeless. She couldn't settle to her gilding. That morning Chloe had asked innocently, "When is Daddy coming back?" She'd thought he was away on business. Those were usually the only circumstances in which they were apart. Rachel had said vaguely, "Oh, not long," and the next question had been, "Can I speak to Daddy on the phone?"

Rachel knew she'd have to reach a decision soon. She'd been away from home two nights now.

She needed to get out of the studio and get some fresh air, so she put on her coat and went outside. It was a fresh day, with a breeze that ruffled her hair, but it was warm in the sunshine.

Last night, talking to Katie about embryo selection, she had really been thinking about Harry. How terribly she was tempted to agree with Daniel that the chance of Harry being a match for Chloe was a heaven-sent opportunity. To give up the possibility of Chloe being free of overnight infusions and blood transfusions, and of being free of fear for the future: could that really be right? And yet, and yet...

She walked on, lost in thought, and found that her feet had taken her automatically to the cathedral. "Come unto me all ye who are heavy laden and I will give you rest." The words came unbidden to her mind. *Yes, that's what I need*, she thought: *rest from these incessant circling thoughts, rest from the agony of uncertainty and indecision.* She went inside, slipped into the first row of seats and sat down.

Instruments were being tuned and musicians were seated in the transept. The acoustics in this huge, empty space were always strange. Today she could hear the chatter of children, with no idea where it was coming from. Her thoughts floated free too, though they were scarcely thoughts, these drifting impressions that mingled the memories of the many times she'd been here, and a yearning for peace. She tried to rest on the stillness and let it absorb her fretfulness and uncertainty.

She became aware of a murmuring behind her. She turned her head and saw a small group of ten or eleven people standing by the ticket desk. Someone said, "Yes, this is for the tour of the Octagon." The group moved away from the desk and passed her as they made their way down the centre aisle.

In all the years she'd been coming here, she'd never been up the Octagon. She'd always meant to. On an impulse she got up, hurried over to the desk, and bought a ticket. She caught up with the others where they stood in the middle of the transept. Brilliant light fell diagonally through the tall stained-glass windows. Rachel craned her neck, taking in the soaring space and, high overhead, the octagonal lantern.

The guide, a man in his sixties, was telling the story, already familiar to Rachel, of how on the night of 12 February 1322, with a noise so loud that the monks thought there had been an earthquake, the original Norman tower had collapsed in a heap of timber and rubble. The sacristan, Alan of Walsingham, had at first despaired, but out of the disaster had come a work of architectural genius and a symbol of the resurrection – of how God could take what was broken and restore it. At the very centre, hundreds of feet above their heads, the guide explained, was the carved image of the Risen Christ; below that, paintings of the heavenly host, cherubim and seraphim; and then a series of wooden panels depicting angels and archangels ran round the circumference of the lantern.

"We're going to climb right up to those panels," he promised. "They open outwards and we can look down on the spot where we're standing now."

He led them to a corner of the north transept where a spiral staircase curled round in the thickness of the wall. They toiled up the steep and narrow steps and emerged onto a landing that was used as a storage space. The models of the nativity, the sheep and the donkey, Mary and Joseph, rubbed shoulders with more domestic detritus: an old kitchen sink, a roll of carpet. Rachel had the sense of seeing behind the scenes, of exploring the secret places of the cathedral.

The tuning of the instruments below resolved itself into the opening bars of a piece of music that Rachel recognized and loved: Albinoni's *Adagio in G Minor*.

"They're rehearsing for a concert this evening," the guide explained.

A second stairway led to an outside walkway. They came blinking out of the dimness into brilliant light. The wind tugged at their clothes and hair.

The sky was huge, dotted with scudding clouds. There was a view to the east and the flat landscape stretched out for miles and miles. Rachel tried to get a glimpse of the *Matilda Jane*, but she was out of sight round the bend in the river. Down into the precinct, figures were walking about and – her heart gave a leap; for a moment she wasn't sure – but, yes, there was Daniel, sitting on a bench. It shouldn't be a surprise; he preferred to get out of the office at lunchtime, even if only for half an hour – but somehow it gave her a jolt, spotting him like that. As she watched, he got to his feet, and crumpled up the bag from which he'd been eating his sandwich. He set off across the grass. Something in the set of his shoulders touched her – he seemed a lonely figure – and she had the urge to call to him, though she knew he wouldn't be able to hear.

There was a hand on her arm.

"Could you take a photograph of us, please?" said a voice with an Australian accent. By the time she'd done that, and the couple had explained that they had arrived from Perth only the day before, Daniel had disappeared.

The tour continued. The group moved in single file along the walkway to the base of the lantern, where they gathered round the guide in the dimness and gazed at huge wooden beams – some nearly one thousand years old, he told them. Then it was time for the third and final climb. The spiral staircase was so narrow that Rachel's coat brushed against the walls. The rope handrail was greasy from the thousands of other people who had hauled themselves up on it, and cool air emanated from the stone walls.

They reached the passageway that led around the lantern. The sound of Albinoni's *Adagio* was distant and muted until the guide opened one of the panels and the music flowed in. He indicated that they should each choose a panel. Rachel opened one, leaned out and looked down. Her fingers closed on the sill. She seemed to be fantastically high up. The figures in the nave were tiny, the whole pattern of the chequered and diapered floor was visible, stretching right down the nave to the door. There was no danger of falling – the sill was chest-high – but she was gripped by vertigo, her fear less for herself than for the little people below who might be injured if someone dropped a camera – or – she put her hands to her glasses, afraid that they might slide off her nose and disappear into the void. And all the time the wonderful music, so sad, but so measured and stately, was swelling and falling, slowly rising to its soaring climax, filling Rachel's head so that there was no room for anything else.

She had no idea how much time had passed when there was a touch on her shoulder. It was time to go down.

The music had taken her so far away that she was scarcely conscious of making her way back down with the others. It wasn't until she was walking out of the cathedral and her phone rang that she came back to herself.

It was Katie.

"Hi," Rachel said. "How did it go, the western blot – "

"It didn't. Nothing showed up on it."

"Oh, no – "

185

"Complete and utter bummer. But I've got an idea what might have gone wrong, and I need to try something out. But that's not why I'm ringing. Will offered to cook for me tonight and I've said yes. So I won't be back until later." As an afterthought she added, "Are you alright?"

"I'm fine. See you later."

As Rachel closed up the phone and put it away, she realized with a little shock of surprise that yes, actually, she *was* fine. She wasn't quite sure how or when it had happened, but at some point during her tour of the Octagon she had made a decision. There was only one possible course of action. She saw that clearly now.

Chapter Thirty-One

"**N**ight-night, love."

"Night-night, Daddy."

Daniel kissed Chloe's smooth cheek, inhaling the scent of shampoo and clean skin. How he'd missed her!

Rachel had asked him to come over and eat with them. They'd done Chloe's infusion together and eaten dinner. Of course, they hadn't talked about Harry in front of Chloe. But Rachel seemed calm and they'd exchanged smiles over something Chloe had said. He was beginning to think that she'd adjusted to the idea that Harry might be his child and what that could mean for Chloe. But still it wasn't going to be easy to tell her what was on his mind.

Rachel had gone up to the wheelhouse and he joined her there. She was craning her neck at the sky.

"It's so clear tonight," she remarked.

He said, "I had a look through the telescope earlier and the central part of the Orion Nebula is coming into view."

"It's ages since we looked at the night sky."

It was something they used to do all the time in the early days.

"Shall we have a look now?" he asked, happy to buy himself some time and prolong the period of accord, though he couldn't delay too long. He had to catch his night flight to New York.

She nodded and got her coat. He hunted for the binoculars. They went out onto the deck.

Daniel had loved star-gazing since he was a small boy and his father had taught him to identify the constellations. He'd started to teach Chloe. As he looked up at the sky, the stars seemed to exert an attraction – almost as though he could be pulled towards them into the vastness of deep space. His head swam.

Rachel shivered beside him. He put his arm round her.

"Where's Jupiter?" she asked.

He located the planet and held the binoculars steady while she slipped in between his arms. She took the binoculars.

"Yes, I see it," she said. "And the moons too. The biggest ones, anyway. Io, Europa, Ganymede and – what is it?"

"Callisto."

"I love those names."

He tightened his arms around her. "I've missed you."

"I've missed you too," she said, turning to face him.

They were silent for a few moments, then Rachel said, "Do you think Nick did that? Do you think he was in the car and just went off and left her? The papers are even implying that he might have had something to do with the accident."

Daniel shook his head. "I don't know. I wouldn't have believed the man I knew was capable of that, but then..."

He didn't need to complete the sentence: the man he thought he knew wouldn't have stolen his best friend's wife.

"That poor little boy," Rachel said.

"Rachel, I've been thinking about Harry..."

"Me, too."

"Look, it's cold out here. Shall we go inside?"

They went down to the galley and sat opposite each other at the dining table. Each waited for the other to start.

Rachel's cheeks were flushed with the cold and her eyes were bright. Daniel leaned forward and took her hands. They were chilly and he chafed them to warm them up.

He said, "You and Chloe mean the world to me, you know that."

She opened her mouth to speak, then seemed to think better of it. She just nodded.

He went on, "All we want is what's best for Chloe. We're agreed on that, aren't we?"

"Of course." She sat calmly waiting for him to go on. He was still holding her hands, but he couldn't read her expression.

He plunged on. "Rachel, listen. Suppose Nick goes on trial and ends up in prison. I've been looking into the legal position. If Harry's my son, he would have been conceived while I was still married to Jennifer and that makes him a legitimate child of the marriage. I could seek custody of him."

Rachel said nothing. He gazed at her, trying to gauge her response.

When she spoke, her voice was full of wonder. "What are you thinking, Dan? As far as Harry is concerned, we are complete strangers. He thinks Nick is his father. No, to all intents and purposes, Nick *is* his father, whatever the results of the DNA test may say. He is the only father this child – who has just lost his mother, let me remind you – has ever known. Are you seriously suggesting that we seek custody of him so that we can transplant his DNA into Chloe?"

He understood then that her calmness was not because she had come round to his point of view. It was because she had already made up her mind.

He felt a flash of anger. "Not just because of that, no!"

"Oh, not just because of that?" She pulled her hands away. "What, then?"

"Rachel, he could be my son. I can't ignore that. It has to count for something. It's not just about the DNA. And if he is my son, I want to be part of his life." The moment the words were out of his mouth, he wished he hadn't said them. He hadn't meant to. He hadn't even known that he thought it.

"Your son?" Rachel said. "Think about this. Jennifer must have known there was a chance that she hadn't conceived Harry with Nick. She could have had an abortion. She didn't. After Harry was born, she could have tested his DNA to see if it matched Nick's – and maybe she did exactly that, we'll never know – but what we do know is that she decided to bring him up as Nick's. And he *is* Nick's."

189

"But Rachel, don't you see – "

She put up her hand to stop him. "It is too late, Dan. Can't you see that? If you'd known when Jennifer was pregnant or Harry was a baby, that might have been different, but you didn't." She enunciated the words one by one. "It. Is. Too. Late."

"But if Nick goes to jail – that alters everything."

She stared at him, disbelief written all over her face.

"Have you listened to a single word I've said? You're a lawyer. Do you think there's a court in the land that would award you custody? There must be relatives. In fact there is a sister, isn't there? She was quoted in the newspaper – "

"But Rachel, think what it means for Chloe. Leave aside the question of custody just for the moment – if there is a DNA match, we can't just do nothing."

"Yes, we can. That's exactly it. Nothing is what we can do, what we ought to do."

He saw the effort with which she was reining herself in.

"But Rachel – Chloe – "

"What effect is it going to have on Nick, finding out that Harry's not biologically his? We can't risk him losing his father when he's just lost his mother."

"It might be Chloe's only chance of a cure!"

"Don't raise your voice. You'll wake Chloe. They're working on it all the time. Katie'll get there in the end, I know she will. And if she doesn't, well, we'll just have to go on as we are."

Daniel caught sight of the kitchen clock. He'd have to go soon. He had to get her to see sense.

He shook his head. "I can't let this go, Rachel."

Her face was stony. "And I can't go along with it. I adore Chloe. I'd sacrifice my own life for her in a heartbeat, but I can't do this, Dan. It's wrong, wrong, wrong."

"Rachel!" He slammed his hand on the table.

"Be quiet!" she hissed.

"OK. OK." He would have to leave it for now, or he would

miss his plane. Best anyway to try to lower the temperature, leave the door open for more discussion. He made an effort to lower his voice, raised a placatory hand. "I have to go. We'll talk again when I get back. I'm hoping I might even be able to fly back tomorrow night. Look, why don't you at least come home – "

"No."

He waited for her to enlarge on that. She didn't.

"No, what?" he asked.

"No, we're not going to talk about it again. I've said everything I have to say. And no, I'm not coming back. I'm staying right here. With Chloe."

She leaned back with her arms folded and held his gaze. This was a Rachel he hadn't seen before – implacable, steely.

As he got up to leave, he felt an answering steeliness in himself. He would go it alone if he had to. For Chloe's sake.

In the meantime, he had a flight to catch.

Chapter Thirty-Two

"Glass of wine?" Will said.

"Great," Katie said, taking off her coat.

Will had offered to make pizzas for her and Minnie, but Minnie already had a date. She had looked coy, so it was probably someone in the lab.

"So – " he said, wielding a corkscrew. "Are you enjoying life afloat?"

She told him that she had Rachel and Chloe with her temporarily.

"Didn't you say they've got a house?"

"On Quayside, yes, but there's a problem with the heating," she said. "They couldn't risk Chloe getting cold, so they're staying at the boat while it's fixed. But it'll only be a few days."

"Did you know them before? Rachel and Daniel?" He poured her a glass of wine.

"No. Actually I've only met Daniel a couple of times."

"I wonder how he's getting on with the lab books."

"Oh, I don't think he talks much to Rachel about his work," she said vaguely. Was he trying to pump her? "Can I help?" she offered.

"Nah, I'm just going to put a salad together. And then I'll put the pizza in the oven. Why don't you relax?"

She sat down on the sofa and looked around the room.

She seemed to exist in two parallel universes. In one Will was a decent hard-working scientist like herself. He was a nice guy, friendly, hospitable, a sweetie, who was helping her to get to the bottom of what had gone wrong with her experiment. In the other universe, Will was a cheat and a liar, and evidence of that might be concealed in this flat. Everything depended on how you looked at things, like those silhouettes that one moment appeared to be a young girl, and the next an old crone. Which was the true picture? Or could they both be true?

She scanned the room, assessing the possibilities for hiding a notebook there. Of course, it might not be hidden as such, because he wouldn't be expecting the place to be searched. It might just be in a drawer somewhere, maybe in that desk over there. That would be the first place to look. Behind the screen that divided the room, she could see the corner of a bed, and beside it, a chest of drawers. But the layout of the flat meant that it would be far too risky to start opening drawers or looking in cupboards, even if Will was in the bathroom or busy in the kitchen.

Will called her to the table.

As he cut the pizza he said, "I've got something to tell you." His face was serious.

She stared at him. Was he going to tell her about the lab book? Surely he wasn't going to own up?

He went on. "I've got an interview at Johns Hopkins. Well, not so much an interview as a preliminary meeting." He named the head of the lab – someone Katie would give her eye teeth to work with.

"Wow! Great! When?"

"Next week – to talk about it – but they've made it pretty clear that they want me."

"But Will, that's fantastic. Tell me more."

"I'd be heading up a team and there's a lectureship attached to it. I've been promised tenure."

"Wow!" She felt a pang of envy.

"And the money. No more scratching around to get basic equipment. There's a huge start-up grant. And I'd been hoping to get to the States. Martha's in New York."

"Oh, so that's her name."

He grinned and then grimaced. "Yep. Just one thing. I haven't told Honor yet."

193

"About the job?"

"Well, neither actually. She doesn't know about Martha either."

"But surely she'll understand, an opportunity like this – "

"She's not going to like it. She's just put in for another grant and it won't have occurred to her that I won't be working on the new project. But I've got to move on. I can't be the lowly researcher to her PI for ever."

"Of course you've got to go!"

He nodded, and bit his lip.

Something occurred to Katie. "Why doesn't she know about Martha? There hasn't been anything..."

He laughed. "Me and Honor? No! But we've been close. Working together all this time. Anyway, she's married. Husband's quite a lot older than her, retired now." His eyes slid away from hers. There was something he wasn't saying. Was it perhaps that Honor *had* been interested in him in that way? That would be awkward, very awkward.

"No," he went on, "I didn't tell her because I knew that if she found out I had an American girlfriend she'd imagine I was planning to leave."

"Which is actually the case," Katie pointed out. She wondered if Will had been looking for a way out for a while.

"Only if it all pans out next week."

"Tell me more about the work."

They were soon deep in technicalities. They ate their pizza and salad, scarcely noticing. The plates with their pizza crusts were pushed to one side. Will was sketching a diagram when there was a buzzing from the direction of the door. They looked at each other wide-eyed. They'd been so absorbed that they'd forgotten where they were.

"Doorbell," Will said.

He got up, and went through into the sitting room.

He opened the door and Katie glimpsed an elderly, grey-haired woman with an anxious expression.

"Oh, Will," she began, then she saw Katie. "Oh, sorry, I didn't realize."

"No, no, it's alright. This is Katie, she works in my lab. Katie, this is Marjorie, my landlady."

"I don't want to interrupt – "

"No, it's alright, we've finished eating. What's the problem? A light bulb?"

She nodded. "In the bathroom. But really – it can wait – "

"Oh, it'll only take me a moment. Katie won't mind." He glanced at Katie for confirmation.

"Of course not," Katie said.

"Well, if you're sure," Marjorie said.

Will went out onto the landing, leaving the door open.

Marjorie was still talking as the two of them went down the stairs. "So kind... my arthritis..."

The talk about Will's new project had pushed Katie's suspicions about the notebook to the back of her mind. But it came to her that now, if ever, was the moment. As soon as Marjorie's voice faded away, Katie leapt to her feet and ran to the desk. She hadn't got long – if the light bulb was all ready and waiting, maybe only a minute or two. The top drawer held a role of Sellotape, batteries, rubber bands – just office supply stuff. The other drawers were equally disappointing – envelopes, paper – no notebooks in any of them. She went to the open door of the flat, poked out her head and listened. There was a murmur of voices in one of the rooms below. She guessed that Marjorie liked a chat, and Will was too nice to rush off. There was nothing nice about taking advantage of that to ransack his flat, but she thrust that thought aside. She darted back in and headed for the chest of drawers behind the screen. Quickly and stealthily, her heart beating fast, she opened the top one: underwear. The next contained T-shirts, the bottom one jumpers. Oh, hell.

She stood and listened for footsteps on the stairs. Still nothing. She looked around and saw something that hadn't been visible from the other side of the room. A bedside table with a drawer in it. Was there time? She went to the door of the flat. There were still voices coming from below.

She went back and edged round the bed. The screen blocked off her view of the door. She eased open the drawer of the bedside table. The first thing she saw was a packet of condoms. She pulled it out further. There was something in there. She stretched in her hand – and closed it on a notebook. She opened it and the date on the first page leapt out at her. Oh, yes –

And that was when she heard the door of the flat close.

"Katie?"

"Over here."

Will's concerned face appeared round the corner of the screen. "Are you alright?" he asked.

She was stretched out on the bed with her hands clasped over her belly. "Stomach cramps," she explained. "Time of the month. Just felt I needed to lie down."

"Can I get you anything?"

"I've already taken some paracetamol. They should kick in soon. But a cup of tea would be nice."

"Sure."

His head disappeared and she heard him go into the kitchen and put the kettle on.

Her heart was beating so fast that she felt breathless. She looked sideways at the drawer. It was open just a sliver. She hoped that Will hadn't noticed. There had only just been time to thrust the notebook inside and fling herself onto the bed. Was he coming straight back? No, he was going into the bathroom now. She heard him bolt the door.

She rolled over onto her side and eased the drawer open. She put the notebook back as she remembered finding it and closed the drawer completely.

She laid back and took a deep breath. So, the notebook did

exist. She had been hoping that she was wrong about Will, but now she knew that she wasn't. And she really didn't want to hang around any longer. She lay back and stared at the ceiling, concentrating on breathing evenly, and wondered how quickly she could escape. She glanced at her watch. Quarter past ten.

Will came back with two mugs of tea. He sat down on the bed. Katie propped herself up on the pillows and he handed her a mug.

"Sorry I was gone so long. Marjorie's one of those people who can't stop talking. She's lonely, I think; her husband died a couple of years ago."

"That's a shame."

His eyes flicked to the drawer of the bedside cabinet for the briefest of moments and away again. Katie would have missed it if she hadn't been so intensely aware of the contents of the drawer. She looked over the rim of her mug and her eyes met Will's. She couldn't read his expression. She couldn't wait to get out of the flat.

She drained her tea. "I really think I'd better be off."

"Are you OK now?"

"Much better, thanks." She handed him the empty mug.

He came out to the car with her and waited while she got in and switched on the lights. He waved a hand and went back to the house.

As she drove off she saw in the rear-view mirror that he was still standing framed in the light from the open door.

Chapter Thirty-Three

"I don't like this," Rachel said. "I think you're doing something dangerous."

She had been waiting up in her dressing gown when Katie got back to the boat. They were sitting at the table in the galley.

"He *could* have noticed that the drawer wasn't quite closed," Katie said, "and that later it was. It was stupid of me. I should have just left it. And then I got spooked. I feel such a fool now. What did I think was going to happen?"

"I think you should tell someone about this. Someone apart from me, I mean."

Katie thought it over. "I know that Will kept a notebook covering the period of the missing lab book when he said he didn't. But is that really evidence of anything?"

"Well, he lied about it, didn't he? And what about the lab book?"

"I don't have any proof that it's a fake."

"A handwriting expert would be able to tell whether it had been written over a period of time or all at once."

Katie groaned out loud. "If I make a fuss and I'm wrong, no need to worry any more about getting a scientific officer post or a lectureship somewhere: I'll be unemployable. And even if I'm right, no one likes a whistle-blower – apart from journalists. Yeah, sure, people pay lip-service to the idea, and the newspapers love a good story, but your colleagues hate you for breaking ranks and you end up being shunted off into some scientific cul-de-sac. Either way I'll be stuffed."

"You can't just leave it, though, can you?" Rachel said. "Not now that you've got this far."

"You're right. Of course you are. I'll have to tell Lyle. I'll ring him now."

She only got his voicemail. She left him a brief message, asking him to phone back.

Katie had been so full of her narrow escape that she hadn't looked properly at Rachel. Only now, as she ended the call, did she notice her red-rimmed eyes.

"What's the matter?" she asked.

"I'm going to be on the boat a while longer. I'm not going back to the house yet. I'm sorry."

"No, no, that's fine, but what's happened?"

"Actually, I might not be going back at all."

"Rachel..." Katie leaned over and took one of the hands that rested on the table. It was warm and a little rough. She squeezed and felt the strength in Rachel's fingers as she squeezed back.

"You don't have to tell me – "

"No, I want to."

Rachel took in a deep breath through her nostrils and pressed her lips together. Katie could see she was working hard to stay composed.

After a few moments, she said, "I feel so humiliated – so confused." Seeing the question on Katie's face, she added quickly, "No, he's not having an affair. At least..." She gave a mirthless laugh. "Maybe he is, at that – an affair with a dead woman. I don't suppose you knew that Dan had been married to Jennifer Blunt, the lawyer who was on the obesity case first?"

Katie shook her head. "Had no idea."

Rachel sighed. "Well, why would you? The marriage ended badly – she went off with Daniel's best friend. I was against his taking the case. I thought it would rake up memories and feelings best left alone."

"And it did?"

"And how," Rachel said grimly. "Jennifer had a little boy, a bit older than Chloe. Daniel thinks he's the father."

Katie stared at her, open-mouthed. "What?"

"They had sex just before the divorce was finalized."

"And you found this out – when?" Katie asked.

"Just a few days ago. Dan only started to suspect last week."

"Ah." That explained a lot.

"I just had to get away and think about it."

They sat in silence for a few moments. Then Katie said, "This means that – what was his name? Harry? – he could be Chloe's half-brother."

Rachel nodded.

"Phew." Katie let out a long breath. "That ups the odds considerably – "

"Of his bone marrow being a match for Chloe's. Yes."

Katie thought it over. "Of course, he'd only be a half-sibling, and even if he is a match, it might not work anyway. It's not a 100 per cent success rate. That's a lot of 'ifs' – "

"But even so."

"Even so."

"He managed to get hold of Harry's toothbrush when he went to look for the lab book and he's sent it off for DNA analysis to see if it's a match for Chloe."

"But surely – that would be a good thing, wouldn't it?"

"Katie, think about it. If Dan turns out to be the father, can you imagine the damage it would do, bringing it into the open? That poor little boy has already lost his mother! Nick is all he has to cling to."

"I see what you mean."

"Dan's been talking about seeking custody of Harry."

Katie stared at her. "Can he *do* that?"

"If Harry was conceived while Dan was still legally married to Jennifer, maybe – oh, I just don't know. But how can he even think of it? We had a row. I told him I couldn't be part of it."

"Whoa. Hang on a minute. Let me think this through. Even if Dan is the father – and even if Harry's a match – why does he have to seek custody?"

"Nick, that's Jennifer's husband, has been arrested. The police seem to think he was in the car and left the scene of the crime. Dan thinks Nick might go to jail. Katie, I think Dan's gone crazy. What's happened to Jennifer, I think it's unhinged him. It's all such a mess. Having a child by this woman..."

"If in fact he has – "

"But that it's even on the cards..." Rachel massaged her temples. She looked up and met Katie's eye. "I don't know if my marriage can survive this."

Katie nodded. She had no answer to the dilemma, which seemed to her so difficult, so knotty, so painful that she had no idea what she would do in Rachel's place. And it wasn't just the problem of what to do about Harry; it was the bombshell of finding that Daniel might have a child by another woman.

Looking at Rachel's drawn face, the frown that was drawing vertical lines between her eyebrows, and pulling down the corners of her mouth, Katie had a feeling it was going to be a long night.

Chapter Thirty-Four

Will was in a psychotic rage, and as he got angrier and angrier he began to shrink and change shape until he was only about a metre high and sort of squarish. Katie woke up gasping. The absurdity of the dream didn't at all diminish the horror. Her rational mind told her that her worries about Will had got mixed up with Chloe's Rumpelstiltskin story, but she was left with a feeling of fear and foreboding.

The boat rocked gently beneath her. Lying there, trying to orientate herself, she smelt coffee and remembered that Rachel was here. They had talked until one o'clock the night before. She yawned, pulled on her thick jumper and socks, and padded through to the galley.

Chloe was eating breakfast cereal and Rachel was taking toast out of the toaster. They both smiled at her and the dream slipped further away.

Rachel poured her a cup of coffee. "I've just been listening to the weather forecast. They're saying there'll be storms and gale-force winds later."

In spite of the late night, Rachel was looking better, more relaxed. It had probably done her good to get it all off her chest.

"Will we feel that much on the boat?" Katie asked.

"Could be a bit rocky."

Katie took her coffee back to her cabin. It was eight o'clock. Too early to try Lyle again? Maybe, but she wanted to get it over with. Then she'd try to forget about it and get on with her own work.

Once again she got his voicemail, so she left another message.

Later, as she walked along the tow path to where she'd parked her car, she saw that already the breeze was lifting the surface of the river into little peaks. The branches of the willow trees were swaying, and a gust of wind released a shower of dead leaves.

She sighed. She wasn't looking forward to the day ahead. This morning she was running the western blot for the final time and she was seeing Paul with the result this afternoon.

She didn't want to run into Will, and took the stairs to make sure she didn't find herself in the lift with him. Instead she bumped into Minnie.

"Hey, Katie. What's happened with the western blot?"

"I'm just about to run it again. Want to come and see?"

"Yeah, why not?"

For the third time it came back blank, but in a sense that was a positive result. Because this time Katie had used a sample that she knew for sure contained her protein. The antibody should have detected it and it hadn't. So the problem lay with the antibody. In all likelihood someone had tipped it out and substituted tap water. Anger flared up. She hadn't lost her touch; someone else had lost it for her. It wasn't just the undermining of Katie as a scientist that hurt; this was research that really mattered. She thought of Chloe, she thought of the anxious faces of the mothers in Paul's waiting room. How could Ian have done this?

"You were right," Katie said.

Minnie was looking at her, aghast. "I wish I wasn't. I know I suggested it, but I didn't really believe – " She was struck by a thought. "Can we be sure it was Ian?"

"Oh, come on. There can't be two people getting up to this kind of thing in the lab – and it couldn't possibly have been an accident."

"No, no, you're right. Well, at least you know now."

"And a fat lot of good it does me, when I can't replace the antibody. There's hardly any grant money left, and – " She looked at her watch. "Oh, blast! I'm seeing Paul in an hour."

"It's not your fault," Minnie pointed out.

"Let's hope he sees it that way."

Her mobile phone rang. She picked it up and saw that it was Lyle.

"This is Lyle Linstrum's PA," said a brisk, female voice with an American accent, "returning your call. May I ask what your business is with Lyle?"

"I'd rather speak directly to him."

Minnie gave a little wave, indicating that she was heading off.

"Was this with regard to Calliope Biotech?" the woman asked.

"Well, yes – "

"Then I have to inform you that Lyle's connection with the company ceased as from six o'clock last night."

"But what – "

"I'm not at liberty to comment," the woman said. "And I don't believe I can be of further assistance to you, so I'll wish you good day."

And that was it: she was gone.

Katie sat back in her chair, feeling as if she'd trodden on a step that wasn't there. What on earth had happened? She booted up her laptop and typed Lyle's name and Calliope Biotech into Google. The first thing to come up was a link to the *Financial Times* with the headline: "Linstrum ousted from own company". Katie clicked on it and skimmed down the report. "The market has been awash with rumours ... share price affected ..." So it was true, hard as it was to credit, Lyle was gone, just like that, dumped by his own company. She could hardly believe it. What to do? She could email Lyle – she had a private email address – or she could try ringing his home in Texas. But it was the middle of the night there. She pursed her lips, considering. What could Lyle do if he wasn't even part of the company any more? She'd have to think about this.

She looked absently at her watch and then looked more

closely. *Oh, no!* She leapt to her feet, closed down her laptop, and grabbed her bag. She was going to be late for her meeting with Paul.

"I suppose I can't be 100 per cent sure it was Ian, but in any case..." Katie shrugged.

"We're up against the same problem."

Paul clasped his hands behind his head and rocked back in his chair.

The silence was broken by the wind rattling the windows. From up here, Katie could see the tops of trees swaying in the breeze.

She waited for Paul to work through the implications of what she had told him. It didn't take long.

He brought the legs of the chair down and put his hands on the table. "OK. There's no way round it. Even if I could magic up some more cash, there's no way of getting hold of any more antibody before your time's up. So no more work in the lab."

She nodded. She'd use the next couple of months for writing up her report. It was laborious and time-consuming and would easily occupy her until her research time ran out.

"You've done some great work," he said. "This therapy could transform the life of some of the kids I see. No more bone marrow transplants, no more blood transfusions and all the rest. But I need a good publishable western blot to keep that research money rolling in. Let's have a look again at that earlier one and see if there's anything we can work with."

She leafed through the pages of her lab book until she found it. They bent their heads over it.

She suppressed a sigh. *She* knew that she had got a result, that this was the band of protein she needed, but would other people be convinced? She waited to see what Paul would say.

"You know, Katie," he said slowly, "this isn't quite as bad as I'd remembered. I'd say this was borderline. You were virtually there with this."

She looked again at the western blot. Was she virtually

there? Was she really? She looked hard, willing it to be not quite so faint, for the edges to be more defined. And the more she looked at it, the more she thought he was right. It *was* nearly there.

"If I got rid of that background contamination..." she said.

He nodded. "Why don't you see what you can do? See if you can clean it up a bit. After all, things are rarely black and white."

Maybe he was right and there was something she could salvage here. It wasn't as if it was her incompetence that had screwed up that second western blot, or even bad luck. It was sheer malice. A bloody-minded streak was telling her that she was damned if she was going to let Ian get the better of her like this. It was only fair that she should have something to show for all her hard work.

"I'll go back to the lab and make a start," she said.

He closed the lab book and handed it to her.

"You do that and I'll get to work on the grant proposal."

Chapter Thirty-Five

It was five o'clock and Katie had been at her bench for two hours. Her eyes were sore and gritty from gazing at her computer screen. It was amazing what you could do with Photoshop. She'd got rid of the meaningless background contamination on the western blot, and the band already looked sharper and cleaner by contrast. The next thing was to tidy the edges so that they were less ragged and indeterminate. There, that was better; it was already much more convincing – and yet, and yet... if only it wasn't quite so pale. She moved the marker on the contrast bar the minimum amount and that helped, definitely. She tried to look at it with fresh eyes. What would she make of it if she were looking at it for the first time? She tried to imagine it on a page in a journal. Mmm, maybe if it was just a tiny, tiny bit darker?

Her stomach rumbled. She hadn't had a proper meal all day. Wasn't there some flapjack in the box that she'd brought over from her old lab? The box was tucked away under her bench. She pulled it out and rummaged in it. Yes, there it was. In reaching for it she disturbed a postcard that was tucked in beside it and caught a glimpse of familiar, italic handwriting. She pulled it out and read it. It brought back a rush of memory. She couldn't help smiling. She'd been so lucky to have Michael as her PI. She had been going through a bad patch early on in her research, had even thought of jacking it in. She hadn't said anything to Michael, but he had picked up on it somehow. She'd found this postcard in her pigeonhole. On one side was a photo of a craggy-featured Samuel Beckett, and on the other side Michael had written that Beckett quote about failing, and trying again, and failing better. That was so typical of him. He wasn't one of those scientists who were interested in nothing but science. He'd once told her that he'd done the first year of a French degree before he switched to medicine. He was always talking about books he'd read, exhibitions he'd seen. How she missed him.

She ate the flapjack – much too sweet, this commercially produced stuff always was – and went back to the screen. But her concentration had been broken. As she edged the marker up and down the contrast bar, Michael kept intruding into her thoughts. What would he say if he could see her now? She thought of the words Paul had used – "clean it up a bit" – weasel words that she couldn't imagine passing Michael's lips. She wasn't cleaning up, or tidying up, or whatever euphemism you cared to use. She could at least be honest with herself about what she was doing. She was manipulating the data, simple as that.

She toyed with the mouse, dragging the marker first one way and then the other. In one direction the band grew paler and paler until it disappeared altogether. Pull the marker the other way and the band grew sharper and sharper. One way it vanished, and with it her scientific career; the other way both of them grew stronger and brighter. Of course, she'd have to be careful not to overdo it, because a perfect image wouldn't be plausible, might even look downright suspicious. Up and down, paler, darker.

She was sure that it worked, that she'd succeeded in transferring her gene, and that they'd lose time and maybe even lives if she didn't produce something publishable that would lead to more grant money. She knew what Michael would say to that: "You think you know, but where's the evidence? Are you on solid ground? If you're wrong, work will continue on a very expensive therapy that could turn out to be nothing but snake oil. And those children and their parents – their hopes raised, only to be dashed – "

But wait a minute, she told the Michael in her head, if

she didn't do it, what was to stop Paul finding someone less scrupulous to manipulate the image – or he could even do it himself? The Michael in her head didn't dignify that with a response. He just raised his eyebrows in that infuriatingly quizzical way that he had. Oh, hell!

She brought the marker to rest at its original position. This was it; for better or for worse, this was her result. And she was going to stick with it. How could she have thought for a moment of doing anything else? She buried her face in her hands. She was tired, so tired.

There was a footstep behind her. She looked up with a start. It was Minnie.

"Are you alright?"

Katie pushed her chair back. "Yep. Well, not really. I still haven't got a publishable result. I thought there was a way round it, but there isn't. Oh, what the hell. Perhaps I've been at this game too long. I hear there are some very good careers in accountancy."

Minnie screwed up her face in commiseration. "Why don't you pack it in now and come and join us? There's a party starting. Will's had some good news."

A version of the old marimba classic "Sway" was playing in the background. The common room was full of the buzz of conversation and the damp heat of a lot of bodies in a small space. Will was shaking something in a glass flask. Seeing him reminded her of her dream: the tiny Will shaking with anger.

He called over. "Hey, Katie! Honor's heard from the patent lawyer. We're home and dry. It's not even going to court. When the other company saw the lab books, they threw in the towel. So let the good times roll!"

She was too taken aback to reply straightaway. In her worry about the western blot, all the business with Will had slipped to the back of her mind. Could it really be that it was all over and settled?

209

She recovered herself. "That's good."

He came over with the improvised cocktail shaker in one hand and a glass in the other. "Good? It's more than good. It's great, it's fantastic." His face was flushed. He was already a bit drunk, she realized.

People were drifting in from other labs, attracted by the rumour of free drinks, and were greeted by Will and his cocktail shaker.

"What'll you have to drink?" Minnie asked. "Will's making margaritas. Or there's some beer."

"You know what I'd really like? A cup of tea."

"You sit down and relax. I'll have one too. Actually, I don't really drink. I'm still stone cold sober."

That was more than could be said for the rest of the crew. Katie pushed past a couple of blokes arguing about the merits of their football teams. She found a couple of armchairs that had been pushed against the wall and sank into one. No one paid any attention to her. She leaned back and closed her tired eyes.

There was a touch on her shoulder. She opened her eyes. Minnie was in the next chair. "Here's your tea," she said, handing her a mug. "What a life, eh?"

Katie nodded.

Minnie leaned closer in so that Katie could hear her. "Don't despair," she said. "Think of Will."

She gestured and Katie turned to look. Through a gap in the crowd she could see Will slumped in a chair, conducting the music with his eyes closed.

Minnie said, "Things couldn't have looked worse for him after that clinical trial went wrong, could they? I mean, someone actually dying. Of course, it wasn't his fault, but still it must have looked as if his work had gone down the pan. And all that stuff with the patent. But now look at him. Turns out the patent's fine and he's got a job lined up in the States."

So that was common knowledge, was it?

"Is Katie here? Katie, there's a phone call for you." It was one of the young postgrads.

"Who is it?"

"Dunno. It came through to the office in the lab."

Who could be ringing her on the office line instead of on her mobile? Katie went to find out.

The voice at the other end of the line was young and nervous. "You don't know me, but I'm Emma Gladwill. I'm Ian's daughter."

"Oh... how is he?"

"Well, he's not having quite so much morphine, so he's conscious more, and talking to us. And he asked me to ring you. Can you come and see him?"

Katie didn't know what to say. Really, she hardly knew the guy, and in the light of what had happened, it was the last thing she felt like doing.

The voice went on. "He said he needs to tell you something. It's very important."

"I really don't think –"

"Oh, please, he's in such a state about it. He says it's very, very urgent and that you'll want to know. Something to do with an antibody?"

It wasn't only dusk that was darkening the vast Fenland sky as Katie drove to Cambridge. Black cumulus clouds were massing on the horizon, and as she drove into the hospital car park, there was a splattering of rain on her windscreen.

Ian's daughter was waiting for her at the door of the ward. She was young, twentyish, and had smooth, honey-coloured hair. She was unmistakably her father's daughter. She looked anxiously at Katie.

"Dad's really sorry," she said.

"That's OK," Katie said. She wasn't going to take it out on this poor young woman.

When she saw Ian, she knew that she wasn't going to take

it out on him either. He was propped up on the pillows, both bandaged hands outside the sheets. His head was bandaged too. He wasn't reading or listening to headphones. He was just staring into space. He didn't see Katie as she made her way down the ward, and only registered her presence when she arrived at his bedside.

His face lit up, only to cloud over again. He looked away.

She sat down by the bedside and laid a bunch of flowers, bought at the hospital shop, on his bed.

"You shouldn't have." He was on the verge of tears and she got a sense of his emotional fragility. His eyes looked huge. His face was thinner, she realized.

"I'm so sorry." His voice was weak. "The antibody. Have to tell you. It's in the top drawer of my desk. Pushed right to the back."

She gaped at him. It took a few moments to find her voice. "So you really did do that? You replaced my antibody with water?"

He nodded. "I'm so sorry," he said again.

"How could you do it? How could you wreck my experiment when so much rested on it?"

"I just wanted to help – to be able to help – to be part of it. I was going to offer to run it again for you. And then when I did it…"

"Hey presto! It would work. Ian saves the day!" She couldn't help herself. When she thought of all that anxiety, all that wasted time…

"It's not too late, is it?" he asked.

It was hard to forgive him for putting her through all that. He moved his hands restlessly on the sheet and his face creased in a grimace of pain.

She softened and shook her head. "No, it's not too late."

He closed his eyes and moaned.

"Shall I get the nurse?" she asked.

He nodded.

212

She looked round. A nurse was already on her way. She adjusted Ian's drip. More morphine, probably.

"You shouldn't stay too much longer," she told Katie. "He'll be getting drowsy soon, anyway."

"Don't go, not yet..." Ian murmured.

"I won't."

He was at least trying to make amends, she thought. She could understand – sort of – what had motivated him in mucking up her experiment: wanting to be important, wanting to be needed. But the other things...

"What about the radioactivity tracked around the lab?" she asked. "Was that you?"

He nodded. "I'm sorry."

She shook her head in disbelief.

"But the gas taps," he said. "That wasn't me. I didn't cause the explosion."

"Oh... OK..."

She could see that he thought she was humouring him. He spoke more urgently. "Really, I didn't do that. Too dangerous." Then he added – and she heard the old Ian: "Wouldn't be such an idiot as to switch the light on if I had." He sighed. His voice grew slower, as if he were having difficulty putting his thoughts together. "Sleeping in my office some nights. After Moira threw me out. Heard someone moving around and went down to the lab. Put my hand on the light switch, and – boom."

He was struggling to keep his eyes open.

"One thing that I can't get straight," he sighed. "Please..."

"What's the matter?"

"The inventory..."

"Someone else can do it," she told him.

"Are you sure? Oh... OK." He was drifting away. "Still haven't found that mouse... have to find that mouse..." There was something else that she couldn't make out. Then he was asleep.

Chapter Thirty-Six

Katie drove back to the lab as fast as she dared. The wind had almost stripped the trees of their leaves and they lay in drifts across the road. On the long stretches of Fenland road, the wind buffeted the car.

She signed into the late book and ran up the stairs two at a time.

In the back of the top drawer of the desk in Ian's office was an unmarked phial of transparent fluid, just where he'd said it would be. She pressed it to her chest, then held it to the light, and gazed at it. She felt almost tearful. One last chance.

Now that there was hope, she was filled with new energy. If she got her starter culture into the shaking incubator this evening... As she set about the routine task, her thoughts returned to what Ian had said about the explosion in the lab. But if it wasn't Ian, who was it? A chilling thought occurred to her. What if it hadn't been an accident that it was Ian who was injured? What if someone knew that Ian was sleeping there and would be first in the lab next morning?

She couldn't think about that now. She pushed on and had just finished with the starter culture when Minnie came into the lab.

She looked relieved to see Katie. "Oh, good, you're still here."

Katie looked at her watch. She was surprised to see that it was nearly ten o'clock. "You don't mean to say that the party's still going on?"

"Everyone's gone now. Thing is, though, Will's had too much to drink and I was wondering if you'd help us to get him home."

"Sure. I was about to leave anyway."

They went along to the common room. Will was asleep in a chair. Minnie and her friend Sam woke him, hoisted him up, and slung his arms around their shoulders. He swayed but managed to stay upright as they staggered along the corridor and went down in the lift. Katie signed them all out, while they waited with Will propped between them.

Katie opened the door so that Will could be guided through, and a blast of cold air hit them. Will uttered an incoherent protest. He tried to shake off their arms and turn back into the building.

Minnie and Sam got a grip on him. He leaned into Minnie and said something to her. Katie heard a note of complaint.

"What's he saying?" she asked.

"I *think* he said he has to see to the mice."

"Mice? What mice?"

"Exactly." Minnie put her mouth to Will's ear. "You're not working on mice," she told him, enunciating slowly and clearly.

He squinted at her. "No mice?"

"No mice."

"Thass alright, then."

"Yes, come on, let's get you home."

Inside the lab, Katie hadn't been aware of the worsening weather. The wind whistled round the building and dragged at their hair and clothes. It was an effort to walk upright. They propped Will against the car, Minnie supporting him, while Sam helped Katie to wrench open the door against the wind.

Will was docile enough as they got him into the passenger seat and strapped him in.

Minnie and Sam got in the back.

As Katie drove off she glanced in the rear-view mirror. Sam was pulling Minnie close. She rested her head on his shoulder. The sight made Katie feel old and lonely. She wished there was someone apart from Rachel to console and comfort her when she got home.

The wind tugged at the steering, and the car swerved. Katie gave her full attention to driving.

Minnie's flat was on the way to Will's, so Katie stopped there first.

Sam said, "I could come and help you get Will up the stairs..."

"No, I can manage. He's not that bad. You go on."

Sam didn't need telling twice. He scrambled out of the car after Minnie. Katie sighed.

She drove off alone with Will snoring gently beside her. She pulled up outside his house. He protested when she shook him awake. She got up and went round to the passenger door. She struggled to hoist him up. He slumped against her, reeking of beer. She got him half way out of the car, only for him to collapse back onto the seat.

"Come on, come on," she murmured, hooking her arms under his armpits again. This time he hung affectionately round her neck while she hauled him to his feet. She had to search his jacket pockets to find his keys.

It was only half past ten, but the house was in darkness. Marjorie had probably gone to bed. She leaned him against the wall while she found the right key and opened the front door. She got him up the stairs by pushing him from behind and then at last they were in the flat. He stood swaying in the centre of the room. She worked his arms out of his jacket and, as soon as it was off, he staggered to the bed and collapsed onto it.

She followed him and he looked up at her with unfocused eyes. He mumbled something. She leaned down to listen. "The mouse," he was saying. "If it hadn't been for the mouse..." He looked at her imploringly. "But it's alright now, isn't it?"

"Yes, yes, it's alright," she said.

"Good, thass good," he muttered. Seconds later he was snoring.

She rolled him over onto his side so that he wouldn't choke

on his own vomit and sat down by the side of the bed to get her breath back. Her eyes strayed to the bedside table. She leaned over and gently eased the drawer out. It contained nothing but the packet of condoms. She wasn't surprised that Will had moved the notebook. Maybe he had even destroyed it?

She tried the drawer in the desk. It was locked. Last time it hadn't been. Will's keys were still in her pocket. She got them out. Just three: his car key, the key to the house and the key to his flat. So where was the key to the drawer? It was probably somewhere in the flat.

She got up and walked around, opening cupboards and drawers, going back every few minutes to check on Will. He was breathing stertorously, but he seemed to be OK. She looked in all the obvious places first. She thought of the movies she had seen where the cops or FBI agents searched for hidden documents. She looked in the freezer compartment of the fridge and behind the books on the shelves. She looked at the back of a photo of Will's rowing team in case the key had been taped there. She was just putting it back on its hook when the theme tune to *The Wire* blared out. She gave such a start that she almost dropped the picture. She looked over at Will. He was still dead to the world and didn't stir.

She traced the mobile to Will's coat and looked at the screen. The call was from Honor. It seemed late for her to be calling. She switched the phone off and put it back in Will's pocket.

Finding the phone had given her an idea. She checked the pockets of the coats and jackets hanging on the back of the door. But no...

Unless she started unscrewing the panels in the bathroom or taking up floorboards, there was nowhere else to look.

She shivered. It was eleven o'clock now and the heating had gone off. The wind was slipping in through the chinks in the old building and a cold draught was playing around her ankles. Before she went, she'd better check on Will one last time. She touched his hand and it was cold. She ought to try to get him under the duvet. She unlaced his trainers and eased them off. He shifted and muttered something, but didn't wake up. What was the best way to do this? She began with his legs. She lifted them up and tugged the duvet out from under them. But she couldn't get it out from under his hip. No, it wasn't going to work. Instead she folded the duvet back so that half the bed was exposed. Then she pulled and pushed at him, until, with a whimper of complaint, he suddenly rolled over, trapping her hand under his hip. As she eased it out, she felt the outline of a key in the pocket of his jeans.

She sat back on her heels by the bed. Will opened his mouth and muttered something that she didn't catch and turned his face into the pillow.

"Will?" she said to check that he was still asleep, her voice sounding horribly loud in the silent flat. "Will?"

There was no response. He started to snore. She climbed onto the bed next to him and laid her head on the pillow so that she could see his face. She slid her hand under his hip and felt about for the opening of the pocket. She got her fingers inside and touched the edge of the key. Will's weight made it hard to get a purchase on it. She twisted her fingers and burrowed deeper. Her face was so close to Will's that she could see pinpricks of blond stubble glinting around his mouth. And then yes, she'd got hold of the key and was easing it out.

There was a heaving beside her and Will flung out an arm across her neck, pinning her to the pillow. She gasped and let go of the key. For an awful moment she didn't know if he had come round or not. Then he buried his face in her hair, muttered something, and was still. She lay there, her heart hammering, waiting until she was sure he was really asleep. She counted to sixty, then felt about until she found the key. As gently as she could, she lifted the dead weight of his arm and slid out from under it. She lowered it onto the bed. He groaned, but he didn't wake up.

She backed away from the bed, her eyes never leaving his face.

Then she was out of sight behind the screen. Her fingers were trembling and it seemed to take forever to get the key in the lock of the drawer, but at last she did it and pulled the drawer open. There was a litter of papers, bills, a passport. At first she thought the notebook wasn't there. But then she found it, right at the back, concealed by a sheaf of bank statements.

She hesitated. If she read it here and put it back, he need never know that she'd seen it. If she took it away, she was burning her bridges. But there was no way she could read this here – not with Will so close, drunken stupor or not.

She put the notebook in the pocket of her coat and locked the drawer. There was a sound from the other side of the screen. She gasped – she couldn't help it – and looked round it, to see that Will had flopped over onto his back. As she watched, he turned over onto his other side, and snuggled his head into the pillow. She went and stood by him. It seemed to her that his breathing had got lighter. He wasn't as deeply asleep as he had been. He was lying twisted round with his hips pressed into the bed. How was she going to get the key back into his pocket? She considered rolling him over onto his back, but she didn't want to leave him like that – he might choke on his own vomit – and anyway, she was afraid of waking him up.

She got on the bed and laid down beside him. She pushed her hand with the key in it under his hip. Will sighed and murmured, "Darling." Katie felt an almost overwhelming urge to giggle. She bit her lip hard until it passed. She managed just to push the key into the top of his pocket and carefully extricated herself.

It was only as she was going down the stairs from Will's flat that she realized she had put the key back in the wrong pocket.

Chapter Thirty-Seven

Soon after the in-flight meal, Daniel fell into a shallow sleep, moving in and out of confused dreams. Someone grabbed his hand and he woke with a start, not knowing where he was – and then an announcement about turbulence came over the tannoy and he knew he was on a plane.

His hand was released. He looked to see who had been holding it. His neighbour was a woman – he was no good at guessing ages, but somewhere in late middle age. She was laughing and blushing.

"I'm so sorry," she said. "I'd dozed off and I thought you were my husband. Actually, I'm on my own this time – been visiting my daughter in Maine and – "

The plane bucked again. Her eyes widened.

His mouth was dry and he had a hollow feeling around his eyes, but he roused himself to say, "It's alright. We're really not in any danger. You said you were visiting your daughter?"

After that it didn't need much more than the odd sympathetic nod or comment to get her talking. It was a welcome distraction for both of them. He heard about the twice-yearly visits and the grandchildren –"we keep in touch on Skype" – and twenty minutes later the announcement came that they were about to land at Stansted.

He looked at his watch. One o'clock in the morning. There would be a car waiting for him and with any luck he'd be home in not much more than an hour.

He said goodbye to his new friend and she went off to the baggage retrieval area. All he had was his briefcase and a small leather holdall. He headed for passport control.

He was exhausted, spent, but he had done what he had set

out to do. And yet, though he had finished Jennifer's work and won the case, he could take no satisfaction in it. He'd managed to put the quarrel with Rachel to the back of his mind, telling himself that he'd deal with it when the case was over. Well, now the case was over and he didn't know what to do, how to make Rachel see sense. But maybe there wasn't anything he *could* do, until the DNA results came back and he knew for sure.

As he walked through the automatic doors into arrivals, he scanned the waiting crowd for his driver. It would probably be Gemma – the company usually sent her – and yes, there she was. His eye had passed over someone else who looked familiar. He looked again. It was Nick. Daniel stopped dead. A man bumped into him and Daniel muttered an apology and stepped over to the side so that he wouldn't impede the flow of people arriving. Nick was obviously looking for someone and hadn't noticed Daniel. A child was clasped to his chest, the little boy's legs round Nick's waist, and his head on Nick's shoulder. One arm encircled Harry, and with the other hand he was stroking the child's glossy fair hair. Harry was bigger than Chloe, past the age really to be carried like that. Nick's legs were braced to take his weight.

As Daniel watched, Nick gave Harry a little shake to get his attention. He let the child slide down his body and set him on his feet. Now Harry too was looking towards arrivals and his face brightened in recognition.

A tall willowy woman was waving. Daniel remembered that Nick's sister lived with her American husband and their children in New York. His heart beating fast, he walked on, averting his gaze. But he couldn't resist glancing at Nick, and at that very moment their eyes met. Daniel felt the contact like an electric shock and he saw that Nick did too. Now Daniel was past the barrier, only a metre or two away from them. Harry was tugging at Nick's hand, trying to go forward to meet his aunt. Nick was still staring at Daniel as though he couldn't believe his eyes. He let go of Harry, who ran to his aunt. She squatted to receive him into her arms.

There were many things that Daniel had thought of saying to Nick if he ever encountered him.

What he actually said was, "Why aren't you still in custody?"

"They released me this afternoon," Nick said.

His eyes were bloodshot. His lank hair fell over his face. He raised a trembling hand, still wearing a wedding ring, to push it back, a gesture so familiar to Daniel that it seemed to summon up all their shared past. They had been such good friends: Scout camp, cycling holidays, travelling around Europe together.

Nick said, "I wasn't in the car. Not when it..." He looked away. "Not when..." He was struggling to control himself. "It was my fault all the same. I was with her just before. We had a row. About Harry. I was so angry I told her to stop the car and let me out. That was the last I saw of her – the car screeching off down the road."

Nick had been so handsome once. Now he looked old and gaunt. Daniel caught a whiff of something sour on his breath.

"If only we hadn't argued," Nick said. "Or if I hadn't got out of the car."

If only... What if... The eternal and unanswerable questions that everyone asks themselves. He thought of saying, "Yes, it *is* all your fault. If you hadn't stolen my wife, she'd be alive now." But suddenly it all seemed a long time ago, the marriage, the betrayal, all of it. That was then, this was now, and he was on his way home to Rachel and Chloe. He couldn't wish any more suffering on someone who was already a broken man.

Daniel said, "If you hadn't got out of the car, you'd probably be dead, too. Jennifer always was a terrible driver."

A flicker of something – amusement? Affection? – crossed Nick's face. "Yeah, she was that all right."

Nick's sister – her name came to him now – Donna – was coming towards them, holding Harry by the hand.

"Well..." Daniel indicated that he should go.

"I'm sorry," Nick said, with a gesture that encompassed it all.

Daniel nodded and turned away.

When he looked back, Donna was embracing Nick and he was resting his head on her shoulder.

"You're soaked!" Rachel exclaimed.

"It's raining stair rods," Katie said, as Rachel helped her off with her coat. "And blowing a gale. There are leaves and twigs and branches all over the roads. I wondered if I was going to make it home OK."

Orlando had come in with her. He gave a chirrup of greeting and shook himself like a dog, spraying water over them.

"Were you waiting up?" Katie asked.

"Not really, I couldn't sleep, but I *was* wondering. I didn't know if I should ring you – here, you'd better dry your hair." She handed her a towel.

Katie was contrite. "I didn't think – but look..." She took the notebook out of her bag.

Rachel stared at it. "You don't mean... that's it?"

Katie nodded. They sat down together on the black leather sofa. Rachel leafed through the notebook, while Katie towelled her hair and told her everything that had happened. Rachel's face shone when she heard that Katie was having another stab at producing a western blot, but she shook her head when Katie told her how she had got the notebook.

"Katie – how you had the nerve... Sooner or later he's bound to realize that the notebook's gone."

"Let's just hope it's later." Katie gave a stupendous yawn. "Oh, I'm tired. It's all catching up with me."

"Are you going to read it now?"

"That's the plan."

"I'll make you some coffee."

"Are you having some?"

"No, I'd better go to bed. But wake me up if you find anything."

***

At first progress was painfully slow. It wasn't like a lab book, where the point was to allow someone to replicate your work and everything had to be crystal clear. A personal notebook was more of an *aide-memoire*, a way of capturing things that would later be recorded more formally. It took a while for her to tune in, to decipher Will's handwriting and to work out what the abbreviations meant, but as she read on, the work came into focus, the process of trial and error that was so familiar. She saw the places where things had gone right and Will had marked them with huge emphatic ticks. She saw where something hadn't worked and Will had had to backtrack. Maybe it was because she was so tired, but she saw in her mind's eye what Will was doing in the lab with an almost hallucinatory clarity as experiment followed experiment in logical sequence. He was good, very good.

It was about half past one when Katie came across a page with two heavy lines scored across it. Those two lines spoke of anger and frustration. Something hadn't worked. What could it be? She struggled to make sense of what was written underneath. What did the abbreviation "m" mean? Will had stipulated ten of them. She got up and stretched, drank a glass of water, and rubbed her eyes. She wondered if Will was still asleep – she hoped he was; she didn't want him realizing that she had pinched the notebook and coming to get it back.

She sat down again and looked at the page. What was it that Will had said earlier? "The mouse. If it hadn't been for the mouse." If so that was odd, more than odd, because he hadn't been doing animal experiments up to now. She read on, every sense alert, because she was on to something, she knew it. This solution for which he had written out the formula, he'd presumably injected the mice with it. That didn't relate to what had gone before either. It belonged to some other set of experiments. She turned over the next page to see what the result was. There was no result. There was a jagged edge where a page had been torn out. She didn't know what was going on, but this must have been a result so memorable – so catastrophic? – that he didn't need or didn't dare to record it. This was it, she knew it.

She looked at the date of the experiment and her heart dropped a curtsey. Surely not. It couldn't be... She fired up her laptop, and typed in the words that would call up the disastrous clinical trial. Links to newspaper articles appeared and she clicked on the first one: "Medical student dies in drug trial". And when she saw the date, she knew. There had been a cover-up alright, but it had nothing to do with when the therapy had been discovered. It was worse than that. Much worse.

Chapter Thirty-Eight

Rain slapped the car window, distorting Daniel's reflection as he gazed out into the night.

He saw again Harry's head on Nick's shoulder, Harry's arms clasped around Nick's neck. He thought of Chloe exhausted after a long day out, the warm solid weight of her on his shoulder, the utter trust of a sleeping child. No instinct of paternity had stirred in him at the sight of Harry. There was no sense of connection. What he did feel was pity. Harry looked so much like Jennifer, the golden child of a golden girl. And he was Nick's child too, whatever his genetic inheritance. Daniel hadn't seen him come into the world or watched him feeding at his mother's breast. He hadn't got up in the night to comfort him, or changed his nappies, or felt torn apart when he was ill. Rachel was right. Nick was Harry's true father. And as for Nick, Daniel could find it in his heart to pity him for the burden of guilt and misery that he carried. Daniel was the fortunate one now – he had Rachel.

It was true that he had married her on the rebound. Perhaps she had sensed that and felt that she was second best and could never compete with Jennifer. Perhaps that worked both ways? Would she have married him if she hadn't got pregnant and wanted a child? But none of that really mattered now. Together he and Rachel had made Chloe. He thought of the texture of his life with Rachel, the way that they had coped with Chloe's illness, the home they had made, and their gentleness with each other. Jennifer had gone, it really was over, and there seemed now to be something flimsy, insubstantial about his marriage to her. They had been so young. He saw now that they had not been well matched. He had been the one who kissed, she had been the one who offered the cheek. He had adored her, but he had never been content in the way that he was with Rachel.

Chloe – Chloe and Rachel... they were his life now. He must have been mad to think for even a moment that he might seek custody of Harry. But the question of whether Harry's DNA matched Chloe's was another matter. Could he let go of that hope? Would that even be right, when it would mean so much to Chloe? That dilemma remained. But he couldn't go it alone. He could do nothing without Rachel. He looked at his watch. It was two o'clock.

He leaned forward and spoke to Gemma. "What time do you think we'll be back?"

"Can't go any faster than this, not in these conditions."

"No, no, I understand."

And it didn't matter anyway, because whatever time he got back, he had to see Rachel. This was too important to wait. He would go round to the boat straightaway. No, he couldn't wait that long. He had to speak to her now, right now, this very minute.

He got out his mobile phone.

Rachel was standing in the doorway to the galley, running a hand through dishevelled hair.

"How are you getting on?" She looked more closely at Katie. "You've found something, haven't you? Something bad."

"There was a clinical trial for the obesity therapy. A student died."

Rachel nodded. "I remember seeing it on the news." She came and sat next to Katie at the table.

Katie went on, "The night before it started, Will ran an experiment that didn't get the result he wanted. I think a mouse had a bad reaction and died. I think this must have been the same procedure that was used in human trials the next day. Will ought to have stopped the trial."

Rachel frowned. "But that doesn't make sense. Wouldn't it have been tried on other animals before the human trial? Why was Will doing that at the last minute?"

"They'd already tried it on primates and it was fine. But earlier on, when Will was experimenting on mice, I think he missed out a stage. He and Honor knew that someone else was working on the same thing and there was a race to the Patent Office. I suspect she was pressing him for results, just like Paul's been pressing me, and he started to cut corners – he didn't do an experiment that he said he had, or maybe he did it, but didn't repeat it. He was certain he knew what the result would be and wrote it up in his lab book as if he'd really done it. It must have nagged at him – he is a scientist, after all, and a good one – and just before the human trials started, he decided he would run the experiment again. He would have thought he was just tying up a loose end. He wasn't expecting a problem. He must have been horrified at the result."

Rachel struggled to understand. "But if the monkeys were OK, why would it matter if the mice weren't? I mean, we're more like monkeys than mice, aren't we?"

"Sure, but it's not as straightforward as that. For one thing, mice aren't that different from us. That's why they're used in experiments. The other thing is that sometimes a person's genetic make-up is different from the norm. They might have a condition that causes them no problems in everyday life – that they don't even know about. But because of it, they might suffer severe side effects from using a drug that's fine for everyone else. That's what happened to that medical student – the antibody was aimed at specific markers and he had those on his heart cells as well as his fat cells. The monkeys didn't share that abnormality, but one of the mice did share it and died."

Rachel thought about this.

"So the trial should have been halted. And if it had been, that student would still be alive."

"Yes."

"What are you going to do?"

"I suppose – the police – I don't know. I was thinking, I know it's difficult, but maybe the obvious person – "

"Is Daniel?"

"You see, he's got the lab book. But I did wonder... He's employed by Calliope – what about client–lawyer privilege?"

"That doesn't mean Daniel's allowed to break the law. He's an officer of the court. That's his first allegiance."

"You're sure about this?"

Rachel rubbed her forehead, pushed back her hair so that it stood on end. "The thing is, if he concealed evidence of wrongdoing, he could end up in prison. He just wouldn't do it, so yes, I'm sure."

The ringing of a mobile phone startled them. They looked at each other wide-eyed. Katie thought, *Will!*

But it wasn't her phone. It was Rachel's.

Rachel took the call and her eyes widened with surprise. "Oh, hi Daniel. No, I wasn't asleep." Her tone was guarded. She walked off into the bedroom and shut the door.

Katie sat at the table, gazing at nothing. She thought of Will in the lab staring at a dead mouse. She could follow his thought processes as if they were her own. He wouldn't be sure that the mouse had died because of the experiment. That was the thing with animals. Sometimes they got sick and died and it had nothing to do with the treatment. Maybe it was just a mouse whose time had come. And there were always blips like this. You could run the same test ten times running and get the same result, then on the eleventh, exactly the same set-up, everything replicated to the nth degree, and it went belly-up. Often it meant nothing.

He would have told himself that the therapy would never have been allowed to get as far as clinical trials if there had been any doubts. He would have tried to ignore the other voice in his head, the one that said that there weren't any doubts because they didn't know that he hadn't run the earlier trial.

She felt cold at the thought of how nearly she had done something that was different only in degree. She had almost decided that because she knew – or thought she knew – what the outcome was, she was justified in tweaking her results. How much more tempting it must have been for Will. If the human trials were called off at that late stage, millions of dollars would be wasted, the whole process set back by who knew how long. And what happens to the promising young postdoc who comes up with a piece of inconvenient and almost certainly irrelevant information on the very eve of human trials? Career death, that's what.

So what did Will do? He culled all the mice and put them in the freezer. The batch of mice might stay in the freezer for years and years before someone thought of incinerating them. When the medical student died in the clinical trial, he would have been horrified. The odds were that the dead mouse had those same markers in its heart cells. She saw Will going back into the lab, removing that mouse and disposing of it. That was why one had been missing when Ian did his inventory.

Rachel came back into the room. Even in her distracted state, Katie noticed that her face seemed softer, she looked somehow younger.

"Dan's on his way home from the airport. Then he's coming straight round to the boat. I've told him what's happened. You can give him the notebook and let him sort it out. He'll know what to do."

"I can understand why Will did it… why he made that decision."

"It wasn't his decision to make. But in any case, it all started to go wrong much earlier than that, didn't it? When he wrote up an experiment that he hadn't really done. You wouldn't have done that."

"Well, maybe not that exactly. But tweaking your results, tidying things up, even ignoring something that didn't come out quite right: I've come very close to doing that. There can't be many people who haven't at least been tempted. There's so much pressure, Rachel; it's so competitive."

Rachel's mouth was set in a firm line. "There's no excuse."

"He was unlucky. It might so easily have been alright!"

"But it wasn't! He is responsible for that young man's death."

Katie was silent for a few moments, then, "No, you're right. Of course you are." She put her head in her hands. "I've just had an awful thought. And how do we know it stopped there? The explosion in the lab. Maybe that was Will? Maybe he thought Ian suspected – after all, he was going around talking about a mouse being missing..."

Rachel put a hand on her shoulder.

"Look, Daniel'll be here soon. Leave it all up to him. It's after two o'clock in the morning. Why don't you go and lie down, see if you can get a bit of sleep? That's what I'm going to do."

Katie shook her head. "I'm too wired to sleep – and that coffee – no, I'll plug on with the notebook. See what he did next."

She read on for a few more pages, then gave such a huge yawn that her jaw clicked. The page blurred before her eyes. There was a tightening across her temples. She put her head on the table and closed her eyes to rest them for a few moments. Outside the storm raged, in here it was warm and safe. The rocking of the boat lulled her. She slipped away into sleep.

Chapter Thirty-Nine

Normally he would have slept in the car, but as they headed north up the M11, Daniel was aware of the wind picking up speed, trees thrashing. He was conscious of tension in the hunched shoulders of Gemma, his driver. He half-expected her to suggest that they stop somewhere and wait out the storm, but she didn't, and he was too anxious to get back to Rachel to suggest it himself.

He thought of what she had told him on the phone. His instinct had been right. Hadn't he known all along that Jennifer had had her reasons for hiding that lab book? She had told Lyle that something was wrong and she had been on her way to tell him about it when she had had the accident. She must have realized that there was a problem with the lab book. Rachel hadn't gone into details, so he didn't know exactly what was wrong, just that Will had known something that meant he should have put a stop to the clinical trial. He had no idea what this would mean for the patent case. What a mess! But it didn't matter the way it would have mattered a week ago. Nothing really mattered, as long as he and Rachel and Chloe were together.

They left the rolling Hertfordshire countryside and bypassed Cambridge. It was as they headed for Ely on the A10 that the full blast of the storm hit them. The wind came roaring across the Fens with nothing to break its force. A plastic carrier bag hit the windscreen and wrapped itself round one of the wipers, flapping frantically as if it were trying to free itself. Gemma had to pull over. She got out, struggling to control the car door. The wind rushed in, ruffling his hair, pulling at his coat. It was like something alive, and he felt a twinge of fear at its power.

Gemma managed to untangle the plastic bag and the wind snatched it away. She got back into the car.

Daniel said, "Are you OK with this?"

She smoothed down her hair and shrugged. "We'll be there in twenty minutes. And it has actually stopped raining."

But a few minutes later there were flashing lights on the road ahead. Gemma exclaimed and braked.

Daniel leaned forward. The headlights caught a man in a high-visibility jacket, and behind him floodlights illuminated the roots of a tree heavy with earth.

The road was blocked.

"Mummy, Mummy, there's a monster!"

It seemed just a few moments since Rachel had fallen asleep. Without opening her eyes, she stretched out her arms, hoping to haul Chloe into bed with her. Sometimes that was enough and Chloe would settle down to sleep beside her.

But Chloe was shaking her arm.

"Mummy, Mummy, there *is* a monster. I know there is, I heard it! It went whoosh! And, Mummy, look out of the window!"

There was a crackling, tapping noise like the sound of a big insect trapped in a lampshade. She opened her eyes. The cabin was full of a whitish-yellow light, as bright as a summer's day. Had she overslept? She squinted at the alarm. It was the middle of the night – and a winter's night, she now remembered. She sat bolt upright, as wide awake as if she'd been dowsed with cold water. Something else was wrong. The boat was moving in a way that couldn't be explained by a high wind.

She jumped out of bed and looked out of the porthole. They were drifting into the middle of the river. The *Matilda Jane* must somehow have slipped her moorings. And now she could hear a muffled roar. The brilliant light was reflected off the water, and it was coming from the wheelhouse. The boat was on fire.

***

It was five by the time the taxi turned onto Quayside and pulled up outside Daniel's house. Gemma had managed to make a detour, driving on small roads round by Wicken Fen and coming out at Stretham, only a few miles south of Ely. Daniel gave her a very large tip. He braced himself and got out of the car, gasping as the wind slapped his face. It was like being plunged into a different element, something hostile, inimical to human life. Pushed and buffeted first one way and then the other, he struggled to his front door. He managed to get his key in the lock and opened the door. He turned and raised a hand. Gemma acknowledged his salute and drove away. She lived only a few streets away, she'd told him on a previous occasion, so the night's work was over for her.

The heating was off and the house had a musty smell. He switched the lights on. Everything was just as he had left it – except, he didn't mind the absence of Rachel and Chloe as much. He imagined the house as it would be in a few hours' time: the warmth, the smell of coffee, the bustle of family life beginning again.

He dumped his bags in the sitting room. He went into the kitchen and got a set of spare keys for the boat and a torch to light his way along the quay. Outside he struggled to stay upright and to make headway, the force of the wind pulling at the skin on his face, whipping his hair around. It took his breath away.

As he passed the Maltings, he discerned through watering eyes an orange glow in the sky over towards the railway station. Somewhere near the *Matilda Jane*'s mooring, a spray of sparks went up like a rocket. The acrid smell of burning reached him.

He started to run.

"Katie! Katie!"

She was awake instantly, her heart beating fast, afraid before she even knew why.

Rachel had her hand on her shoulder. "There's a fire in the wheelhouse!"

Chloe was standing beside her, wide-eyed and open-mouthed.

Katie looked for the fire extinguisher. She'd noticed one earlier in the galley. Rachel read her mind.

"It's too late for that. We mustn't open the door!"

"Then how – ?"

"The roof light. In my bedroom. Come on."

As they ran into the bedroom and shut the door, Katie thought, *Fuel tanks. Almost certainly under the wheelhouse.*

Rachel pulled a fold-up aluminium ladder from under the bed.

She said, "There's something else. She's slipped her moorings. We're drifting in midstream. I *can* swim..." Her eyes dropped to Chloe. "And Chloe's had lessons, but..."

"Lifejackets?"

"In the wheelhouse."

"I've trained in life-saving. I can get her to shore."

She saw the doubt in Rachel's face. There was no time to explain that Katie had swum for her school, had worked as a lifeguard at the local swimming pool in university vacations.

"I can do it. Trust me." She was already stripping off her thick socks and her jumper.

Rachel reached up and tugged at a handle on the roof light.

For a terrible moment it seemed to stick, then it swung open and a current of cold air came in.

Rachel unfolded the ladder and hooked the curved edges over the windowsill. "You go first. Then Chloe."

Katie went up the steps and emerged on the roof of the boat. The wheelhouse was blazing like a beacon and the water was lit by a lurid light. The wind hit her, and she stumbled. She saved herself by dropping to her hands and knees. She turned to receive Chloe. Rachel followed her up and all three were on the roof, Chloe sandwiched between them.

235

There was an ominous creaking somewhere and the air was scorching hot.

Katie put her mouth close to Rachel's ear. "I'm going into the water. Pass Chloe down when I give you the signal."

Rachel nodded.

Katie clambered down onto the walkway. She sat down and hung there for a moment, backside on the edge, arms braced, readying herself. Then she took a deep breath and let go.

The water closed over her head. The shock of the cold tightened her chest. She bobbed up, gasping. Her heart was thumping and she was afraid of blacking out. She forced herself to relax and let the water buoy her up. There was a brackish taste on her lips; the water was gritty.

She looked up. Rachel was on the walkway, with Chloe between her legs, her arms hooked under Chloe's armpits.

Katie waved to her.

Rachel tried to lower her down, but Chloe was protesting and struggling, trying to turn and climb back into the boat.

"Chloe, Chloe, come to me," Katie shouted, treading water.

"Mummy, Mummy! Orlando – where's Orlando?"

"Rachel, drop her!"

Rachel's face was set, her mouth was open, and her teeth were gritted. Wisps of smoke were curling round her head.

"Mummy!"

"Rachel! Just drop her!"

And Rachel did.

The wind pushed him this way and that as he forged ahead, tossed about like a swimmer in a rough sea. He prayed that it wouldn't be the *Matilda Jane*. Perhaps it was the boatyard, or one of those boats that were laid up for the winter – yes, that was more likely – and he felt an anticipatory sense of relief.

The wind dropped briefly, and in the sudden silence his footsteps thudded on the pavement. Then he was rounding the bend past the pub. The wind roared again, shifting direction, and it was as if there were hands in the small of his back, propelling him forward. The path curved to the right after it went under the railway bridge. He could see the fire, flames that illuminated boiling clouds of smoke, but he couldn't see where it was coming from.

And then he was round the bend and oh, no, it was the *Matilda Jane* that was burning. And she had drifted from her moorings, carried by the current into the middle of the river.

Above the roar of the wind, he heard a siren.

The tow path was crowded with shadowy figures outlined against the orange glow of the fire. He grabbed first one shoulder, then another, but they were all strangers. He elbowed his way through, stumbling, gasping.

As he neared the boat, waves of blistering heat came out to meet him. In the din of crackling flames and the confusion of smoke and flickering light, he couldn't make out what was happening.

A man shouted, "That's it. Got her."

A bulky figure was kneeling on the tow path, blocking the way. Daniel grabbed its shoulder. "Please – my daughter – "

The person looked up. It was Daisy from the boat next door. "Dan – it's alright."

"Chloe – "

"She's here. She's safe."

He saw now that Daisy was clasping something to her. She released her grip and between the folds of a blanket he saw Chloe's face. She saw him, too. "Daddy, Daddy!" She struggled out of Daisy's arms and he snatched her up. She was soaking wet and reeked of smoke. He knew he would never let her out of his sight again. But –

"Chloe, where's Mummy?"

Daisy shook her head. Dan thrust Chloe back into her arms and moved forward. More people were coming along the tow path, converging on the part nearest the boat, then falling back as the heat of the blaze hit them. The siren was very loud now, filling the night.

A woman's voice shouted, "I've got to go back!"

It was Katie. She was being embraced – no, held back – by a man that he recognized now as Frank. Frank had his arms clasped round her. She was swinging her arms impotently, trying to free herself.

Daniel ran to them. "Where's Rachel?"

"He won't let me go back in!" She was sobbing.

"I keep trying to tell you," Frank shouted. "Someone's already gone back in!"

"Where is Rachel?" Daniel said again.

Katie was dressed only in a T-shirt and pants, and water was running in rivulets down her. The wind dropped and he heard behind him the crackling and roaring of the flames, and then the voice of someone shouting encouragement: "Yes, you can do it! Come on, come on."

A man was kneeling by the edge of the water. As Daniel ran towards him a spectacular shower of sparks burst from the burning boat and the wind flung them wide. He ducked his head and caught a whiff of singed hair.

Out there in the river, a dark head as sleek as an otter was moving slowly towards the bank. Daniel flung himself down next to the man on the bank. They stretched their hands out over the water. Rachel was tiring, but she struggled doggedly on, closer and closer, and then he had her hand, and they were hauling her in.

He held her in his arms as she knelt on the riverbank, her face wet against his, her body trembling. She pulled back. Her teeth were chattering and she couldn't speak, but he knew what she wanted to say.

"Oh, my darling, Chloe's safe. Katie as well."

She hung on to him, shivering, and there seemed to be something else she wanted to ask him or to tell him.

But then the paramedics arrived and they took her away, and Chloe as well.

238

Chapter Forty

It was daybreak by the time Daniel came home. Rachel, Chloe, and Katie were still in hospital, being treated for smoke inhalation and hypothermia. He hadn't wanted to leave. He would have liked to sleep in the chair next to Chloe's bed. But Chloe was asking about Orlando. She wouldn't rest until Daniel said he'd go back and look for him. Rachel had told him how she and Chloe heard Orlando yowling and Rachel had realized that he was trapped. She couldn't let him be burned alive. She had gone back and opened the door to the saloon. Orlando had rushed in and so had the smoke. Rachel had almost been overcome, but there'd been someone else, a man, who had somehow got on the boat and had hauled her up the ladder. She didn't know what had happened to him – or to Orlando.

Daniel got a taxi back to the house, and fell asleep for ten minutes in the back. Once home, he stripped off his ruined suit and put it straight in a black bin bag. He ought to feel hungry, he hadn't eaten since the in-flight meal, which seemed to have happened in a different life, but he couldn't face the thought of food. He was jet-lagged and exhausted, but he was still fizzing with adrenaline. He made himself a cup of strong coffee with plenty of sugar and went to the bathroom. He looked in the mirror. The creases in his face were lined with soot, his hair was stiff with ash, and he stank of smoke. He stood for quarter of an hour under a hot shower, and had a shave. Then he got dressed and went outside. The wind had dropped and only shreds of cloud remained. Mist was rising from the river. There was a crispness to the air and the light was bright. He looked at his watch. Ten o'clock.

He retraced the route of the night before, reliving the horror of realizing that Chloe and Rachel were on the burning boat. *Thank you, thank you for letting them be all right*, he thought, though he didn't know who he was thanking.

The *Matilda Jane* had been towed back to the bank, and the area around her had been taped off. There were people in white suits busy around the boat, and a couple of police officers standing on the bank outside the taped-off area. Out on the river was a police dinghy, and in it, a man in a wetsuit.

Daniel's first thought was that the damage could have been worse. At least she was still afloat. The wheelhouse had gone, of course, but the front of the boat seemed relatively undamaged. With patience and hard work, perhaps she could be restored. The main danger to Chloe and Rachel and Katie had not been from the fire, but from the smoke. If Chloe hadn't woken up... but better not to go there.

He wondered if the notebook had survived. He ought to try to find out.

Frank was on his narrow boat, inspecting some damage at the end that had been nearest to the *Matilda Jane*. He raised a hand in greeting.

"How bad is it?" Daniel asked, nodding towards the boat.

"Nothing much. Bit scorched, that's all."

"The insurance'll cover it. Your boat as well as ours."

Frank made a gesture of dismissal. "Never mind that. How's the little one?"

"She'll be fine. And Rachel and Katie. Being treated for smoke inhalation. It's not serious. But Rachel's very upset about Orlando – "

Frank gave a snort of laughter. "Orlando? He's asleep on our bed. He swam ashore on the other side. The police found him mewing over there a while ago and brought him back in their boat."

"Thank goodness for that."

"Used up one of his nine lives, that's for sure. Arson, it

must have been. Only an accelerant would have got that fire going so fast."

"There was someone who helped Rachel get off the boat – "

"Ah." Frank cleared his throat. "Yes, well. I saw Rachel go into the water and someone go after Rachel – dunno who it was – but I didn't see them make it back to the bank. But what with the smoke and that, I can't be 100 per cent certain. Maybe he got out on the other side, like Orlando. The police are checking now – "

A mobile phone rang with a little fanfare that was followed by a tinny rendition of a tune that Daniel couldn't quite place.

He looked at Frank.

Frank shrugged. "Not mine."

"Nor mine," Daniel said, looking around.

A light flickered among the dead leaves at the side of the path. He bent down and, clearing the leaves away, picked up the phone. It vibrated in his hand.

"Answer it, I would," Frank offered.

As Daniel put the phone to his ear, he remembered what that tune was: the theme from *The Wire*.

A woman's voice, unexpected, yet familiar. "Will? Will? Where are you?"

"Will's not here."

There was a silence, then: "Who is this?"

"Honor? This is Daniel, Daniel Marchmont."

"But where's Will? What are you doing with his phone?"

"I've just picked it up. It was lying by the side of the tow path."

"The tow path! But what – ?"

"There's been a fire – our boat – "

Frank laid a hand on his arm. "Dan – I think they've found something."

He looked round. There was a new alertness in the people clustered on the riverbank.

"I've got to go, Honor. Honor?" There was no reply. She had already ended the call. He put the phone in his pocket.

A police diver was doing a one-armed backstroke as he towed something to the shore. Two men reached down, grappled with something heavy, struggled to lug it out of the water.

"So I was right." Frank shook his head as the body emerged from the river, water streaming off it. "Poor bloke."

They laid the body out on the grass. Someone covered it with a tarpaulin.

Daniel and Frank watched in silence.

A police officer came over to them. "Perhaps one of you two gentlemen can identify this man. He's most likely a member of the riverside community."

Frank climbed off his boat and bent down to look. "No," he said. "Never seen him before. He's not one of us."

Then it was Daniel's turn. He looked down at the face, wiped clean of expression, the hair dark with water, plastered to the skull. He'd known, really, since he had answered the phone. Dark spots appeared before his eyes. He swayed. The woman put a hand on his arm. "You alright?"

"I'll be OK in a minute."

She held his arm while he waited for the dizziness to pass.

"You know who he is?"

Daniel nodded. "His name's Will Orville. I don't know where he lives, but he works for Calliope Biotech."

The woman bent down and gently drew the tarpaulin over his face. Now that the dead man had been named, a respectful silence fell. It was broken by a commotion behind them. Daniel looked round. Honor was running down the tow path.

She reached Daniel's side and stared down at the shrouded body. "Oh! Oh! Oh!"

He had never heard a sound like it. The hairs went up on the back of his neck. It brought home the fact of death to Daniel, more than Will's blank face or the limp hand that curled from under the tarpaulin. A young man was dead and a woman was wailing.

Honor fell to her knees. She was about to fling herself on the body when Daniel grabbed her elbow and the police officer grabbed the other. They hoisted her to her feet. She went on wailing, words tumbling out in a disjointed stream.

Daniel wanted to cover his eyes, to be somewhere else, anywhere else. At the sight of this strong woman stripped of her self-control and dignity he felt an embarrassment so intense that it was like shame.

The shock had unhinged her. That was what he thought at first, but gradually the sense of the words sank in.

"Why why, why?" she moaned. "Stupid, stupid, stupid... you fool."

There was anger there as well as pain. Perhaps that was a natural response, except that – a chill settled on him as he realized...

"Why did you come here, Honor?" he demanded, pulling her round to face him.

She looked at him as if she didn't know who he was. Then he saw that she had taken in what he said. She gestured to the body.

"How did you know to come here?" he asked again. "All I told you was that I'd found the phone – and when you got here, how did you know this was Will? His face is covered."

Over Honor's shoulder he saw the police officer's eyes narrow, her face grow alert as she too waited to hear the answer that Honor was groping for. "I don't know – I – "

"What happened, Honor? I know about the notebook. That's survived," he lied. He was close enough to see her pupils dilate. That had hit home.

She said, "Will... I guessed that he was going to do something – when I heard about the boat – "

"I don't think so, Honor. Will died rescuing my wife. Why would he do that if he'd set the fire in the first place? Did you realize that, Honor? Did you know that Rachel and Chloe were on board? I hope you didn't!"

She shook her head, but her eyes were darting everywhere as if she were searching for an answer.

Daniel went on. "But Will knew and he rushed over here. He guessed that you'd stop at nothing to get the notebook back, and he was afraid of what you might do. He was too late. By the time he got here, the boat was already on fire. He couldn't let innocent people die to protect your secret. And now he's dead."

Chapter Forty-One

Katie made her way along the hospital corridor to where Rachel and Chloe were in the same room. Chloe had got into bed with Rachel and was snuggled up beside her, asleep.

Daniel had come in earlier and had told Rachel and Katie what had happened. Katie still hadn't taken it in. How could Will be dead? All that energy, that brilliant scientific mind – it couldn't be just gone, snuffed out. She couldn't shake off the thought that if she went to the lab, he would be there at his bench as he'd been when she first saw him.

She sat down next to Rachel. Rachel stretched out a hand and Katie clasped it. Rachel's eyes went to her sleeping child and back to Katie. She smiled. She had thanked Katie more than once, but even then words hadn't really been necessary. There would always be a bond between them.

Katie reached out to stroke the sleeping child's hair.

"How is she?"

"Fine, now that she knows Orlando is alright. Wanted Dan to bring him into the hospital. Actually, she'll see him this evening. They've said we can go home."

"Me, too."

"You'll come home with us, Katie?"

Katie hesitated, but then, "No," she decided. "I think the three of you should be alone together. I've still got a week to run on the lease of my flat and most of my stuff's still there. And Minnie's also offered to come and stay with me, if I don't want to be alone. Spoilt for choice, really. But, oh Rachel, what are you going to do about the *Matilda Jane*?"

"The damage isn't as bad as it might have been, Dan says.

At least she's still afloat. It'll take time, but I'll fix her. And nothing really matters as long as Chloe is alright."

"I wonder what'll happen to Honor's lab. No sooner do I arrive than the place collapses around me. To lose one lab may be deemed a misfortune. To lose two..." Katie gave a shaky laugh. "I feel like Typhoid Mary."

"The rot set in long before you arrived, Katie."

"But if I hadn't started to dig around..."

"Don't think like that," Rachel said firmly. "It's not your fault. No one could have imagined that Honor would do what she did."

"There was a lot at stake. Her whole career, her reputation, and Will's career as well. Perhaps that was the worst thing for her..."

"You think she did it for him?"

"Maybe..." Katie shook her head, lost for words.

They sat in silence for a while. Then Rachel said, "There's something else, isn't there, Katie?"

Katie nodded. "Last night. I went to see Ian. He admitted that he'd been sleeping in his office. That was why he was in the lab that night. He swore, though, that he hadn't switched on the gas taps, and I believe him. But if he didn't, who did? What if it was Honor?"

"She blew up her own lab? But why?"

"Ian had discovered that a mouse was missing. He must have mentioned that to Honor, without realizing the significance. If he went around telling people... someone else might have realized, or he might have got to the bottom of it himself. But the thing is, Rachel, Honor knew that Ian was sleeping in his office. She let that slip when we were talking in the canteen. And if she knew, why hadn't she put a stop to it? Maybe because it meant that he would be the first into the lab that morning."

"Do you think Will suspected?"

"If he did, he redeemed himself, didn't he? Realizing that

Honor was going to do something drastic last night, when he told her that the notebook was missing, then trying to get to the boat first – he risked his own life – "

Katie thought of the photos of Will surfing and skiing. He'd been a risk-taker, always one for bold, decisive action, and that was part of what made him so attractive. It had led him to make the wrong call over the dead mouse and the clinical trial, but it had also led him to jump into the water to rescue someone from a burning boat. Had anyone told Martha yet? And at that thought she couldn't hold back the tears. A large drop spilled over and fell onto the bed. She rubbed her face with the back of her hand.

Rachel reached for a handful of tissues from the box by the bed, and handed them to Katie.

"I expect we'll find out more at the inquest," Katie said. "He must still have had a fair bit of alcohol washing around in his system."

"All the same," Rachel said, "it was a good thing, a brave thing. That's what we need to remember."

Back in the ward, Katie found Minnie sitting by her bed, reading a copy of *Nature*.

"Hey, Katie, there's something here that would suit you down to the ground: a job heading up a research project into haematological cancers in Oxford."

For a moment Katie wondered if it wouldn't be a relief to just leave it all behind, the hundreds of pinprick frustrations of her life as a scientist, the uncertain prospects, the failed grant applications, the long days in the lab, the weekends and evenings disrupted by checks on cultures for experiments that failed anyway...

Then she thought about Chloe. She thought about the woman in the supermarket with the caliper. She thought of the vaccines for polio and measles and mumps and TB and diphtheria. She thought of all those who hadn't let themselves despair when their experiments failed, who just went on plugging away regardless. She thought of the antibody waiting for her in the lab. Would it work this time? Maybe. Maybe not. She remembered Samuel Beckett's advice to fail again, fail better.

"Oh, what the hell. Give it here," she said, reaching for the journal. "When's the closing date?"

Epilogue

Daniel rolled over and looked at the alarm clock. Nine o'clock. Rachel was still asleep beside him. He had brought her and Chloe home the day before.

He got up to look at Chloe. She was breathing peacefully, her face a healthy colour, apparently no worse for her experience, though who knew what the longer term effect of those traumatic events would be. He couldn't bear to think how it all might have ended.

Chloe's duvet didn't need rearranging, but he did it anyway, tucking it up round her chin. He watched her sleeping face a little longer.

He went downstairs, and put on the kettle for tea.

Honor had admitted to setting fire to the boat, but she'd claimed that she hadn't known Chloe and Rachel were on board. She had been desperate to destroy the notebook – and if Katie got in the way, so much the worse for her. The notebook had survived, but so badly damaged by smoke and water that it was virtually illegible. However, Katie was willing to swear an affidavit about the contents. And the lab book itself could be examined by handwriting experts to determine whether it had been written over a period of months or if it was a fake that had been written up in a matter of hours.

The future of Calliope Biotech did not look good. The company could be sued if it could be proved that Will and Honor had known the research was flawed and had not called a halt to the clinical trial. No doubt the work would be carried on elsewhere, but what a waste Will's death was. And as for Honor: with the loss of Will and of everything she had worked for in her long and distinguished career, her life was in ruins. Her mental state was deteriorating and Daniel wondered if she would be fit to stand trial for setting fire to the boat.

As he was pouring water into the teapot, he heard the clatter of the letter box.

He went to pick up the post and saw an envelope with a typed address. He wondered if this was what he had been waiting for. There was no logo, but given the nature of the company's work, he didn't expect that there would be. He went back into the kitchen and slit the envelope with a knife. He didn't take the letter out, just flexed the envelope so that he could see the letterhead. Yes, it was from the DNA testing company. He put the envelope down on the kitchen table and turned to make the tea.

A sound at the kitchen door made him look round.

Rachel was there, yawning and pulling her dressing gown around her.

Her eyes fell on the envelope. He saw her putting two and two together.

"Is that – "

"Yes."

He came over and picked it up.

"Have you read it?" she asked.

He shook his head, and went into the sitting room. Rachel followed him. He went over to the wood-burning stove and opened the door. He was about to thrust the letter inside, when Rachel said, "Wait."

She put a hand on his arm and looked into his face. "Are you sure, Dan? Really sure?"

He held her gaze. "I'm sure."

He wedged the letter in, angling it so that it touched the few glowing embers from the previous night's fire. For a few moments nothing happened, then a tiny orange flame nibbled the corner. The edge of the envelope grew black. Rachel slipped her arm round his waist and he pulled her close.

They watched the fire flare up and the paper shrivel.

Soon it was nothing but ashes.

Acknowledgments

It is true: if you want something done, ask a busy person. This novel required a lot of research and I couldn't have written it without the support and generosity of a number of people. For any mistakes that remain I am, of course, solely responsible.

So thank you to:

My old university friend, Gary Moss, who again and again shared his knowledge of patent law with endless patience, and kindly read a draft of the novel.

Dr Paula Bolton-Maggs, haematologist and sister-in-law, who helped me to choose a blood disease, and combed through the last draft for me.

Dr John Olsen, who allowed me to shadow him in the lab and explained various scientific procedures to me – as many times as it took – as well as reading and commenting on a draft of the novel.

Dr Angharad Watson, who advised me on the details of the obesity therapy, and what might go wrong in a clinical trial. She and her husband kindly read a draft of the novel.

Dr Sandrine Soube, who gave me a wonderfully vivid picture of the ups and downs of the life of the scientific researcher, and introduced me to others who could also help.

Dr Jemma Lace-Costigan, who shared with me the frustrations and rewards of scientific research, as well as discussing some aspects of the plot.

Dr Alison Graham, who allowed me to shadow her in the lab, and made valuable suggestions.

Professor Rob Wynn, who spared time from his demanding schedule to talk to me about bone marrow transplants.

Christine Poulson

Dr Helen Crimlist and Dr Beverley Howson, who gave me advice on some of the medical aspects of the novel.

Dr Rachel Jones, who over lunch in Leeds told me about life as a young patent lawyer, and followed that with suggestions by email.

Alistair Breward, who took time to tell me about the world of the venture capitalist.

And then there are my non-scientific friends and readers:

I cannot imagine writing anything without the support and feedback of my dear friend, Sue Hepworth.

I want to thank everyone at Lion Fiction, but especially Tony Collins, Sheila Jacobs and Jessica Tinker.

Thanks also to Jo Burn, Becky Dewitt, David Poulson, John and Chris O'Nions, Lisanne Radice, Amanda Rainger, Pauline Wainwright and Jonathan Waller, who all gave me valuable support and assistance, and last but not least, my husband, Peter Blundell Jones.

LOCAL POET

Rob Seaton killed a woman

Rob doesn't know Laney Grey. But when she steps out in front of his van and dies on impact, his life will never be the same.

The police declare him innocent, but how do you deal with the guilt?

He has to know who she was, why she chose to die, and why he had to be part of her death.

To understand her, he must learn to read her poetry. To know her, he must unravel the mysteries of her past.

As Laney's dark secret starts to come to light, and Rob's innocence is questioned, he must discover the truth.

But truth comes at a cost... will Rob be the one who has to pay?

ISBN: 978 1 78264 230 5 | e-ISBN: 978 1 78264 231 2

THE CANTALOUPE THIEF

**"The worst thing about being homeless
is being looked right through."**

It's ten years since wealthy matriarch Alberta Resnick was found stabbed to death in Georgia. Local reporter Branigan Powers sets out to investigate the city's only unsolved murder.

Branigan knows that the homeless often have information, but are rarely asked. She gets in touch with Liam, a pastor who runs a shelter. As they start to ask questions, secrets begin to surface. Then homeless people start dying.

Clearly the killer won't stop until all tracks are covered. But what the killer doesn't know is that someone is watching, someone who is used to being ignored and unseen...

ISBN: 978 1 78264 192 6 | e-ISBN: 978 1 78264 193 3

GAME, SET AND MURDER

**It's the first day of Wimbledon.
And a dead body is lying on Court 19.**

Newly-promoted detective inspector Angela Costello recognizes the dead man as Croatian champion-turned-coach, Petar Belic. A double grand-slam winner, Petar was famous, and much loved.

However, Petar had an ex-wife who wanted him back; a girlfriend who wouldn't let him go; a business partner with secrets. Then there was the temperamental leading Brit, Stewart Bickerstaff, whom Petar had been coaching.

D.I. Costello deduces that only one person could have committed the crime. Unfortunately she has no way of proving her suspicions...

ISBN: 978 1 78264 072 1 | e-ISBN: 978 1 78264 073 8